Bernice Rubens was born in .... and later read English at the University of Wales, of which she is now a Fellow.

Her writing career began when she was thirty and around the same time she started work in the film industry. For some time, Bernice alternated between writing novels and making films. For the last ten years she has concentrated solely on writing. Her novels to date include the Booker Prize Winner *The Elected Member* and *Five Year Sentence* which was shortlisted for the Booker Prize. In 1987, Bernice was on the Booker Prize jury and she has also won the Welsh City Council Prize for *Our Father*. Two of her books have been successfully transferred to film; *I Sent A Letter to My Love* and most recently *Madame Sousatzka*, directed by John Schlesinger and starring Shirley Maclaine.

Bernice's other love, apart from writing, is playing the cello. She has two daughters.

BERNICE RUBENS

Autobiopsy

An *Abacus* Book

First published in Great Britain in 1993 by Sinclair-Stevenson
This edition published in 1994 by Abacus
Reprinted 1994, 1995 (twice)

Copyright © Bernice Rubens 1993

The moral right of the author has been asserted.

A CIP catalogue record for this book
is available from the British Library.

ISBN 0 349 10568 5

Printed in England by Clays Ltd, St Ives plc

Abacus
A Division of
Little, Brown and Company (UK)
Brettenham House
Lancaster Place
London WC2E 7EN

To
Liza Williams

PART ONE

Chapter 1

When I say that my friend Walter Berry was the greatest novelist of our time, I am not exaggerating. Even the meanest of critics acknowledged that fact, and during his lifetime too. So that, when he died, his death made little difference to his sales or reputation. His sudden absence from the literary scene occasioned a general sorrow, but also a sigh of relief from his fellow writers who hoped now for some recognition that there were other novelists at work besides the great Berry.

I shall miss him terribly. He was my mentor and my friend. He was old enough to be my father, and in many ways he fulfilled that role, a role that had been poorly and cruelly played in my growing-up years. Late as it was, for it was not until my aging teens that I met him, I welcomed Walter as my substitute father. He respected what small writing gift I possess, and he encouraged me in my work. He was an enabler, was Walter. He enabled my talent, as well as that filial love that I had for so long and so painfully suppressed.

Besides being a genius, Walter was a very good man. Affectionate, generous and humane. No fault could be found with him, and I suppose that the only decent thing left for him to do was to die, and to leave the field clear for others in his profession. This he had done in his fair-minded way, and I noticed how those, envious of his reputation, could now freely praise his work as they would the work of any foreign writer. For neither the alien nor the dead spell rivalry.

On hearing of his death, I went straightway to his home. Mrs Berry had phoned me early in the morning, shortly after he had died. I ran all the way to his house, my heart pumping its breathless sorrow. I hoped to discover some explanation there, one that would be found untenable and therefore dismissed, and Walter would be alive again. But on arrival I was shown to his bedroom, and there he lay, his arms crossed on his chest, his head resting sideways on the pillow with the stillness of one undeniably gone. I stared at him and noticed how I trembled. Anger had suddenly overtaken my sorrow. How dared he leave me when he had been at such pains to nourish my need of him? I wanted to kill him, to re-dead him, and I actually raised my hand to strike him, but Mrs Berry caught it mid-air and held me close and let me weep my fury away.

'I'll leave you with him a while, Martin,' she said.

Looking back now, I sometimes wish she hadn't, for what I had in mind could never have been done in her presence. Or in anyone else's, for that matter. For it was private. And solitary. And terrible. You see, I was not prepared to let Walter go. Not wholly, that is. But I needed tools for what I had in mind.

I rushed from the room, and told Mrs Berry that I had an appointment and that I would be back within the hour. She told me that I would be welcome at any time. I kissed her. It was the first time I had done so in all the twenty years or so of our acquaintance. She took it as a token of a sorrow shared, but in truth my kiss was one of cunning gratitude, that she was allowing me free access to a death vigil.

Within the hour I had returned.

'Sit with him a while,' she said. 'I have so many things to attend to.'

I shut the bedroom door. Had there been a key, I would have locked it, for now my sorrow was laced with fear of discovery. I went straight to the bedside and laid my tools on the counterpane. Or rather, my tool. For I needed only one. A suction-pipe. Because what I had in mind was to syphon off Walter's brain.

You may be curious as to my trepanning technique, and you may well doubt that such venture is possible at all. But whether you like it or not, you have to take my word for it. It *is* possible. And I did it. But I am wary of telling you how.

4

And for good reason. For who knows into what irresponsible hands such knowledge would fall? How lacking in touch those hands may be, and how ham-fisted their powers of selection? Why, were the world to know how I set about my cunning brain-picking, a plague of plagiarism would infect the universe and nobody would have to think for himself for ever more. Publishers would be besieged with novels, all of them purloined. And not only novels. For painters, composers, architects, scientists, inventors – all of them would get on my trepanning wagon. All they would have to do all day is sit there and use my technique. On the relevant skulls. Thus readers would be obliged to dine on the crumbs from *Middlemarch*'s table and on Shakespeare's unused postscripts. Psychiatrists, already in a conning profession, would compound their swindle with Freud's afterthoughts. Poets would fleece Milton's blind visions and composers would concoct Vivaldi's fifth season or the completion of Schubert's *Unfinished*. And painters would dine off Van Gogh's lunatic ravings, for there is no more fertile an imagination than that which dwells in a mind disturbed. Grand larceny and pillage would erode our creative world and the results would be judged only by the cunning and disguise of their piracy. No. I shall not reveal my technique. I used a simple tool. A suction-pipe. Let me leave it at that.

I was not interested in the brain's physical make-up, the gristles and the jellies, for these, no doubt, were no different from those of any illiterate man in the street. They would come, of course, as part of the whole package, but they could, I thought, like offal, be discarded. The matter that *mattered* to me had nothing to do with jelly or gristle. It was the grey stuff that I was after, the ideas, the thoughts, the sheer lunacy of that wonderful imagination. I have to admit that I was not without scruple. Not so much for the legality of the exercise, but for its questionable ethics. I told myself that what I was about to do would be to the ultimate benefit of mankind. But I would not be fooled. That 'benefit to mankind' plea I knew to be a handy excuse for all manner of spurious experiment. Besides, I had absolutely no intention of sharing my findings with anybody. I was on my own, and I would have to take the consequences.

I looked at my friend and muttered an apology. I thought I saw a smile skim across his face, but perhaps I thought so because I needed his understanding. I took up my syphon in a trembling hand, and laid my cunning thumb on its button. I offered up a prayer for forgiveness. Then pressed. Slowly and gently. I knew that Walter's brain, in its lifetime, had been teeming, and no doubt a deluge of invention lay within. So my extractions had to be measured, else a flood would ensue. I realised that the last thought that the great Walter Berry had entertained on this earth would be the first to emerge from his fertile brain, and as I withdrew my thumb – oh so very gently and with such baited, awe-filled breath – I wondered what earth-shattering thought had been the great man's final signature. What feverish notion had his last breath bequeathed? What mind-blowing perception had orchestrated my friend's death-rattle?

And this is what it was.

Shit! My chest hurts. Why does she have to wear that terrible yellow dress? That colour's enough to kill you.

Which clearly it was. My old friend Berry had gone out in a blaze of yellow, blinded by his wife's sunflower sorrow.

I was stunned. This was not what I had expected at all. I felt like a shameful eavesdropper and it crossed my mind that perhaps I should forgo my private pursuit. But at the same time, I conceded that my friend, like any ordinary citizen, was entitled to trivia and to thoughts below the standard of his reputation. There would be many of them and I would have to take them in my stride. And at my leisure. Yet my friend's funeral was scheduled for a week hence, certainly not long enough to drain that febrile mind of all its fancies. There was only one solution. I had to excise the brain entire. But for that, I needed more tools. I patted Walter's head, and noticed that

6

the smile had disappeared. I hurried out of the house, pleading yet another appointment to Mrs Berry, and promising my
swift return. At home, I collected some fine carpenters' tools –
woodwork is a hobby of mine – and on the way back to my
friend's house, I dropped into a chemist's to buy some make-
up. I told the counter-assistant that it was for my wife, though
I had none, and I could have sworn she winked at me as if she
had heard that excuse before. A pancake foundation was all I
wished. Flesh-coloured, I told her, and the transaction was
swiftly completed. Then, armed with my bag of tools and
camouflage, I hurried back to the death-chamber.

Mrs Berry let me into the house, then left quickly for the
airport where she was to meet her daughter, who was cutting
short her holiday to attend her stepfather's funeral.

I was alone and glad of it. I could take my time. And though
I did, and took the utmost care, I was surprised at how quickly
the operation was performed. There was no threat of fatality,
of course, and I suppose that assurance allowed me to work
swiftly and with confidence. When the extraction was complete, I applied the pancake powder with the sponge provided,
and that small camouflage covered up all evidence of theft. I
took a last look at my friend. Though he was fully clothed,
brainless, he looked suddenly naked. I turned my face away. I
was elated and ashamed, both at the same time. So I hurried
from the room and hastened to my own quarters, where I
locked my loot in my freezer. I decided to do no more
investigations until after the funeral. A small scruple of
decency nudged me into this postponement, though I must
admit that I regretted the delay, and that often during the
waiting week, I opened my freezer simply to view my precious
quarry.

On the day of the funeral I woke up in a nervous sweat. I am
not a believer, but I feared the 'Wrath of God'. It was a phrase
that I'd picked up from my father. He had threatened me with
it along with his trouser-belt. Because the former could not be
proved, he simulated it with his belt, and I bear the marks of
its buckle on my back to this day.

I ascribed my nervousness to the coming occasion. I denied

myself breakfast for I wanted to avoid the freezing compartment of my kitchen. I arrived early at the church. It was already crowded and I saw that many mourners were directed to an annexe where a tannoy had been installed to relay the service. As a close friend, my seat had been reserved in the main body of the funeral chapel. I was happy to notice that it was in an advantageous position, close to the television cameras, from which point I could view the arrivals and recognise the celebrities amongst them. And there were many. The whole of literary London had turned out for the occasion. The cameras began to roll, and I noticed how the mourners adjusted their faces, urging the ready-baked tears from their eyes with that half-mast sorrow that is reserved for public view and has little to do with private grief. When most of the congregation had settled and the organ fade-out threatened the onset of the service, Mrs Berry entered the chapel. At her side was her daughter Amanda, trailing her son by the hand. Amanda was dry-eyed, solemn, and of starched upper lip. Walter's widow was draped in appropriate black, a colour broken only by a single yellow rose that she carried before her. I smiled to myself. Clearly, after all her years of marriage, Christina Berry had never cottoned on to her husband's citron aversion.

The chief mourners took their seats in the front pew and the service began. One after another, the writers came forward and sang my friend's praises. The eulogies were manifold and on the whole sincere, though I thought many of them were too studied, over-researched, as if many drafts had gone into their making. I tired of them and of their florid repetition and, as discreetly as I could, I studied the faces of the assembly. Many of them I recognised as Walter's close friends, but others were perfect strangers to me. I was puzzled because, as an intimate of Walter's for many years, I considered that I had met most of his circle. I wondered whether he had led a secret life, peopled by those strangers in the chapel. Then I realised that, in the course of my brain-draining, such a life would be revealed to me, and I could not help but smile. One of the strangers caught me at it, and I quickly fashioned the smile into a grimace of pain, a look more appropriate in the circumstances. But I have to confess that, inside myself, I felt a surge of joy. I could not mourn Walter because, for me, Walter was not dead. He was alive, that is, the better part of him, and safely at home in my freezer.

I was anxious for the service to finish. I was itching to go back to my kitchen and to take the syphon in my hand. But I would be obliged to go back to Walter's house after the service. I would be obliged to commiserate with the family on their loss. But I would be at pains to disguise that their loss was undeniably my gain.

'I shall miss him terribly,' Christina wept on my shoulder.

A lot more than he shall miss you, I could not help but think, and I realised with a certain unease that, with one single syphoned thought, I had already discovered more about Walter than his wife would ever know.

The party was subdued, as was fitting for the occasion. I noticed that those strangers in the chapel were nowhere in evidence in Walter's home. They must define Walter's extra-mural pursuits, I thought, and once again, I itched to be back in my kitchen. But common courtesy dictated that I linger.

The guests were mainly writers and their wives. Or, in some cases, their husbands, for Walter had cultivated the friendship of many women writers who were legion at the time. I noticed how their husbands hung in their shadows, and I pitied them. Clearly they had each been lacerated in chapter and verse, and I wondered why they didn't unite in authoress genocide. I would never put up with it, I thought. Marriage was something to be avoided. The occasional affair perhaps. That's enough for me. But never a relationship. Connection, that's all I needed. And in one-night stands. That way no woman could get a sentence out of me.

I mingled amongst the writers. They knew me as Walter's close friend, and they were always welcoming. I was a little nervous of them. They were established and well published, while I had but a single novel to my name and a block on the second that had lasted for many years. The talk turned to the question of Walter's biographer. Clearly there would be no shortage of publishers anxious to commission such a book. The problem was who should write it. The question had never arisen during Walter's lifetime. He was always writing and he had died mid-sentence. Like all writers at work, he had considered himself immortal, so he had entrusted nobody with the telling of his posthumous tale.

'It all depends on Christina,' one of the writers said. 'Without her consent, there would be no access to his note-books and letters.'

'I doubt,' another writer offered, 'that dear old Walter had very much of a private life to hide.'

I listened carefully to their discussions and I felt uncomfortable, for each of their contributions fed my sense of absolute power. For I was on the brink of knowing everything about Walter Berry, perhaps even more than my friend himself. And what's more, I didn't need any of his letters or note-books to prove it. Not even the novels, though I had read them all. And certainly I didn't need Christina's permission. For I had the Berry oeuvre entire in my freezer. No-one on earth was more equipped than I to write Walter's story. His autobiopsy, as it were. Let all those writers scratch about the note-books and letters to winkle out the lifestory of my friend. Only I could reveal the absolute truth of that life, for only I had the key to its very essence.

I took a glass from a passing drinks tray and gulped at it in an attempt to still my gnawing sense of power. It did little to soothe my itch to get back to my kitchen. But I tarried. To leave would have been discourteous. I hung around till many of the guests had left, and I drank far more than was good for me. I had no wish to be left alone with Christina and her daughter. Fortunately, other relatives were present, Walter's two brothers amongst them, and they would share the burden of mourning. Besides, I was nervous in Christina's company. When she looked across at me and smiled, I felt like a thief. An invader. In truth, I did not like myself very much. But work, I knew, would lift my spirits, even though that work was of a dubious kind. In time I took my leave, promising to visit again soon, though in my heart I doubted whether I would have the courage for a further encounter. I hurried to my car and I noticed how my thumb was trembling, syphon-poised.

Chapter 2

A flow of indecipherable verbiage tumbled out of Walter's brain on my second syphoning. I could make neither head nor tail of it. I attributed its waffle to a possible pre-death delirium, and that his last moment of clarity had been reserved for the moment of death itself. But, undaunted, I pressed on, gently and slowly, and soon, out of the gibberish, a few words took shape.

> *Please God. No afterlife. No second*
> *encounters. I could not face him again.*
> *Please don't manoeuvre it in Your cunning*
> *way. Already in this life, I die of shame. Is*
> *one death not enough?*

I whipped my fevered thumb off the button. I was shocked. I was indeed opening a can of worms and for a moment I wondered whether I had the stomach to carry my friend's guilt. But my curiosity overcame my fear and my thumb trembled once more.

> *No more fear. No more fear. Free for ever*
> *now from accusation.*

I made to remove my quivering trigger, and as I did so, another thought emerged.

I'm a little short on silver linings.

I had to sit down. The whole enterprise had begun to frighten me. That small and frozen globe of knowledge was clearly a minefield. I was sweating. I needed air. I replaced my quarry in the freezer and left the house. I needed a breathing space. I needed pause. I needed, above all, to sit quietly and have a serious board-meeting with myself. I shut my mind to all thoughts until I reached the river bank. I took some time to find a comfortable and secluded spot, postponing a decision which I knew would affect my whole life. At last I settled down and opened my reluctant mind to resolve.

First, I had to come clean with my motives. I had to cast aside all mitigation and finally to confess to myself that I was nothing more than a nosey-parker. But indeed I had cause. I had already unearthed enough information to warrant my curiosity and it would have been an act of sheer masochism not to satisfy it. I was human, after all. And in that failing lay perhaps another motive – I was coming squeakingly clean. Did I perhaps hope to purloin some of my friend's seductive ideas and appropriate them to my own work? Was I a thief, as well as a Peeping Tom? But that too I construed as human. Yet there was something else that troubled me. It was the *manner* of my snooping. I was staring through an open window, as opposed to a narrow keyhole. I was viewing the climax without having savoured the foreplay. I was prying the wrong way round. I thought of Walter and his sometimes scathing criticism of his contemporary writers. How many of them who had nothing at all to say, would fashion a technique of saying it, hoping that the technique itself would camouflage the lack of profound thought. Writing a novel backwards was one of these techniques and I realised suddenly that that was exactly what I was doing with my dear friend's thoughts. If for no other reason, I owed it to Walter to turn his brain upside down. Or the right way up. Depending on how one viewed the state of modern fiction. I owed my friend *chronology*. I would pay my dues. I would start at the beginning.

I hurried home. I hoped that my respect for calendar would

offset my meaner motives, and that, in that light, Walter would forgive me, and in time perhaps, I could learn to forgive myself. I opened my freezer and very gently held Walter in my hands. And caressed him, too, as I would never have done in his lifetime, though a passive caress always lay adrift between us. I turned the brain the right way up and stroked the virgin surface where no syphon had yet trod, and I felt like the very first moon-walker. And I trembled. I laid my syphon on the surface. I was about to discover the very first thought of that child who would grow to be a master. In view of my knowledge of his very last thought on this earth, I was prepared for a trivial first. So I was surprised when, after my virgin plundering, the following thought emerged.

It's not my fault that I'm not a girl.

The meaning of Walter's last thought had been abundantly clear, and moreover, further clarified by Christina's funeral rose. But I could make neither head nor tail of this primal thought. And if I could, God knows where it would lead. Yet I knew it was seminal. To such a thought attention must be paid. Attention by way of research and investigation. But I am a man lazy by nature and the prospect did not please me. Yet if I were not prepared to investigate, my friend's thought-patterns would be meaningless. I stared at Walter's world and wondered how I could profit by it. The thought crossed my mind to defrost and bury Walter once and for all, and to return to my painful and now aging writer's block. I dared to recall how many years had passed since I had penned a line. Twelve almost, a block creeping into its teens. Then a thought nudged me, gently at first, and then struck me with a force so joyous that I laughed aloud. I would write a novel based on Walter's thoughts. I would use each one as a signpost to the plot, a plot of Walter's secret life. Bugger the research. Let others make do with biography. My story would be the truest form of fiction ever written. Walter, as I have already pointed out, was an enabler, and the bequest of his skull, though purloined, had broken my long-standing and dreary writer's block. I was elated. I had to celebrate. I had to treat myself a little.

So I went to my piano. Another hobby of mine. Between the woods and the ivories I was able to while away a good deal of my time. I used both pursuits as postponements to writing, and in the course of my age-long writer's block, I became an expert carpenter and no mean pianist.

I rationed myself to one movement of a Schubert sonata and then I settled down at my desk. Then rose again. I had to return Walter to the freezer. I had enough material to get myself started. Then I returned to my desk. I decided I needed coffee. Another postponement. That done, I forced myself to sit down. I prayed for the phone to ring or for someone to come to the door. But all was silent. I had absolutely nothing else to do with my life but to make a start on a novel. I picked up my fountain-pen. There was still a chance, I hoped, that the ink had run dry. But the black dye oozed with urgency. It was not to be denied. So I threw in the sponge and registered myself as one of the working novelists of the time. Thank you Walter.

UNTITLED

Chapter One

Mrs Berry was planting the first of the primroses when she went into labour. She knew the pains. This child would be her third. And the last, she prayed. She wasn't particularly fond of children.

She preferred to look after her garden. Flowers and vegetables didn't answer back. In her garden she exercised complete control. She stood up wearily and went to the phone. Tom would have to come back from the office and see to the boys when they came home from school. She could get herself to the hospital. She hoped this one would be a girl, or Tom would insist on trying again. But she would put her foot down. Three was enough. Of whatever gender.

By the time Mrs Berry reached the hospital, her labour was well under way. She was taken straight to the delivery room and helped to put on a white hospital gown. Then white socks to balance the temperature of her extremities. The sheets were white and the pillows, and the nurses' starched aprons, and Mrs Berry, being a woman of order, was pleased with the whiteness of it all. When the doctor arrived to examine her, he wore a pair of white rubber gloves, and that pleased her too. The colour reminded her of the lilies that she had left unbedded in the earth. If it was a girl, she decided, she would call her Lily. But little Walter, being a breech baby, proclaimed his gender before any formal introduction. Mrs Berry made no attempt to hide her disappointment.

'Blast,' she said when they told her, and certainly her curse lay within little Walter's earshot. Poor little Walter. It was not a promising beginning.

He arrived home to a cool reception. Both his brothers had wanted a little sister, and Mr Berry was too disgusted to make any comment at all. In his infant years, Walter was fed, changed, and generally seen to. He was the passive object of his mother's dutiful attention and his father's out-and-out indifference. His growth was an offensive inevitability.

His crawling years were spent largely in the garden beside his weeding mother, so that an eye could be kept on him. One day, Mrs Berry, in an unaccountable fit of maternal aberration, cuddled him, and he screamed so loudly for his release, that she never attempted it again. Because, for little Walter, a gentle touch, leave alone a cuddle, was quite outside the norm, and his little body rejected it for the sake of its own survival. He was alone most of the day, caged in a play-pen, where the bars kept an eye on him. He rarely cried, for he knew that crying would draw attention, and he had learned to do without it. The family had cast him in the role of outsider. And he had obliged them. He would fend for himself. And as he grew into movement and speech, he . . .

I sensed that I was running away with myself. I had to stick to the facts, or, to be more precise, the thoughts. A certain license was allowed me, to be sure, but I was not entirely free to invent my own fiction. Even if I had been able. This was Walter's story and I had to refer to his guidelines. I made for my freezer, but on the way, I could not resist the final movement of the Schubert sonata. I was entitled to a treat after all. And more coffee too.

After all my postponements, I reached for my syphon and resumed my explorations. For a while, the thoughts were monosyllabic, parrot-like, the monkey-language of imitation.

Wet. Baby. Boy. Red. Green. Yell . . .

It was clear that Walter had choked on that liverish hue. There followed a stream of such imitation and it seemed that Walter had a voracious appetite for vocabulary. It was probably the only gift his mother could give him. Gradually one word became two. An adjective surfaced and later on, a verb. That was the turning-point. The *doing* word. The whole sentence could not be far behind. And then it came. Loud and clear. And it fairly floored me.

> *Always in the garden. Always in my pen. I*
> *am a bird in a cage that hangs on the*
> *branch of a tree.*

I was stunned. I thought *I* had invented the garden. I thought I had *imagined* Mrs Berry's hobby. Then, swiftly, I recalled one of Walter's lessons. Never research, he had advised me. Write your book and do the research later. Simply to see if you've got it right. And more often than not, you have.

I was beginning to feel like a real writer. I gave swift thanks to Walter and syphoned on. I had no clue as to how old Walter was at the time of the caged bird thought. I did notice though, a small shrinkage in the brain which indicated that some Walter years had been syphoned away. And then my deduction was confirmed in his next decipherable thought.

> *I am ten today, but nobody takes any*
> *notice. When I grow up I want to die.*

This poor thought saddened me, and suddenly I missed Walter terribly. The idea that he had first to grow up before he could decently die, that it would be almost rude to do otherwise, was a childlike one, but the very notion of death on his tenth birthday, hinted at a past of accumulated despair. And what followed seemed to validate that thought.

> *My father is kissing a lady who is not my*
> *mother.*

I felt ready now to resume my novel. I refrained from further syphoning which might have blunted my powers of invention, and after another coffee, I had a go at a very short Scarlatti sonata, one of the first, and there are five hundred and fifty-five of them. Enough to see me through to the end of my autobiopsy. I took my pen and picked up where I had left off.

> . . . and as he grew into movement and speech, he found ways of cutting himself off from a family that clearly didn't want him. He took long and solitary walks through the fields that surrounded his house, and other people's gardens, untended by his mother's obsession. He climbed trees and freely hung from the branches where once he had swayed as a caged bird. One morning he awoke, knowing it was his birthday. He was ten years' distance from innocence. He wondered whether anybody in the household would acknowledge it. And if not, should he

draw attention to it himself. Breakfast passed with no reference to the day, and Walter was too proud to hint at it. From the small conversation around the table, it was clear that friends were coming to dinner that evening. His parents' friends. A celebration that had nothing to do with his birthday. Though he had expected nothing from his family, he could not deny his disappointment. School was a relief. He had friends there. William, his best friend, was waiting at the gate and Walter could not help but off-load the burden of his first decade.

'It's my birthday today,' he said.

'What d'you get?'

The question scudded like an arrow. Walter hesitated. He regretted having mentioned his birthday at all. Then, suddenly inspired, he listed those things that he had wished for. He was selective and cunningly omitted those that for some reason were unobtainable. 'I got a wireless from my aunt, and an Arsenal football, and a torch, and a Swiss army knife.' He thought it would be politic to omit the bicycle, for that, more than all the others, would have to declare itself.

'Lucky you,' William said. 'Aren't you having a party?'

'I'm going out with them tonight.'

'Where?'

'It's a surprise,' Walter said quickly. 'I'll tell you tomorrow.' By the morning he would have dreamt up a night on the town. And one that could not be investigated. He decided not to mention his birthday to anybody else, and even to try and forget it himself. But William spread the word about, and he was obliged to repeat his present list to all and sundry.

'You forgot the Swiss army knife,' William interrupted. 'And you didn't tell me about the cricket bat.'

'I forgot,' Walter said, and he realised that, to be a good liar, one had to have a good memory. He decided to train that sense of recall, for he sensed that his life would be a mendacious one, and a good memory would be its handiest support.

At playtime, his friends surrounded him and tossed

18

him ten times in the air, and that tossing was the only tangible celebration that marked his tenth birthday.

That evening Mrs Berry insisted on an early night for the boys. She blackmailed them with crisps and chocolate. As she doled out Walter's ration, she slapped an extra packet of crisps on his bribe.

'That's because it's your birthday,' she said.

Walter's little heart swelled with gratitude. Despite the meanness of her offering, she had, at least, acknowledged his day. At her reminder, his brothers too, Hugh and Peter, offered their votes, and even donated an off-key rendering of 'Happy Birthday'. Walter went gratefully to bed. It took little to satisfy him, and he fell asleep almost immediately, lulled by the sudden, if belated attention he had drawn.

But later, he woke up, nagged by a raging thirst. That extra packet of crisps had turned out to be less of a bonus. He had a craving for a glass of milk. He crept out onto the landing and heard the hum of conversation from below. He looked at the clock in the hall. 12.15. His birthday was over, and if he were caught, he could expect no allowance. He knew that the stairs to the hall creaked, so he slid silently down the banister, then lowered himself into the carpeted hall. The kitchen door was ajar. His only remaining hurdle was the opening of the refrigerator door.

But that door was blocked, together with the milk within. Leaning against it was a lady. She wore a yellow dress. A stranger in a yellow dress. Walter could not see her face, for it was shielded by his father's very own. Walter withdrew from the kitchen threshold, so that there was no chance of his being seen, but he kept the terrible sin in his line of vision. He watched, appalled and fascinated.

The kiss was noisy and full of water, and he hoped that they could not hear it in the dining-room. He watched as his father lowered his one hand to the stranger's thigh, keeping his lips on hers all the while, and as he raised the stranger's yellow skirt and fumbled with himself, and a great rod emerged.

Walter turned away and tip-toed back into the hall. He climbed the stairs, careless of their creaking, and went to the bathroom where he had to be satisfied with a glass of water. Then he sat on the rim of the bath-tub, and wondered how he ought to be feeling.

Hatred was in order. Anger too. That was for his father, and the stranger lady, whoever she was. Pity was in order as well. Pity for his mother. But that feeling he could not summon. On the contrary. Serves her right, he thought, and he was thrilled with the deception. He wondered whether he should tell his brothers, but decided against it. He wanted something of his very own. Something that no-one else had. A secret. A secret so terrible that its divulging value was supreme. It gave him a certain power over his mother and he would not shrink to use it at the appropriate time. He smiled. He couldn't have hoped for a better birthday present.

At breakfast next morning, there were no signs of any change. Walter took some delight in staring at his father with what he hoped was a look of accusation. Mr Berry was unnerved.

'What are you staring at?' he shouted.

'I wasn't staring. I was day-dreaming.'

Nevertheless, Walter continued to stare at him, and his father was obliged to leave early for the office. Walter was pleased with the results of his manoeuvre. He would continue to give his father a bad time. It was fun. He skipped all the way to school and slowed down only when he saw William at the gate, standing there, awaiting his story of his night on the town.

'I didn't go out,' Walter said, without even waiting for William's questioning. 'My mother fell down and broke her leg.'

It was his biggest fiction to date and it was probably in that moment that the ten-year-old Walter decided that there was nothing he could do with his life other than to become a novelist. He looked forward to home-time and to staring at his father.

But that night his father came home from the office very late. So he stared at his mother instead. Though he had to admit that the maternal target was less fun. But tomorrow was Saturday and he would have a whole weekend to day-dream in his father's face.

He stared through breakfast, lunch and supper. His father remained silent, as if afraid of making an issue of the affront. He maintained that silence throughout the Sunday breakfast and lunch. But in the middle of Sunday supper, Mr Berry blew. He rose from the table, his face varicose-flushed, and dared the question.

'Why d'you keep staring at me, you bully?'

'Don't you *know*?' Walter asked. His tone of surprise was laced with innocence.

Then Mr Berry knew that, somehow or other, his peccadillo had been discovered and he reached across the table and punched Walter's face into an angry nose-bleed. The black eye would not blossom until the morning. Mrs Berry stared at her husband, bewildered by what seemed to her an unwarranted display of rage. But she did not rise from her seat. She simply reached for her handkerchief and passed it to her youngest and unwanted son, and told him to tidy himself up. This passivity on her part did nothing to assuage the outrage that boiled in Walter's heart. He wondered whether now was the time to spill the beans. Whether this was a propitious moment. He heard his brothers giggling and it was their laughter that finally spilt his secret. With what was left of his sight, he stared at his mother.

'I saw him,' he said, and he was surprised at the strength in his voice. He sensed that he must get his secret over quickly in case that strength left him. He took a deep breath but he never took his eyes off his mother. 'I saw him, with a lady who came to dinner that night. On my birthday,' he hastened to add, hoping that would deepen the shame. 'Against the fridge,' he went on. 'And he was kissing her, and he had his thing out and he stuck it into her and he was doing her.'

Now it was all out. All of it, and he felt suddenly weak. He looked at the astonished faces round the table and felt that it would be politic to go to his room and to leave his so-called family to deal with the chaos he had wrought. He got into his bed, and but for his shoes, fully dressed. He ached to sleep, but first he had to fashion a tale for William that would explain away his black eye. He heard his brothers go to their rooms, giggling still. They had clearly been sent from the table. He listened to the echoes of raucous argument from downstairs, but he was too indifferent to eavesdrop. And too tired too. He fell quickly asleep, leaving the house to smoulder in its own cruelty.

In the morning, Mr Berry did not appear at the silent breakfast table. The question, 'Where is Dad?' burned on each boy's lips, but both Peter and Hugh were fearful of the answer. But not Walter. He considered that he had already burned his boats and he had nothing more to lose. And he had, after all, initiated the drama. He was entitled to know its dénouement.

'Where's Dad?' he almost shouted.

'He's gone,' Mrs Berry said.

'To the office?' Hugh dared.

'He's gone for good. And he won't be coming back.' Mrs Berry rose from her seat. She was trembling. Hugh and Peter cowered. But Walter stared at her. She turned on him and slapped him across the ear. 'And it's all your fault,' she screamed at him.

My phone rang, and I was glad of it. Whoever it was, it was a well-timed call. I had come to the end of Walter's last thought. I had validated it as well as I was able. Guided by the dress colour of his father's mistress, I had elucidated his life-long aversion to yellow. I needed a break, and I picked up the receiver with gratitude. But it was a call I could happily have done without. My mother. When I hear her voice, my stomach curdles. But I know that it is *my* stomach, and *my* guilt. No doubt her stomach is fluttering too, and no doubt with her fear of my reaction to her voice. For I have fed that fear in her, already well-nourished enough by my father. She must notice how my voice drops a few decibels on hearing hers. I'm sorry for all that, but I cannot help myself. Things are not good between us, and haven't been for some time. I often wish I had a brother or sister to share the burdens of siblinghood. But as an only child, I must bear them alone.

'How are you Martin?' she said.

The use of my name should betoken affection of some kind, but from her mouth, its tone is accusatory. At least, that's how I read it. My poor mother. In my ear, every word she says is loaded.

'I'm fine,' I said, which I would say to her in any circumstances, for it is a reply that does not require further investigation.

'I haven't seen you for nearly two weeks.' Her voice is gentle and oozes the epic blackmail of frailty.

'I've been busy,' I said.

'Busy doing what?'

I parried. If I were to say, 'Look Mother, I'm syphoning off a man's brain,' she wouldn't have put it past me. She has never thought too highly of my character. One doesn't risk the truth with my mother.

'I'm writing,' I said. I didn't have to tell her how or what.

'Writing?'

My mother didn't have to say very much. The mere tone of one single word carried its own myriad sub-titling.

'Yes,' I affirmed. 'Writing.'

'That's nice,' she said. Then after a pause, 'When are you coming to see me?'

'I'll come now if you like. I'll come for tea.' I don't know why I said it, but I had nothing else to do and I needed a break. Besides, a weekly visit was obligatory and I would go and get it over with.

My mother lives in fine style. My father sees to that. Money, since he has it in plenty, is the easiest way to ease his conscience, and this he gives her with some relief and my poor mother doesn't have the freedom to refuse. Thus her dependence on my father is assured. She is in his thrall, as she was when she was married to him. On my way to her house, I rehearse my answers to the questions I know she will ask. She will first talk about trivia, the price of butter, or how difficult it is to get good service nowadays. Thus she will warm to her major theme, and after a decent interval, she will ask whether I have seen my father. She will ask that question in a nonchalant tone, throwing off its urgency, for it is indeed urgent enough and it is the only answer of mine that concerns her in my weekly visits. I sometimes think it is the only reason that she wishes to see me.

I pulled into the driveway and rang the bell. The chimes got on my nerves a little. Violet, the trusty maid of long standing, opened the door.

'Good afternoon, Master Martin,' she said and she held out her hands to take the hat and the coat that I did not wear. I felt I was in another century.

'Madame is in the drawing-room,' she said.

I made my way there through the large marble hall.

'Hullo Mother,' I called. I was determined to be cheerful.

She didn't answer of course. It's not done to shout and I had to wait until I reached her chair before she would acknowledge me. She rang a little bell on the table, a signal for the tea to be brought, then she looked up and smiled. I kissed her forehead. That's about as far as I've ever been able to go.

'How are you Mother?' I asked. 'You look well.'

'I'm the same,' she said.

And indeed she was. Exactly the same as she has been every year for the whole fifteen years since my father left her. The years and the bitterness have aged her, and when I look at her face, I try not to pity her. For that pity would only serve to ignite a rage against my father with whom I have achieved a relationship of comfortable indifference.

Violet brought in the tea-tray. The silver-ware of my child-hood and the Spode china. Little has changed in the house where I was born. Where I was father-beaten and mother-bribed. I thought of Walter then, and for the first time I realised how similar our childhoods had been. 'Walter died,' I told my mother. 'Two weeks ago.' Thus I postponed the chat about the price of butter and service, and she was thrown a little.

'I know,' she said. 'I read it in the papers.'

She made no comment after that. I resented the fact that she did not utter a word of sympathy for my loss, yet she knew that Walter was my closest friend.

'Is that too weak for you?' she said, pouring the tea, and without waiting for my reply, 'I don't know what they do to tea nowadays. It doesn't have the real tea taste it used to have.'

'Nothing is the same, Mother,' I said. I prepared myself for further questioning. And it came soon enough. But first she passed me a buttered scone as a sweetener. Then came straight to the point.

'Have you seen your Father?' she said, pouring her own tea the while.

'No,' I said. Which was true. 'I had to arrange Walter's funeral. I was too busy.' I was determined to force a little sympathy out of her. But nothing was forthcoming.

'Did you speak to him then?' she persisted.

'Yes.'

She did not ask how he was. She was not supposed to show an interest in his welfare.

But I satisfied her. 'He's well,' I said. 'He's going on holiday,' I offered. Then regretted it, for it was like another knife in a fifteen-year-old wound. I have a streak of cruelty in me and my mother is a favourite target of mine. I cannot help myself. I need to punish her. I need to punish her for her weakness. For her fear. For not leaving my father because she was afraid. For ratifying his ridiculous expectations of his son because she feared his disesteem. If there is a villain in this piece, it is my father. Yet with him I have an adequate relationship. A relationship compounded less of affection than controlled contempt. You see, I had won the battle with my father. The lines were drawn. He wanted me to go into his thriving accountancy business. I simply refused. No argument. But with my mother, there was no concrete battle between us. No concrete cause. It was like fighting an echo.

25

Like warring with the descant of my father's continuing disapproval. My father poured scorn on my writing ambitions. The phrase 'creative accounting', was never far from his lips, as if my imagination could be adequately fed by an income-tax return. And my mother would nod, without smiling.

'You're a great disappointment to me,' he would say, over and over again, and I only had to view the buckle-scars on my back to care not a fig for his disappointment. And to gladly do without his damned approval. But my mother had left no visible scars, and words and cruelty were still viable between us. Or at least on my part. My mother maintained the blackmail wall of silence.

'Those are nice scones,' I said, attempting to change the subject. 'Did you make them?'

'Violet made them. You know I don't cook any more.'

I heard the dire sub-titling and I was anxious to get away. I had done my duty, yet there was no relief in it. When I left, I would resolve to do better next time, but since this was a decision I took after almost every visit, I knew myself to be unreliable. I kissed her once more on the forehead, and I fled, not even bothering to say goodbye to Violet or to wait for her to see me to the door. When I reached home, a pall of depression overcame me and I went early to bed and dreamed of files and ledgers.

Chapter 3

I slept late the next morning to compensate for my frequent and fearful midnight wakings. I got up, refreshed, and went straight to my kitchen. After coffee, I felt no need to procrastinate. Scarlatti could wait. I was anxious to go a-syphoning. I enjoyed that aspect of my pursuit more than any other. It was as if Walter was doing the work for me, which in a way he was, giving me the guidelines to the next episode in his story. I was excited. I wondered, as I had wondered before, whether I had invented what turned out to have actually happened. And my dear Walter's next thought confirmed it.

> My mother shouts at me all day. She
> thinks I am her husband. She was my
> father's doormat and now I am hers. If I
> ever grow up, I vow I shall never have
> children.

And he didn't. That much I knew. Amanda was his step-daughter. Christina Berry had been married before and she and Walter had no further offspring. So Walter had kept his vows. I syphoned further. A string of unintelligible waffling emerged, but much of it I deciphered as weeping. For thoughts can weep too, without words. But soon the cause of his tears wept its words aloud.

> I have slept all night with Death and I
> think I have caught it.

I was puzzled. Did Walter mean that he had trapped Death and conquered it, or did he think that death was a disease which, during the night, he had contracted? Both possibilities offered up much speculation and both were generous sign-posts to the direction my novel should now take. So I put Walter back in the freezer and once again picked up my pen.

... 'And it's all your fault,' she screamed at him.

Hugh and Peter giggled with relief. They formed a united front of innocence against their younger brother's palpable guilt. They said nothing and their very silence accused him.

'It's all your fault,' his mother said again.

Walter was bewildered. Perhaps all this was adult logic that he was too young to understand.

'But *I* didn't do it,' he protested.

The brothers broke their silence. Or at least one of them. 'But you *told*,' Peter said.

Again the logic defeated him, for now it clearly wasn't an adult one. So his father's doing was not the crime. It was his son's telling of it. But whoever was to blame, he understood that a great deal of damage had been done. The damage of division and family break-up.

Over the next few weeks, this division was manifest in sundry ways. Each night the boys were sent early to bed. Mrs Berry's continual and outraged weeping brooked no argument. The house was restless and full of noise. One night Walter lay awake and listened to a new, echoing din from his parents' bedroom. Drawers and cupboards opening and shut, and the furious dropping of offending hangers. In the morning the cause of all the nocturnal cacophony became clear. On his way to school Walter passed the dustbins in the lane at the back of the house. And there, fully exposed, with no attempt at disguise, were all the trappings and the trimmings of his father. A shirt-tail spilt over the black plastic, an odd tie and sock had loosened their moorings, and a new tweed jacket was severed at one elbow, as if his father had been an amputee. And that, no doubt, Walter thought, was what his mother wished him. For a moment he pitied his father and had no wish to stare at him any more. His mother had buried him once and for all. Perhaps now there would be some purchase in staring at *her*.

When he came home from school that day, he found locksmiths at work on the windows and doors.

'So that your father can never come back,' Mrs Berry growled at her children. 'He'd have to be a magician to get into this house.'

Their home was indeed a fortress, Walter thought, and his mother had only succeeded in imprisoning herself.

For the most part of the days that followed, there was silence, broken only by the sound of Mrs Berry's strangulated sobbing which the children heard on their return from school. Hugh and Peter accommodated their pain in non-stop giggling, but Walter sobbed on his own in sympathy, because he was convinced that he was the cause of his mother's tears. By whatever logic, they had all told him so. Each morning he would pick up the post and lay it at her place at the breakfast-table. Some letters, he noticed, were addressed to his father. Others were official looking, with windowed envelopes. At breakfast his mother would sort the post, and those addressed to her errant husband were ostentatiously torn in two, in a kind of display, so that the children were left in no doubt as to their father's status. The others, the official ones, she put aside, clearly to read after the children had left for school.

Sitting at his desk, his teacher's voice a background drone, Walter wondered what his mother was doing. Whatever it was, he knew that it was tear-stained. She was perhaps opening the letters that she'd kept for her privacy. Perhaps she was on the telephone abusing his father to her few friends. Or perhaps she was scouring the house for any contaminated vestige of him. And sobbing all the while. He heard his name called. And sharply.

'Berry! What is the answer?'

'To what?' he said in a dream.

He was sent to the headmaster's study.

'What's the matter with you Berry?' Mr Lucas asked. 'Lately your teachers have been reporting that you seem in another world. Is anything troubling you?'

'My father died,' Walter said without hesitation.

The headmaster was somewhat taken aback. 'But . . . but you're at school. And your brothers too.'

'It's not *their* father,' Walter said.

'But surely you're all of one family.'

'But it's *me* he left. It's me he's left with her.'

'Who's her?' Mr Lucas asked, careless of grammar.

'My mother.'

This was all beyond the headmaster's understanding. The boy seemed to him to be talking in riddles. He was known amongst the staff to be a boy of vivid imagination, but Mr Lucas found it more comfortable to think of him as an outright liar. He felt suddenly angry.

'How did your father die?' he asked.

'Overnight.' Walter's answer was prompt. 'He was gone in the morning.'

The riddle was compounded. 'When was the funeral?' Mr Lucas shot at him. There could be no conundrum in the answer to that question.

'Now,' Walter said at once, 'and it will be going on for a long time.'

The headmaster was once more flummoxed. He threw in the sponge and decided the boy must see a psychiatrist. But before making that arrangement, he thought he might phone Mrs Berry and in a series of oblique questions, discover whether she was, or was not, a widow. He dismissed Walter and dialled the Berry number.

The phone was answered scarcely before the first ring had faded and the acknowledging voice was clearly bereaved. Its tone was low and hopeless and for a moment Mr Lucas sensed that Walter had indeed told the truth.

'Mrs Berry,' he said, 'I'm a little worried about Walter.'

'What's the matter with him?' Mrs Berry said with slight irritation.

Walter was the last person she intended to worry about.

'He's behaving very strangely. He actually told me his father had died.'

'Rubbish!' Mrs Berry screamed. Her riposte was like gunshot in his ear.

'Then there's no truth in it?' Mr Lucas asked.

'Of course not.' Mrs Berry actually managed a laugh though the headmaster thought it a shade hysterical. 'He's very much alive. I just spoke to him in his office. And we shall be going out together tonight,' she added for good measure. For she would scotch any rumours that her treacherous youngest son had planted. 'No, he's not dead,' she repeated. 'He's very much alive and kicking.' Her voice faltered on this last phrase as she heard its sad truth, and the life and the kicking from which she was now excluded. She would deal with Walter when he came home.

The headmaster, for his part, was satisfied. He now had no need to resort to the school psychiatrist whose profession, in any case, he didn't trust. Young Walter Berry was an out-and-out liar, and that was the long and short of it.

Mrs Berry was waiting for Walter to come home from school. She derived a sneaking pleasure from the waiting, and the rehearsal of how she would deal with him. She went out to meet him at the gate, then dragged him into the house, for her onslaught was not for neighbours any more than was her cuckolding.

'Your headmaster phoned me,' she shouted at him. She defined her witness straight away. 'You told him your father was dead.'

'Well he is, isn't he. In a way. He's gone, and he's not coming back. You said so yourself. *And* you buried his clothes,' he added for good measure.

'How dare you say your father is dead,' she said. 'Is that what you would like?'

'Wouldn't *you*?' he dared ask her. He spoke to her as one of equal years and it was that that riled her. That and the near truth of what he had said and his wisdom that he should know it. So she hit him for his insight, and

31

Walter became a child again, not understanding how his mother could defend a man who had treated her so shabbily. He was angry and he stared at her, his fixed gaze his only weapon. But guiltless as she was, it made no mark on her.

The silence continued to reign in the house, with the same morning ritual of letter-shredding. Then one day, for no reason that Walter could ascertain, his mother was kind to him, and that kindness continued for many days. Then at last she brought some news to the breakfast-table that in some way, in Walter's mind, might have given her kindness cause.

'You're going to boarding school,' she announced. 'Not you, Walter. Just Hugh and Peter. I need one of you at home for company.' She attempted a little laugh at this last thrust, a giggle that pleaded with him for his understanding.

Walter was crestfallen. He envied his brothers that they could escape from the terrible silence of the house. He would not miss them. For all the connection they had with him, they need not have been there at all. But what frightened him was the prospect of being alone with his mother, and of how she would use him. He knew that his company was the last thing she sought. All she needed was a target, a butt for her fury, her resentment and her downright need for revenge. His future terrified him. He pleaded with his mother to let him go, not so much to the boarding school but out of the prison that she would make for him. But she refused, blaming his father who, she said, was not willing to foot the bill for three sets of school fees. She lost no time in shifting the blame where she pretended it belonged, and that would be the pattern of her bitterness for the rest of her life.

It had been some weeks since the children had seen their father. They missed him, even Walter, and they longed for a visit, but all were afraid to suggest it to their mother. Walter, as the doer of everybody's dirty work, was delegated to make the request. He met with a flat refusal. Not loud, but whispered, which rendered it irrevocable. He did not ask again.

Hugh and Peter were shipped off to their boarding school with no paternal farewell. Mrs Berry and Walter stood together on the station platform. Hugh and Peter were at pains to hide the joy and excitement of their escape, else it hurt those they left behind. Not Walter, but their mother, whom they were sorry for, so they resorted to their time-honoured cover-up for everything – the giggle – and they giggled their farewells as the train shed the platform. It had long been out of sight, but still they stood there, the unwilling mother and her reluctant son. Then suddenly she turned and took Walter's arm. 'Let's go to a restaurant and treat ourselves to lunch,' she said. That kindness again, but this time it sounded ominously serious.

Walter's dining-out experiences had hitherto been confined to fish and chip shops and ice-cream parlours. This was to be his first experience of a proper restaurant, and Mrs Berry was at pains to choose a classy one. It was indeed the treat she had promised, but Walter was so acutely aware of her kindness that he had difficulty in savouring it. She was trying to compensate him for his father's unwillingness to send him to boarding school. He knew that, and he could not help fearing the price he would have to pay for the treat and he wondered whether there were more treats to come and whether their prices would escalate. What relish he tasted from the lavish food, which the waiter placed before him, he was at pains to hide from its donor. He concentrated on it, taking it slowly, making of it an event, one that would absolve the need for conversation. Few words had passed between them. Yet he dreaded that she might ask him to elaborate on the tale that he had told, that tale from which all chaos had erupted. He would have no difficulty in repeating it. That yellow dress pressed against the refrigerator, and the red rod that had pierced its hue, was an image that was forever imprinted on his retina. He knew it would blur his vision till the end of his days. But he did not want to express it. Words only served to reinforce the image, to dazzle him, and even to re-awaken in his parched throat that thirst that he could not assuage. That thirst that he had gone to the kitchen to slake, and its quenching that the yellow dress had denied. Even now, with his mouth full of chicken, he felt the thirst come upon him, and he heard her question, that first instalment of her kindness-price.

'Tell me again what you saw in the kitchen,' she was saying.

He swallowed. 'I've told you already,' he said. 'I don't want to tell you again. I don't like to think about it.' He went quickly back to his chicken.

But his mother persevered. 'Of course you don't, Walter,' she said. 'It was too disgusting. Her and him. And what he did to her. And what she let him do.' If Walter wouldn't tell her, she would take the filthy words out of his mouth herself. 'Isn't that right?' she almost shouted.

He nodded. Her shrill embarrassed him. But his silence riled her.

'Well isn't that right?' she repeated.

'I suppose so.' He wondered how much longer she could milk the subject. Surely by now it had run dry. And from the silence that followed, he knew it had, and its dryness had cracked into the bitterness that gnawed at her heart and brought tears to her eyes. Walter knew they were there, but he did not want to look at them, else they would move him to pity. He knew that if he fell into that trap he would be forever her prisoner. His appetite suddenly waned. He could barely finish his chicken and he could not be tempted to a dessert.

'I don't wonder you've lost your appetite,' his mother said. 'That talk about your father. He has spoiled all our appetites.' Thus she included him in her own rejection and that dictated the ensuing pattern of their relationship.

The house was different without Hugh and Peter. It was even more silent and more of a prison. Walter felt himself in solitary, a condition that would not have troubled him had not his mother continually disturbed it. He looked forward to school as never before, for it was an escape from the manic kindness of his mother. Weekends were purgatory. Once he dared to ask her if he could visit his father. He waited for tears, and hoped, as he always did, that they would no longer affect him. But despite their frequency and regularity, he was never to be immune. And through them, she gave him her 'No'.

'But *when* can I see him? He's my father. Whatever he's done.'

'So you're on his side,' she accused him.

'It's got nothing to do with me. It's not my business,' Walter said. 'I'm entitled to see him.'

She turned away. 'You'll see him when the divorce is settled. The Judge will decide.'

'Is he coming to Parents' Day?'

The phrase made her shudder. It was a nightmare phrase that had disturbed her sleep ever since the notice had arrived. In her infrequent and abrasive communications with her husband, she had taken care not to mention it. If his absence was noticed, she would say that he was away on business. But she knew that he was cunning enough to enquire of the school, since Parents' Day was a yearly event and took place shortly before the end of term. She dreaded such a meeting for she feared her replacement would be by his side. He was cruel enough for that. To masquerade her as a parent, and thus replace her two-fold. She shivered at the thought of it.

'Does he know about it? Will he be coming?' Walter insisted.

'Of course he knows,' she said.

'Where does he live?'

'I don't know.' It was one of the very few truths she had told. For indeed, she had no idea where her husband was living. Her contact with him was on his office telephone. She had swallowed her pride and enquired of the woman's husband. He had, after all, sat at her dinner table. But he, pride-swallowing too, had no idea of his wife's whereabouts, and presumed that wherever they were, she and Mr Berry were together.

'If he's there, I'm going to talk to him,' Walter said. He hoped his voice wasn't threatening.

'Only if he's alone,' his mother said. 'If that slut is with him, I forbid you to go near. D'you hear me, Walter?' she raised her voice. 'I absolutely forbid it.' She put her arm around him to offset her angry tone. 'Shall we go to the pictures before supper?' she said.

'I can't. I've got homework.' He had already finished what little homework he had but he couldn't tolerate another kindness. He wondered why he insisted so on seeing his father. He didn't like him very much. He never had, and his dislike had nothing to do with the manner of his departure. No. He was insisting on seeing him merely on principle. A son had the right to see his father whether he wanted to or not.

He went early to bed that night, but he could not sleep. His mother's sobbing echoed up the stairs. And her pottering. Her endless pottering. He hoped his father wouldn't come to Parents' Day, and if he must, he prayed fervently that he would come alone. He rehearsed how he should behave towards him. Should he smile or should he glower? Should he kiss him or spit in his face? Or should he just stare at him? But most of all, should he say and do as *he* pleased, or was he obliged to be his mother's mouthpiece? He turned and tossed in his bed, racked with his dilemma. After a while he heard his mother climb the stairs. Quickly he closed his eyes and feigned sleep. He heard her open his door and creep over to his bed. Then he felt her lips on his cheek and the sour and sorrowful smell of whisky as she withdrew. He waited until he heard the door close then he let his hot tears flow from his aching heart.

Mrs Berry had always looked forward to Parents' Day. Her boys had done well at the school. Even Walter had given no trouble, so there was no embarrassment in confronting their teachers. And she had had her husband at her side. It *looked* right, and others' opinions were of the utmost importance to her. But this year it would be very different. There would be no glowing reports on Hugh and Peter and God knows what embarrassments she would have to endure regarding her youngest, unpredictable son. And she would have to face them alone, with others watching her and wondering why she had no support. It was this latter that troubled her the most, and she rehearsed to herself what excuses she could make for his absence should he decide not to attend. Illness was a possibility. It was also wishful thinking. But the conversation that would ensue would embrace prognosis and sympathy, and both were too complicated to handle. She decided she would say he was out of town on business. Undiscussible. Then she had to entertain the possibility that he might after all, attend. If he were alone, she would nudge to his side to give a public appearance of togetherness. She dared not think that *she* might be with him. She could never rehearse that eventuality, and she set about busying herself with preparation. She poured herself a drink. She was slightly disturbed at the growing frequency of this habit. She looked at her watch. It was ten o'clock in the morning. He'll come back and I'll give it up, she thought. She would not let it worry her. She fortified herself more than adequately, and then she got on with her dressing.

At school the boys were lined up in the assembly hall. It was their last practice of the school song, that with which they would greet the parents. Walter was nervous. He was anxious to get it over with, then he could hide himself in a corner and watch for the arrival or otherwise of his father. But after the rehearsal he was not able to get away. He was called to the headmaster's office. There was a message for him from his father.

'Your father rang, Berry, to say that he would be late and that you should wait for him,' Mr Lucas said. 'I suppose your mother would wish to be told. I shall leave that to you.'

Did he know, or didn't he? Walter wondered. As he was leaving, 'Are you alright, Berry?' Mr Lucas asked.

'Yes Sir,' Walter said quickly.

He went into the playground, debating to himself whether or not to tell his mother. When he saw her arrive, he quickly hid himself. She was smartly dressed and that pleased him. And it moved him too, for nowadays she rarely took care with her appearance. He noticed too how wary she seemed, how she searched among the faces in the crowd and he knew it was not himself that she sought. He decided not to give her his father's message. He feared her sad and terrified reaction. He moved in her direction. I'll be kind to her, he decided. I'll try and make it up to her. Thus they colluded with kindness, a kindness they both knew was not for its own sake. She stooped to kiss him and he wondered at her strong peppermint breath. He escorted her to the assembly hall and suggested a seat in the front row. But she preferred the back, she said. Sitting in the front would give her neck-ache, but Walter knew that she wanted a vantage point from which she could view the arrivals. He left her sitting there while he went to join the choir. He himself was in the front row, being one of the smallest of the boys, and he had a good view of her and her wary searching. He kept his eye on her during the whole of the school song rendering, by way of remote protection. During the headmaster's speech, he kept his eye on the door as he knew she was doing, though more relaxed now, thinking that it was too late for her errant husband to put in an appearance. At the end of the speeches, she even smiled, and walked amongst the other parents.

Around about the hall, teachers stood and made themselves available. Walter jumped down from the platform and rushed to her side. And as he did so, he saw his father enter from the back of the hall. And mercifully he was alone. He stared at him for a while, then saw that his mother was already in conversation with his English teacher. He went to her side.

'Mr Berry not with you today?' Mr Harringay asked.

'No,' his mother said. 'He's abroad. On business.'

Walter gasped. 'Away' would have been enough. 'Abroad' was taking matters a little too far. His father was very much a stay-at-home. Well, almost. He doubted whether he even had a passport. He saw his father moving in their direction.

'Look Mum,' he had to interrupt. 'He's come back.' His father was a coward, he thought. He was engineering an encounter with witnesses present, so that no row could erupt. He knew his wife's concern for public image. His mother started, but quickly regained her composure. As he reached her side she said without looking at him, 'I was just telling Mr Harringay that you were abroad. I didn't expect you home so soon.'

'Well I'm here, aren't I,' his father said, not without scorn, and Mr Harringay wondered at their coldness towards each other. Walter wandered away. He wanted no part of it. He had seen his father, if not spoken to him. But that was enough. He went to join his friend. William was avoiding his own parents' encounter with the headmaster.

'I won't half get it when I get home,' William said. 'My report's terrible.'

'How d'you know?'

'Old Lucas told me.'

'I don't care,' Walter said. And meant it. 'Mine are always terrible.'

'Look,' William said with sudden enthusiasm. 'Your folk are having a good old row.'

Walter looked up. William was right. His mother was mouthing words hysterically and prodding his father in the chest. He looked at his father's face and knew that he could blow at any time. It was the same look he had worn in the staring days. Walter waited for the clap of thunder. And then it came.

'Bitch,' his father shouted, and his voice could be heard across the hall, and as if that were not enough, he gave her a mighty shove so that she crumpled to the floor.

'Cor blimey, what's going on?' William said, salivating with the prospect of an event.

'They're rehearsing for a play,' Walter said. 'They rehearse everywhere. Amateur dramatics.' His voice faded in its own disbelief. Not even the gullible William would buy that one.

Walter went over to where his mother lay. Already there were many gathered around her prone body, helping her to her feet. Of his father there was no sign and there was some relief in that. She was upright by the time he got to her side and he took her arm. He thought it best to get out of that place as quickly as possible, away from the comment, the sympathy, the shame and the humiliation. Nobody would ever forgive anybody. Ever again. Such was their mood, mother and son, as they crossed the forecourt of the school. A taxi cruised towards them and Walter hailed it. It was a gesture he had never made before, and it seemed to jettison him into manhood. He was in charge. He gave the driver their home address, and ushered his mother into the cab. She began to cry, which was embarrassing enough, but at least it was better than words. When they reached home, he suggested she go to bed. He didn't want a post-mortem.

'Take this,' he said, pouring her a glass of whisky. 'It'll help you sleep,' he said. He knew she would not pour one for herself in front of him. She grasped it with pathetic gratitude and swallowed it in one gulp. Walter pretended not to notice. He hoped she would go to bed soon.

'What will you do today?' she asked.

'I'll find something,' he said. 'I'll listen to the wireless in the kitchen.' Normally such a pastime would have been forbidden, but he felt that he held all the cards. She would deny him nothing.

'Then I'll go up,' she said. 'I'll come down later and make you something to eat.'

'Don't bother,' he said. 'I can get it myself. You just sleep.'

He heard her bedroom door close. She was probably

throwing herself on the bed and weeping. He felt very much burdened and alone. He wished he had a friend to talk to. He even wished for the company of Hugh and Peter, so that they could at least share the responsibility. For that is how he saw it. There was no-one else to take care of her. He didn't know how he could face school on the following day. Words of the fight would have reached the ears of every pupil, and almost all the teachers had witnessed the event. There was no invention that he could offer. The plain truth had been laid out before them. He would be ill, he decided. He would feign a headache or a cold. He was good at sneezing. It was a simple matter of holding one's breath and one's nose at the same time. And if his mother would not be fooled, he would simply put his foot down and refuse to go. Ever, ever again to that school. They'd have to find him another one. He was in charge now, and they would do as they were told. For a fleeting moment, he understood his father, and perhaps all fathers. Husbands too, and the power invested in them. He felt suddenly tired, exhausted by the emotional draining of the morning. To sleep during the day was an adult licence, forbidden to children, unless they were ill. He was not ill, but he had certainly known the rite of passage to adulthood, so he curled up on the couch and fell asleep.

He woke with a start. It was dark in the room, but he could just define the outline of his mother. She was standing at the cabinet and pouring herself a drink. It was a little time before he could gather himself into his whereabouts, and into the terrible reality of his waking.

'What are you doing?' he mumbled.

She started. 'A drink will cheer me up,' she said. 'I've made you supper.'

He realised how hungry he was. He hadn't eaten since a meagre breakfast.

'What time is it?'

'Bed time. Eat your supper and go to bed. You have to be up for school in the morning.'

41

The word was a thunderbolt. 'I don't fell very well,' he said.

'It's only because you're hungry. After you've eaten, you'll feel better.'

Walter got up and switched on the light. His mother gave a little cry and covered her face with her hands.

'What's the matter? Why are you hiding your face?'

'I've been crying,' she said, 'and I look terrible.'

Her skin was blotched and swollen. Her make-up was smudged, striping her face with reds, blues and blacks so that it looked like an abstract water colour. Walter said nothing. He was half sorry for her and half angry that she had so displayed herself. He went straight to the kitchen and ate seriously and with much concentration, to take his mind off the unthinkable. Later he went to bed. He did not wish his mother goodnight. He could not face her face again. But he called his goodnight from the stairway and he heard her muttered and indifferent reply. Once in bed, he hummed softly to himself, trying not to think of the morning, and when he heard her at his door, he feigned sleep, and as he felt her kiss on his forehead, he was etherised by the whisky smell on her breath. He was not tired. Despair, not fatigue, overcame him, and for once he didn't hear his mother's sobbing and pottering from below.

In the morning Walter woke in a sweat. His sheets clung to him and his limbs ached. He wondered whether he was imagining his sickness and he tried to get out of bed to see if it was real. But his legs would not hold him and he fell back between the sheets and purred with delight. He would not have to go to school. When his mother came to call him, she saw at once that he was indisposed. She took his temperature, and it merited at least one day in bed and perhaps even the doctor.

'Would you like to go into my bed?' she said. 'Then you could listen to the wireless.'

'Yes,' he said quickly. That would be a real treat. He did not construe it as one of her 'kindnesses', neither did he think of its possible consequences, else he would have stayed firmly where he was.

'D'you want something to eat?' his mother asked.

'I can't. My throat is sore.'

'I'll bring you a hot drink and aspirin. It'll bring down the temperature. Now get into my bed. I'll come up soon.'

He decided that he would not take the aspirin if it meant that it would bring his temperature down. He wanted a temperature for ever, or at least until his father came home or he was sent to another school. He settled into his mother's bed, taking care to lie in the middle so that he could not be accused of taking sides. He switched on the wireless at the bedside. His favourite. An early morning story. He no longer felt pain in his limbs. He just prayed that his temperature would hold. He did not have to think of school any more, and for the first time in many weeks, he was almost happy. Not even thoughts of his mother entered his head, and each time she appeared with her kind tray, he saw her as an intruder. His temperature mercifully held throughout the day. He had no appetite and he began to accept that he was really unwell. He had wished illness upon himself and his wish had come true. That was something for a young boy to marvel at, and to wonder to what use he could put that gift in the future. So after some serious thought, he wished for his father's permanent absence, his mother's eventual happiness and for himself to be ensconced in a happy boarding school, miles away from the lot of them.

Towards the evening his temperature began to discomfort him and he gladly took the aspirins his mother offered. She said he could stay in her bed if he liked and they could listen to the wireless together. He felt too weak to argue, and when she climbed in beside him, he shifted over to his father's side. He knew instinctively that it was a wrong move, but he needed the space between. Only one more night of this, he thought, then the school would have broken up for the holidays and he could wish himself well again. And Hugh and Peter would be home, and perhaps they would tell him stories

43

of their new school and maybe he would tell them about the fight. Yes, he certainly would tell them about the fight. Then they would have to share his burden.

On the day that the school term finished, Walter made a miraculous recovery. He moved back into his own room and though he kept his ear tuned for the sobbing, he heard nothing. But Mrs Berry was putting on a good face for the return of her sons. Sobbing was for Walter's ears and now, for two weeks, her 'kindnesses' would be suspended.

Together they went to the station to meet the boys. It was a happy home-coming and Walter hoped that it would remain so. Mrs Berry had prepared a special welcome-home meal, and they sat around the table laughing and telling tales, as if nothing at all, and nobody on earth, was amiss. When Walter went to bed that night it struck him that throughout the whole day, neither Hugh nor Peter had once giggled.

And so it continued throughout the holiday until the day that they were due to return to school. Walter had told them nothing about the fight. There had never been a right time, and he didn't want to upset the peace of the household. During the holiday he had grown much closer to his brothers and he had forgotten the black and ominous days and nights of their absence.

On the last day, they spent the morning packing. Their train did not leave until the evening. In the afternoon they said they had to return some books to the library. For some reason, Walter didn't believe them, but Mrs Berry was not one to doubt their word.

'Don't be late,' she said. 'You don't want to miss your train.'

Walter was troubled all afternoon. He was tempted to go to the library himself, in order to check on them. But he feared he would not find them there. Then he would have to face the truth of his instinct, and the consequences of that truth, those he would have to bear alone when Hugh and Peter had gone and were well out of earshot of the sobbing. He wished they would come home. And quickly.

Their train left at eight o'clock and it was already past six. Mrs Berry was restless, calculating the distance from the library to the house, for it did not occur to her that they might have gone elsewhere. In her anxiety she went out to the front gate, as if her presence there would accelerate their return home. And then she saw them coming down the street, and she wondered why they occasionally stood still and looked at something they were holding in their hands. She shouted at them, and on seeing her, they quickly hid the objects of their attention in their jacket pockets. And ran towards her. But she had turned and gone back into the house. She knew that an explanation was in order, and that was best done indoors.

'What's that you had in your hands?' She came to the point right away. 'Show it to me.'

Hugh and Peter looked at one another. They were clearly frightened.

'Show it to me,' she shouted at them again.

Then, for the first time in the entire holiday, Hugh and Peter started to giggle. And Walter knew that whatever they had in their pockets was, in one way or another, unlawful.

The boys brought out their loot and laid it on the table. Two yo-yos. Nine nine nines, each of them. The Rolls Royce of the toy. Walter gasped. He had had dreams of owning such a yo-yo but it was much too expensive a toy to expect.

'Where did you get them?' she whispered. She did not suspect theft. They were not the sort of boys to take risks. She whispered the question because she half knew and dreaded the answer. They could only have come from one source.

'Dad gave them to us,' Hugh said, shamefacedly.

'Where did you see him?' The sobbing had begun.

'At his house,' Peter giggled.

'How did you know where he lived?'

45

'He writes to us at school.'

'Was she there, that slut?'

The boys were silent. Not even giggling could cover their confusion.

'Well was she there or not?' Mrs Berry persisted.

'She's only another person, Mum,' Peter said.

'She's quite nice really,' Hugh had the stupidity to add.

Mrs Berry crumpled. She had ceased sobbing. It seemed that there was no sound on earth that could express her pain. Only the internal thunder of her throbbing heart. Walter went to her side. He sensed she might die of her pain. And indeed she was wishing herself dead, for this was the worst of times. She had lost the status of wife and that had been painful enough. But the status of motherhood was not on offer. Never. Never. Yet now she was threatened with its loss.

'We must go to the station,' she said tonelessly.

Walter held her arm on the way. His brothers lagged behind. She shivered as she walked, aching with her wretchedness. Her sorrow had become physical.

The train was waiting on the platform when they arrived. Hugh and Peter suddenly rushed to her, and in a gesture, never before seen, they held her close and the helpless giggle was not far behind. They held her until it was time to board. They said their farewells clinging to her still. Perhaps they were stung by an omen of tragedy. It was only when the train guard started closing the doors that they loosened their hold and climbed quickly aboard. They waved from the window as the train pulled out. Mrs Berry tried to offer them a smile, but she no longer knew how to make one. As the train pulled round the corner of the track, it seemed to Hugh and Peter that their mother had shrunk and that when they next came home there would be nothing left of her.

They walked home in silence. Walter held her arm all the while.

'I think I'll make an early night,' she said.

Walter thought for a moment. Then, 'Can I sleep in your bed?' he asked. He was careful with his choice of

46

words. 'Can I' implied that she would be doing him a favour, though in his mind it was 'Shall I', as a favour to her.

'If you want,' she said. Nothing about her cared any more. Her walk had become a nonchalant slouch, and she seemed heavy on his arm. Whatever sight surrounded her and whatever people, she had clearly had enough of it all.

He made her a cup of tea when they got home, and from the kitchen he heard the clink of bottle and glass. When he brought in the tea, she told him he should go to bed. He was happy to oblige. He could better cope with his own despair than with others'. Upstairs in her bedroom, he lay on the treacherous sheets of his father's side. He considered the notion of hate, both towards his father and his brothers, but he could not think clearly. He lay in a paralysis of depression. He willed sleep, and mercifully it came quickly. He did not hear his mother creep in at his side nor smell the fumes of her sorrow. During the night he woke for no reason and listened to her surprising snore. He let it lull him to sleep again, and he dreamed of yo-yos.

In the morning, he awoke to a silence. It was never like that. Even after his father and brothers had left, he could still hear the pottering downstairs. He looked at the clock on the mantelpiece. Half past nine. It was late. By half past nine, or much earlier, breakfast was over. He turned round in the bed and the noise of his turning was like thunder. He saw his mother lying beside him and he wondered why she was still sleeping. He also wondered whether she always slept like that. With her eyes wide open. He'd never caught her sleeping before. He hoped she would sleep a while before waking to terrible recall.

He got up and went down to the kitchen. He passed through the living-room and noticed the empty whisky bottle on the table. And something more. Another bottle. Empty. Echoing the empty whisky and shrieking its hollow descant. He paused for a moment, though that moment seemed an eternity and the silence in the house

47

was screaming. He paused to make the reluctant connection, then he streaked upstairs calling 'Mum, Mum,' with each step of the climb, and screaming it in her ear at the bedside. He shook her. He pleaded with her to wake. 'Please, please,' he begged. He kissed her face all over, expecting to sniff those sad vapours of her grief. But he smelt nothing. And again he feared the terrible connection. He smelt nothing because there was no breath in her. He remembered a film he had once seen, when someone, the hero, put a mirror to a lady's mouth to check whether or not she was breathing. He rushed to the bathroom, calling his mother all the time. The only portable mirror was his father's, one that he used for shaving. He noticed that it was cracked, but it would do for what he had in mind. He placed it close to his mother's mouth and nostrils and he prayed for mist. He left it there for the time-span of at least ten breaths, using his own breathing as a count. Then he looked at the mirror and saw only his own magnified and cracked face, through a glass that was cruelly clear. In panic, he began to shake her, calling her all the time, begging her to open her eyes, ignoring the fact that they were already wide open. The shaking exhausted him and he broke into hot and laden tears that refused to be shed. He held her still and took her hand and stroked her face and called her name.

And at last he made the final and appalling connection.

Chapter 4

The first person I thought of when I finished that chapter was my mother. I needed to see her, and moreover, I *wanted* to see her, and I have never felt that need or desire before. I recalled Mrs Berry and her catastrophic cuddling. I counted my blessings and dialled my mother's number.

She could not disguise her pleasure at my unexpected call. After all, I had visited her only a few days previously, and it was not my wont to be so frequently in touch. She asked me what I wanted, with a touch of anxiety in her voice. I assured her that all was well.

'Then why are you phoning me?' she asked.

'Just to say hello.' How could I tell her that I was phoning simply to make sure that she was alive, that she would not die before giving me time to forgive her, or her to forgive me, or for both of us to forgive ourselves.

'Well hello,' she said, and I heard the smile in her voice. 'When are you coming to see me?'

Why did she have to spoil it? Why could she not be satisfied with a small step of approach? Why was she so greedy for the vaulting leap into reconciliation?

'I'm busy,' I said. I was short. I wanted her to know that there had been no change in me. That each of my visits was a reluctant one, that my irritation towards her was still in full and spendid flower.

'Well come when you can,' she said, her voice a cascade of disappointment.

'I will,' I said, and quickly put the phone down.

The last chapter of Walter's story had depressed me unutterably. I had no doubt that it was true. The thought that I had syphoned was clear proof of its authenticity. And I recalled that last thought that I had withdrawn from Walter's mind before I had turned my friend the right way up! 'No more fear,' it had said. 'Free for ever from accusation.' My friend had clearly committed some monstrous sin, but in the light of his wretched childhood, whatever it was, whatever the nature of his terrible shame, could be forgiven. It seemed to me nothing short of a miracle that Walter had survived at all.

I was loathe to continue with my syphoning. At least for the time being. That last thought of his had taken it out of me. When the phone rang, I thought it was my mother and I picked up the receiver with little appetite. But to my relief, it was Christina Berry. I felt badly that I had not been in touch with her since Walter's funeral. She had gone totally out of my mind for, delving as I was into Walter's childhood, the notion of a Christina Berry was not yet viable. She invited me to tea the following afternoon. Walter's brothers would be down from Yorkshire. I accepted eagerly. The visit would be what Walter had called post-novel research. I would go to tea to see if I'd got it right.

I almost fell into the trap of calling the brothers Hugh and Peter and would have done so had not Christina pre-empted my greeting and introduced George and Graham, Walter's brothers from Yorkshire. I was a little disappointed, but how was I expected to divine their names? Walter would have forgiven me. But they looked exactly as I had imagined them. Honestly. Tall, gaunt and boring. You have to take my word for this. I'm not a descriptive writer, so I can show you no proof. But indeed, in my eyes, they had grown up in exact relation to my image of their boyhood faces. I was tempted to plunge in at the deep end, and to ask them about their childhood, their boarding school, their father, and especially the manner in which their mother had died. But swiftly I decided against it. If their tales had not coincided with mine, I might have been disappointed. I might have felt I'd been cheating. I had to convince myself that I was writing a novel, and that my version of Walter's story was *my* truth, and that was the only truth that mattered. So in my mind, I did an about-turn. Far from delving into the past, I would do what I could to steer the conversation towards the present, and if necessary the future, any time in fact, as long as it was post-Walter. It was not difficult. When I arrived, George was in the course of telling Christina how they proposed to sell their farm and perhaps move closer to London. From my delicate and carefully chosen questions, it transpired that they shared a farm between them, that they lived together and that neither of them had ever married. Theirs had been a miserable life, I thought, and I wondered whether of all the three children, theirs had been the greater guilt. After all, in my terms, in *my* truth, they had been the primary cause of their mother's death. Walter had simply been in on the kill. But that was my story. I remembered then how Walter had once said to me that he often left in the middle of a dinner party because the table-talk was interfering with the conversations he was having with his fictional characters. I was beginning to feel the same and I was anxious to get away and to continue with my syphoning. Christina seemed in a happy enough mood though it was barely two months since Walter had died. I noticed that the colour of her dress was green and it seemed to prove that she was learning to live without him.

'I would love you both to move to London,' Christina said. 'We could see more of each other. And then you could help me sort out Walter's papers.'

And then the most extraordinary thing happened. They giggled. George and Graham giggled. Both of them together. I swear to God they did. If I'd been right about nothing else, I'd hit the bull's eye with the giggle. It was a magic moment indeed. Walter used to talk about these occasional magic moments, how, what one wrote on page three or so, and without any conscious reasoning, would find its inalienable logic thirty or so pages later. My logic had surfaced in a God-sent giggle. I was elated. Now I wanted to stay, in the hope of further validation.

The doorbell rang and Christina rose to answer it. For a while I was alone with George and Graham and I was tempted to ask them to giggle again. But I refrained. Logic must not be abused. Shortly Christina returned with Amanda and her son. I reckoned that little Simon was about six years old, and was clearly the love of Christina's life. Though I had known Amanda since she was a teenager, I knew very little about her. My conversations with Walter usually took place after supper, by which time Amanda had gone to bed. I watched her grow up and remarked on her beauty. She must have taken after her father whom I had never met, and knew nothing about, since there was little of Christina in her. Walter had doted on her. She was a mere baby when he and Christina were married. Amanda had never known her father. He had died two months before she was born. But Walter had loved her as his own. I rejoiced with her when she married and some two years later I commiserated with her on her divorce. Now she lived alone, it seemed, with Simon. Despite affectionate overtures to her from Christina, I noticed a distinct coldness on Amanda's part. Perhaps it was a projection of my own maternal friction, but nevertheless it disturbed me. And not only was she cold to her mother on her own behalf, but she seemed to extend that aloofness to Simon, discouraging him in his intimacy with his grandmother, and it was hurtful to see Christina's bewildered pain when Simon was encouraged to move away.

'Don't disturb your Granny,' Amanda covered up, though it was clear that all Christina wanted from life, was little Simon's disturbance. So I played with Simon myself, and Amanda seemed pleased, encouraging me the while with remarks to the effect that I would make a good father. But I was aware of Christina's displeasure and hastily withdrew from the play. I sent Simon to his great-uncles for pastime. Whatever the conflict consisted of, I wanted no part of it. George and Graham did not giggle again, but once was all that I needed, and shortly after Amanda's arrival, I took my leave, saying I would come again soon, and this time, meaning it, for I felt there was much to be gleaned from that sombre drawing-room.

I was anxious to return to the novel. The giggle was a great spur. The joy of writing which, during my writer's block, I had strongly and defensively denied, now filled me with overwhelming gratitude. I owed it all to Walter and I would do my best to do him proud.

When I reached home, I indulged in my usual postponement programme. I made coffee, I read the early evening paper, and for a while, I fingered Scarlatti. Then into the kitchen and more coffee which I drank leaning against my freezer. I knew that there would come a time, and pretty soon at that, when I would have to open it, so I sipped slowly. Over the years I have developed nothing short of a talent for slow drinking. A Scarlatti sonata dictates its own pace, but with a cup of coffee you yourself are in control. I lingered over it, to its last infuriating drop and then, having nothing more on my programme to delay me, I opened the freezer door. I don't know why, but each time I held Walter, I asked for his forgiveness. I suppose in a way I must have felt I was cheating. But writers are thieves by nature. Some actually steal others' *stories*, hook, line and sinker, whereas I suctioned only thoughts and these were not necessarily ideas. They were but clues. It was I who directed them and gave them shape and colour. Nevertheless, I murmured my regrets to Walter, as unnecessary, I thought, as Boswell's possible apology to Johnson.

I put Walter on the kitchen table, and took up my syphon. I did not expect a joyous thought. His last had been concerned with courtship of Death, and I expected that to be the tone of what followed. So I was surprised at the first decipherable thought, for it smacked of levity.

Who stole the first petrol-cap?

I was deeply sympathetic to that thought, for some years ago one of my own petrol-caps had been stolen and I had no scruple in nicking another of similar size. So there must be one man on earth, or woman perhaps, who is solely responsible for an undulating wave of car crime. Walter's was a happy thought, and certainly a change from his Death-wooing. But it was not a thought that gave much of a directional clue, so I syphoned further.

> *People are cruel to animals. Especially*
> *horses. They make them run races even*
> *though some of them are handicapped.*

I liked that one. Clearly the young Walter was going through a meditative phase. But still no signpost to my novel's development. And then a possible light appeared.

> *I won't tell anybody about it. I think I have*
> *invented it. It's so absolutely wonderful*
> *that I shall keep it to myself. In any case, I*
> *think it is a sin.*

I smiled. I too, thought I had invented self-abuse. I too thought it was a sin. Until I went to boardingschool and found myself amongst a herd of time-honoured sinners. Perhaps Walter did too. No real signpost that, so I syphoned on. And then it came. A positive direction.

> *I shall go again tonight. Into her*
> *Shakespeare and into her loving.*

A signpost indeed. I put Walter back in the freezer and took up my pen.

... and at last he made the final and appalling connection.

After their mother's death, the three Berry boys moved in with their father. And the yellow dress. Mr Berry refused to mourn his wife. Her manner of quietus had outraged him. Suicide was a criminal legacy to leave one's children. He grew to hate her with as much passion as once he had loved, and he hardly waited for the grass to grow on her shameful grave before he married his yellow substitute. After their marriage it was inevitable that Walter should join his brothers at boarding school, since Mrs Yellow found the prospect of a living-in Walter faintly resistable. Walter was glad to go. He would have welcomed any means of escape from that house which his father called home. The new Mrs Berry instructed the boys to call her 'Auntie' but Walter wouldn't dignify her by any name at all, and if he had to call her attention, he would address her as 'you'. To his father he did the same, and with the same hatred in his heart, and each was glad to see the back of the other. Hugh and Peter adjusted to their new situation with greater ease, though their giggling was now continuous, and had nothing to do with laughter. But in the train on their way to school, they sobered, even to the extent of making fun of 'auntie' and they let Walter join in with their mockery.

Walter was excited. And nervous too. He knew that he was a loner, and ill-adjusted to groups. He hoped he would find a William at his new school, a loner like himself who, for form's sake, sought out another. But Haydon Lodge was no place for loners. You joined in or you got out. For the whole duration of six years at the school Walter Berry did neither. He found an alternative. He simply survived. At times he was viewed as a hero; at others, as a craven coward. He was indifferent to both labels. He went his own way, a lonely route, but peopled by his ample invention. Of his brothers he saw very little. Their Houses were geographically apart. But on holidays, in their adopted home, he was close to them.

Walter noticed how each time he came home, Mrs Yellow had faded a little. Her natural zest was diluted, and was now taken neat from a bottle. But unlike his mother, who had been at pains to hide her addiction, this one was quite brazen with her booze. She would pour out her sustenance in front of the boys, and with greater exhibition in front of her husband, and Walter often considered whether his father was not good for women.

Was he perhaps having someone else on the side, and if so, what colour was she?

One Christmas, when the boys came home from school, Mrs Yellow looked so washed out, it seemed she had been put through the wringer. She was too drunk to make any festive preparations, and Mr Berry took the boys to a hotel for their Christmas dinner. That holiday marked the last of Mrs Yellow.

On their next home leave, they were greeted by what his father called his 'housekeeper', a young man of pale and frail features, who looked incapable of keeping himself, leave alone a house. He laughed a lot, and was embarrassingly familiar. He was an actor, he told the boys, and temporarily 'resting'. Hugh and Peter giggled, and Walter asked no questions. All three of them knew, without knowing. But at least Terry, as he was called, didn't drink and the house had never looked so spotless. And most surprising of all, their father had never been so content. There was no sign of his erstwhile rages, and a welcome warmth and affection had appeared, as if from nowhere. They returned to school bewildered.

And then everything in their lives changed. On September 3rd, 1939, war was declared. Hugh and Peter had come to the end of their school days, and though deferment would have been possible, they were conscripted together into the army. They giggled their way into their uniforms and Walter pitied them. He could imagine no greater hell than conscription, than the inescapable barracks of crowded men, and he resolved to claim conscientious objection when his turn came. He hoped he would land in solitary. It wasn't that he was against the war. In his young way, he believed it had just cause. But he preferred to fight it on his own. Terry was exempt for the call-up on account of his flat feet and poor health and Mr Berry pulled a few strings to keep him in his service. Walter went back to school alone, and though he was used to seeing little of his brothers during term-time, he suddenly, and for the first time in his school life, felt very lonely.

There were changes too at the school. Some of the masters had been called up to service to do their bit for king and country, a fact made much of by the headmaster at the opening assembly. The national anthem was sung and the choir wallowed in patriotic fervour. A Union Jack was found and flown defiantly from the headmaster's study. Haydon Lodge could be relied upon to do its bit.

Part of the school's war effort, though they had little choice, was to be the employment of women teachers. And there were other diversions too. There were breaks in the humdrum routine. Gas-mask drill was one of them, and the orderly march to the shelters, another. A cadet corps was formed, but joining it was voluntary and Walter was happy to sit on the sidelines. There was a buzz in the school of great expectations, of falling bombs and conflagrations. But the countryside around Haydon Lodge remained unchanged. Once, on passing a farm on the way to the playing-fields, the boys were shunted to the side of the road to give way to a couple of trucks. They heard singing coming from the inside, women's voices, unharmonious, but full of cheer. The backs of the trucks were open, and the boys caught their first glimpse of the Women's Land Army. They choked back their sighs and their whistles, but some of the more daring ones actually responded to the girls' waves and though they knew that they were never likely to be any closer to those winsome haymakers, it was comforting to know that young women shared their own environs.

And then one day, that gender actually landed on their own doorstep. Two young women, fresh from university, who, in normal times, would never have graced the prestigious portals of Haydon Lodge, arrived to take up their duties, as English and Maths teachers respectively. Miss Freeman was the first, and Miss Thwaite the second, and if they were not yet friends, they would surely, faute de mieux, soon have to be so, if for nothing else than to form a united front against a natural staff-room hostility.

But the pupils were overjoyed. Hitherto, their only whiff of womankind had come from Matron, that same guardian who had treated the homesick needs of many of their fathers. She was stern but kind, and there was something essentially forbidding about her motherly manner. For many boys, she was home from home. But the whiff of Freeman and Thwaite was altogether different. It was newly minted, yet it had an odour of vintage. In comparison with the closeted lives of the Haydon Lodge boys, Freeman and Thwaite had lived. They had been dancing in their time, and openly smoked cigarettes, had frequented restaurants perhaps, and had heard the air-raid warnings of the big cities. They smelt of smoke and chimneys, late black-out nights, and lazy mornings, and in the healthy, disciplined and unpolluted air of Haydon Lodge, they were a refreshing eye-sore. The boys welcomed them with metaphored open arms, but keeping their distance and feigning nonchalance. Even the youngest ones had already learned that 'hard to get' was a sure invitation into a woman's arms. But Walter had no notion of such technique, nor even an instinct for it. He kept his distance out of sheer shyness.

He was sixteen years old at the time of the women's invasion. And he was ready. At least, that's how he felt himself to be. But he was not sure for what. The sight of the women and their daily presence, generated feelings in him that were hitherto unknown, and galvanised his physical being into a new and bewildering awareness. His old habit of staring once more took hold, but this time he did not use it as a weapon. His staring had no intention in mind. He simply could not help himself. It was Miss Freeman who drew him most. She was not as pretty as Miss Thwaite but it's possible that Walter was drawn as much to her subject as to her person. For over his school years, he had grown to love words, their sounds, their rhythms and their cadences, and often in his solitary times, he would read aloud and savour the music of language. Miss Freeman had a beautiful voice, and often, as he stared at her, he had the feeling that she declaimed solely for himself. He heard a personal declaration in the love poetry that she read, and he hid his

58

blushing face as others around him shifted in their seats, in muted and tone-deaf giggles. His progress in English in that first Freeman term surprised even himself. He knew that she was pleased with his work, though she was careful not to over-praise him. He was grateful for that, for his class-mates would have isolated him even further. When she asked him to come to her study to discuss his homework, she did so when they were alone, during a chance meeting in the corridor.

'I'll give you a cup of tea,' she smiled.

Though his knees were melting, Walter made it fitfully to the end of the corridor. There he stopped and stilled his breath and trembling body. And in that moment he knew that, to all intents and purposes, his school-days were over.

It was a Friday, a day that echoed the emptiness of the weekend to come. Many of the teachers took their week-ends at home, and some of the prefects enjoyed privileged leave. At five o'clock, when he made his way across the courtyard to Miss Freeman's study, the car and bicycle-park was almost empty, and the early winter dark had fallen. He knew that all his life he would remember this night, and he savoured each of its sights and sounds. There was little of either, but the sheer emptiness of the school yard, and its silence, was memorable. He heard his own footsteps as they took solemn leave of his adolescence. He counted each one and knew that they were irretraceable. When he reached the door of Miss Freeman's study, he began to tremble. He thought he ought to be thinking about how he should behave. He knew instinctively that her invitation had nothing to do with his homework. He would take his cue from her, whatever that cue might be, and he hoped that she had some experience in these matters. Then he hoped fervently that she hadn't, and he trembled further with a gnawing pang of jealousy.

He stiffened his knees and knocked on the door. She did not call, 'Come in,' but after a short while she opened the door herself, and her startling appearance confirmed

59

that Walter's homework was not on the agenda. She had unpinned her hair. Her daily classroom appearances were always chignonned, and though she wore the same school dress, her look was many miles from the classroom.

'Come,' she said. 'I've made you tea.' She put her hand on his shoulder and steered him into the room. His flesh burned through his blazer beneath her touch. At that moment he thought of his mother and he couldn't understand why. Nor could he understand the hot tears that had insisted on his cheeks, such a flow of them, all those tears that over the years had been sent back to where they came from. When his mother had died, he had kept the tears at bay. His witnessing had been enough, and the tears had frozen. He wondered whether he should apologise for them, but he felt too that an apology would diminish the statement that they were making. That now, the tears were right and proper. And in their own time.

Miss Freeman put her arm around him and sat him on the settee. 'Tell me,' she said.

He poured it out, never having spoken about it to anybody before. And he saw it all in colours. In a curdled rainbow. The yellow dress, the red rod, the white pills, the brown liquid cry for attention, and the terrible grey of choking sobs. And in the final frontier, the pale parabola of death.

Miss Freeman listened, and with such concentration that she dared not interrupt her hearing even with a sigh. And when it was all over, she took him in her arms. She kissed his face, his brow, his eyes, his cheeks. And then his lips, sucking out of his mouth that sour taste of Death that he had retched on for so many years, and in its place she gave sweetness and hope and then poured it into his whole body, delving his young and virgin well and guiding the fountain of his joy. No words passed between them, and when it was over she cradled his throbbing.

'I love you, Miss Freeman,' Walter said. And he knew in that moment that never in his life, would he love so passionately again.

60

Chapter 5

At the end of that last chapter, I was obliged to take pause for thought. Not to consider what was to follow. I wasn't worried about that. I knew that one sentence would generate the next. And so on and so forth. I had faith in that. Indeed a writer's block is brought about by a simple loss of that faith. But Walter, in his purloined bequest, had restored it to me. No, it was not the matter of what was to follow that gave me pause. It was my sheer astonishment at what I had already written. I had written about love, a subject that I had hitherto dodged with fear. For what did I know about love? I, Martin Peabody, who all his life had avoided the theme and the practice thereof. From time to time the challenge of love had been offered me, but I had never risked its taking. Thus, I had concluded that my lack of experience in the love market disqualified me from expressing its matter in writing. Yet, good or bad, I had actually written a scene of love. I recalled how Walter wrote on such varied subjects. Every novel of his, and there were many, was different, yet he could not have had personal experience of his whole wide and varied range. I remember his telling me that all fiction is about pain, joy, anger, envy, fear and courage, and that everybody in their lives had experienced most of them. Every theme on earth is about one or some of them, he would say, and if you are a writer, you can write about anything, and set it in any country and at any time. Well, certainly Walter had proved that this was possible. And now I had gone a little way to proving it myself.

I decided to celebrate with two Scarlatti sonatas. Not only did I play them through, as is my wont, I actually practised them and, after an hour, I was note perfect in each. I realised that my piano 'treats' had lost their aura of hobby, and threatened to become serious pursuits. I was not troubled by it. The function of the piano in my life was to give me pleasure and if that delight was curbed at any time by practice, I would revert to my normal playing and turn a deaf ear to its inadequacies.

I was not ready yet to re-open my freezer. I was not postponing. I was simply becoming aware that there was another life to be led. That my own had become very circumscribed, and that outside my self-made confines there was society and all that that entailed. I would invite Christina to supper perhaps, and Amanda too, if she were free. And perhaps other friends whom I had neglected since Walter's death had launched me into the solitary life. I rang Christina at once, and arranged an evening on the following Friday when Amanda would also be free. To make up the numbers I invited a close friend from my university days and had perforce to invite his wife, though I found her as faintly resistible as my friend did himself. I was excited. I had not entertained for many months though cooking for friends was always a pleasure for me. I sat down and prepared a menu. I knew Christina was a hearty eater, but I had no idea of Amanda's palate. I decided on asparagus, followed by a boeuf-en-croute, a dicey dish, but worth the risk in its making. A lemon syllabub would follow and my mouth watered as the fare flowed from my pen. Shopping was another treat that I had neglected of late. I do not favour supermarkets. They are too swift, and the pleasure of shopping is too soon completed. No, I favour a number of small shops; a corner greengrocer, a reliable butcher, and my local general store. I spent a good part of the following day in my shopping expedition and that evening I practised yet two more Scarlatti sonatas. Before I went to bed that night, I looked in the mirror. On the whole I avoid mirrors, and I hadn't seriously looked at my face in a long while. But I knew it had changed, and radically, since my writing-block days. It looked younger somehow, and happier. I must ring my mother I thought, not knowing why, but then decided against it, sensing that a conversation with my mother would wrinkle me once more.

I spent the following day cooking, and listening to music as I did so. But my mind was on my novel and I had to turn down the radio to stop it interfering with my thoughts. Occasionally I went to my desk to make the odd note, random ones, for the opening of the next chapter depended entirely on Walter's subsequent thought. But random and irrelevant notes kept me in the business of writing, thus feeding my growing belief in myself. Again, as so often since his death, I muttered my thanks to Walter. I could repay him only with words.

On Friday I rose early and made my final preparations. All was finished by the end of the morning and I thought I might spend the afternoon a-syphoning. I did not need Scarlatti or postponement of any kind, and I went straightway to my freezer and gently withdrew my Muse. I contemplated the sphere for a little while. Despite my withdrawals, it had retained the shape of a perfect circle, though a little shrunk, as was to be expected. The last thought I had withdrawn had been seminal, for it marked Walter's passage into manhood, and I suspected that shortly I would discover those thoughts that pertained to his writing career. There had been the odd jottings, which I confess I have not troubled you with, because they were not germane to my story. Thoughts are often random and without connection or relevance, but when they are turned into writing, they are sifted and refined and I considered that sieving process part of my self-imposed commission. I inserted the syphon and gently pressed my thumb on its trigger. This time there was no waffle to ignore, for the thought emerged without any tangled preamble.

> He did not go to war. The war came to him.

That was a signpost indeed, for it determined the backcloth of my ensuing chapter. Tomorrow I would make a start on a new episode, in which I would invent the 'He' to whom war came.

It was almost eight o'clock and I was a little nervous. It had been so long since I had entertained guests at my table and I fussed with the pre-prandial drinks to give myself something to do. I listened to the bell of the first visitor with a mixture of relief and panic. It was Stephen, with his wife Florence in tow, or more to the point, the other way round. Stephen hovered in Florence's wake, barely visible, since her large frame practically filled the doorway. She was behaving as if it were she who was my friend and that Stephen was on the fringe of that friendship. So I made a point of greeting Stephen first, and effusively, and offering to her but a formal acknowledgement of her presence. Stephen had been one of my closest friends in my university days. We had both read English, a fairly useless pursuit, since anyone of any reasonable intelligence would do it anyway. A degree in English led to few careers, and teaching seemed to be one of them. Stephen took that option and I was about to do the same when, of a sudden, my father left my mother for what dear Walter would have called a Mrs Yellow. My mother would sneer at the phrase, 'to take to the cleaners', but she was not above practising the art, and my rich father was happy enough to oblige. He felt deeply guilty about his adultery, and money, if you have it, is the easiest way to assuage a bad conscience. Part of that mitigation was a generous allowance in my direction, and as a result, it is possible that the teaching profession lost a very valuable asset. But I don't think I would have lasted very long in a classroom for I had already caught the writing bug. And besides, I had just met Walter.

I called them both into the living-room. I asked Stephen how he was.

'He's fine,' Florence told me before Stephen had a chance to open his mouth, and I was heartily pleased that I wasn't married. I didn't ask after Florence's health. She looked as if she had enough for both of them.

The doorbell rang again, and with some relief I welcomed Christina and Amanda and wondered at the same time whether it had been a good idea to invite anybody else. For I wanted the Berrys to myself. I wasn't looking for clues. Signals from the Berry quarter might have misled me, I simply wanted to maintain a link with my old friend. I brought them into the living-room, and offered drinks and introductions all round. Amanda took one look at Florence and shuddered. It was not a good beginning. I steered Florence into Christina's orbit, and Amanda into Stephen's, and I stood in the centre like a master of ceremonies to see that all went well. Florence took no time at all to colonise Christina, who was cowering beneath her grilling. I felt mean and at a loss. Then I was suddenly inspired. I would ask Florence to help me in the kitchen. Like a good host, I would bear the burden of her alone.

She was surprised at my request, but glad enough to comply. She rose immediately, leaving Christina's timid responses in the air. I thought I might boss her about a bit and give her a taste of her own medicine. So I gave her sundry orders and I was stunned by her obedience. And her silence. Moreover, she was smiling happily. She was clearly a changed woman. All she needed in her poor life was a little acknowledgement, and that I had given her. If at that moment I had asked her, I think she might have married me. She did more than I asked of her, even washing the saucepans that I had put aside. If I hadn't stopped her, she might well have embarked on a spring-clean. I sensed she was taking me over, as another Stephen, as if she had it in mind to live for as many people as she could.

I called my guests into dinner. 'Are you comfortable?' I said to the general assembly. Once seated at the table, opposite Stephen, Florence reverted.

'We're all fine,' she said, and I was tempted to ask her to wait at table.

I had seated Amanda by my side. I wanted to get to know her a little, and until now my Muse had given me no clues regarding Walter's step-daughter. I asked after Simon. 'He's well,' she said, 'but don't talk about him,' she added in a whisper, 'or Mother will get out the photographs and bore us all silly.'

If she had said this last with a smile, I would have accepted it as something of a family joke, but she was utterly serious, and I recalled the tension I had witnessed between her and her mother on account of her son, and I decided that little Simon was no suitable subject for conversation. But I wondered at it, and hoped that in time my Muse would give me a clue.

Florence was in the driving-seat once more. She was informing the table of Stephen's overloaded teaching duties, and how his headmaster did not appreciate his work. How he had missed out on promotion because of envy. The list of Stephen's misfortunes was endless. I looked at my friend and I couldn't understand why he remained silent and still. If Florence had been my wife, I would have drowned her. But not only was he silent. He even smiled at her, and I began to think he deserved everything he was getting. I turned my attention back to Amanda. I asked if she had a job.

'Not a real one,' she said. 'I'm sorting out Walter's papers. Frank Watson is doing the biography and I'm his sort of researcher.'

I pricked up my ears. Frank Watson had never been an intimate of Walter's, but he was an undoubted admirer of my friend's work. He was a dull academic, and for that reason I thought he was a poor choice. He would never, for instance, admit the concept of magic into the making of fiction, and that was what Walter was all about.

'Will it be his life as well as his work?' I asked.

'No. Only his work,' she said quickly. 'We insisted on that.'

But I'm doing his life, I thought, and I was relieved that there would be no poaching on my territory, imaginary as it might be. There were many more things I wished to know about Amanda, but this was no time for personal questioning. It crossed my mind to take her for lunch one day, but I quickly dismissed the idea. For lunch wasn't just lunch. It could lead anywhere, and I was nowhere near ready for that no-man's-land. I regretted it. But lunch had never been my scene. It entailed too many imponderables.

The hors d'oeuvre had been dealt with and I made to collect the plates. But Florence beat me to it and I followed her into the kitchen. Once there I automatically gave her orders and she complied with painful docility. She placed the croute on a platter and neatly settled the vegetables around it. I stood aside, allowing her to take it to the table. But she handed it to me.

'You take it,' she said. 'It's yours. It's all your own work.'

She really was not so bad, old Florence, I thought, but I was puzzled by her strange and sudden turns of behaviour. I noticed that neither Amanda nor Christina was speaking to poor Stephen. I suspect they had all cottoned on to Florence's management skills. To communicate with Stephen, one would have to go through Florence and neither of them thought it worth their while. So good host as I was, I proposed a change of seating for the main course. I relinquished Amanda and took Stephen in her stead, but I was careful, too, to place Christina on my other side. Which left Amanda and Florence saddled with each other. But I had little choice. I carved the meat to sighs of congratulations and when everybody was served, I turned my attention to Stephen.

I spoke to him almost in whispers, to preclude Florence's interference.

'How's the Jacobean book going?' I asked him. I knew that he was working on the subject of decadence in Jacobean drama.

'Things are not what they seem,' he whispered back.

My expression questioned him.

'I'll tell you later,' he said, under his breath.

I didn't know how to follow such an exchange, so I turned my attention to Christina and wondered what I could say to her. But she opened the conversation herself.

'I miss him terribly,' she said.

'Of course you do,' I consoled. I put my hand on hers. 'We all miss him.' I was lying. I rarely missed Walter. How could I, since he was almost always by my side. I felt a bit of a heel not being able to share in her sorrow. But at least she wasn't wearing yellow. Not a trace of it.

'Amanda tells me that Frank Watson is doing the biography,' I said.

'That's right. I think Walter would have approved,' she said. 'Frank was a great admirer. He'll do Walter justice, I'm sure.'

I agreed with her, whatever justice meant. Watson would do no more justice than I, but at least I had the excuse of fiction. I turned once more to Stephen.

'Is it really so bad, your school?' I asked.

67

'No. It's a good school, I suppose. I just don't get on with the boss. I'm thinking of changing anyway. I'd like to get out of London. Maybe a boarding school.'

'Well I hope it's a kind one,' Christina said. 'Poor Walter went to one, where he spent the most miserable days of his life.'

I wanted to kiss her. Perhaps my novel was not so much fiction after all. I allowed that Walter had never told her about the delectable Miss Freeman.

I noticed that Amanda was making great efforts with Florence, but clearly Florence wasn't listening. Her ear was cocked to others' conversations, waiting for a gap in which to offer her judgement. I couldn't fathom her.

It was still early when Florence announced she wished to leave. I noticed with some concern that she had suddenly aged. Her face had fallen and there was a tired pallor about her, so unlike the picture of radiant health she had presented on her arrival. Even her voice had lost its resonant peal. I was about to ask her if she felt unwell, but thought better of it, fearful of the conversation that would ensue. Stephen said he would bring the car round since he was parked a little distance from my house. I offered to go with him, and I excused myself from the company.

Once in the street, he stopped and touched my arm. 'She's dying, you know,' he said.

I was shocked, and I didn't know how to respond. There were questions I wanted to ask, but in the light of Stephen's prognosis, they seemed irrelevant. But he enlightened me.

'It's cancer. Her behaviour is strange. Its the medication. She has two months. At the most.'

Then I said I was sorry. And I was. And mostly for Stephen. 'We must keep in touch,' I said lamely.

Later that evening, when they had all departed, I recapped, as far as I was able, on Florence's every movement, gesture and remark. There was no doubt that, unpleasant as it had been most of the time, she had made an indelible impression. And that was the nub of it. That was all she had wanted to make. She had wanted to ensure that, with affection or with dislike, she would not be forgotten, and for the sake of that sad need of hers, Stephen had allowed himself to be subsumed. I felt very sorry for both of them.

It was in this post-mortem mood of mine, that I recalled Amanda. That woman bothered me. She was still very attractive, and I felt a strange link with her. Perhaps it was because both of us had mother problems, though they probably stemmed from very different sources. Perhaps one day, I would invite her out to lunch, but first I had to get on with Walter's story. It struck me then that I was using my novel as postponement in the same way as I had used Scarlatti and woodwork. My priorities were changing and the change unnerved me. I must get back to my fiction, or lose all anchorage.

The following day, after breakfast, I went straight to my desk. I had copied Walter's last thought into my note-book and I noted that my book was due to go to war. I read the last sentence of my previous chapter, and I set to work.

. . . that never in his life, would he love so passionately again. Had it not been for Miss Freeman, Walter might have run away from Haydon Lodge. Now nothing in the world would have tempted him outside its gates. His last two years at the school made up for all the misery and isolation that he had endured before she came. He went frequently to Miss Freeman's study, and one weekend, they even dared a hotel together. He did not consider that the affair would ever end. After he left school, he assumed that they would pursue an open courtship. And perhaps he might even bring himself to call her by her christian name. For still, even in their moments of blissful climax, it was always to 'Miss Freeman' that he declared his love.

But Miss Freeman knew otherwise. Walter's school-leaving would mark the end of the affair. Their love was a pupil/teacher one, and, as such, it must eventually flounder. On the day that Haydon Lodge broke up for the summer, Walter went to Miss Freeman's study for the last time. He was elated. He'd been offered a place at London University after he'd fulfilled his military service. But there would be some time before his papers arrived and until then he could spend time with Miss Freeman without fear of discovery.

Miss Freeman was gentle with him. 'It doesn't belong outside,' she told him. 'It's over.'

He refused to believe it. He pleaded that he still needed her. But she was firm. She bade him goodbye without regrets. There were other Walters at Haydon Lodge. Miss Freeman was a teacher in every sense of the word. And always would be.

Walter thought he would never recover from such a rejection and he left school that day in tears of anger and frustration. But even on the train, on his way back to London, his heart lightened. He began to see the logic of Miss Freeman's argument. He saw a certain freedom in it, and he was sad that he had left her with such a display of rage. He marvelled at how quickly he could recover and by the time he reached London, Miss Freeman had become a soothing and loving memory.

The year was 1944, and London, along with other big cities, suffered frequent bombing. Many Londoners had moved out to the country. Walter's father had compromised. He and Terry had moved into the suburbs, to the green belt as it is now known, an unserious bomb depository. Walter had not seen the new house and he looked forward to it. He looked forward too, to seeing Terry, whose occasional ill-spelt letters had cheered his days at school. His father rarely wrote to him, but Terry kept him au courant with the news. Of Hugh and Peter who were both in Italy and in the same regiment. He'd sent him drawings of the new house, but they were like a child's, complete with boxed windows and gingham curtains. There was a neat little car in the hedge-clipped driveway, even though, due to the petrol restrictions, his father had long since been car-less. The front door was framed in climbing ivy, and Walter knew, without having been told, that the doorbell was a series of chimes.

Which indeed it was, and he listened to their pealing as he waited for the door to open. Terry answered, complete with gingham apron.

'Welcome, welcome,' he said, kissing Walter on the cheek. 'I'm cooking. A welcome-home dinner. Your dear father's in a mood, I can tell you. Lost an account today. I said to him, you lose one, you get another. But does he listen to me? You know your father.' A short pause followed. 'But *do* you know your father?'

Terry laughed. He was a tonic in the house. But for Terry, Walter would never have come home.

His father, despite his lost account, was delighted to see him. He did not seem in any way depressed. Terry was given to hyperbole, and in any case his role was to cheer people up, whether they needed it or not. His father had changed radically, Walter thought. He seemed gentler and less demanding. Terry had tamed him, or perhaps he was simply happier.

Despite stringent rationing, Terry had prepared a sumptuous dinner, and Walter knew better than to ask where it all came from. The talk was easy, Terry holding the floor for most of the while. He read aloud the letters from Hugh and Peter, lacing their banalities with all the theatrical flourish he could muster and Walter could hear not a giggle between the lines. Suddenly he missed his brothers. After the war, perhaps they could all be a real family. Terry too. He understood what Terry was. He had seen Terrys at boarding school. There was a master too, a Terry of a kind, and Walter wondered whether his father would fall into that category. The thought did not bother him; it intrigued him rather. All evidence in the house pointed to a similar labelling, but the thought that his father was one of them, was too ridiculous to contemplate. He was grateful for his father's affection, unshown in his boyhood days, and he decided to settle for that without questioning its cause.

After dinner, Terry went into his doodle-bug routine.

The doodle-bug terror had only recently hit London. It was an unmanned missile, a lethal weapon, maiming both mind and body. You could hear it coming from a distance and it buzzed overhead with a droning sound. At that moment one prayed for the drone to continue, for if the noise cut out over your head, you knew that your life was over. Terry had turned the event into a cabaret act, playing both the bug, and the worthy citizens in its path. It was a hilarious turn, and no doubt Mr Berry had seen it a dozen times, but he joined in the laughter with Walter though he was cautious enough to add, 'But it's not funny.'

Walter decided to spend most of the summer at home. He had two months' grace until his call-up papers arrived, so, with his father, he joined the local Home Guard and at night did fire-watching duties. But there was little to do, for in their suburb all was quiet, and at night he listened to the rhythmic stutter of the anti-aircraft fire piercing the skies over London.

There had been a few days' lull in the bombing. It was a Sunday and Walter thought that he might go into town. Lately his mother was often in his thoughts, and always with a certain remorse. He wanted to visit her grave and to tell her he was sorry. He wanted to tell her that he now understood, that as he grew up he had learned how she had suffered. He wanted to kneel at her grave and shed those tears that had been her entitlement at her pill-strewn bedside.

When his father asked him where he was going, he did not hesitate. 'I've never been back to Mum's grave,' he said. 'I'd like to go there.'

'D'you mind if I come with you? I haven't been either. Terry says I ought to.' There was pleading in his voice. And an apology. 'It's too late, I know,' he said, almost to himself.

Walter took his father's arm. 'We'll go together,' he said.

The sun was shining.

'A fine drying day,' Terry said. 'I'll take advantage. I'll wash the nets.' He promised them a good supper when they came home. 'You'll need cheering up a bit,' he said.

They took the bus into town. They spoke little to each other on the way. Their destination was bond enough between them. They bussed through the centre of London. There were many people about and all of them seemed to be in a hurry. They looked worried and miserable. The lull in the bombing had not fooled them. Yet they took advantage of it, grasping the daylight, as if that too was rationed.

'I'm glad we moved out,' Walter's father said. 'Where we live the war seems to have passed us by.'

They changed buses at Piccadilly, and took another to the cemetery in north London. It was going to be a long ride and Walter now felt the need of conversation. There were so many questions he wanted to ask, but he had to be careful with their framing. They must not smack of judgement.

'Do you ever think of Mum?' he asked. He asked it as gently as he was able, and his father did not take the question amiss.

'I'm never *not* thinking of her,' his father said. 'Not a single day passes without a thought of her. I made mistakes. Terrible mistakes. But I was young. There were so many things I didn't understand.' He looked out of the window. Bomb craters lined the roadside and single half-attached house-walls stood astonished. Nobody walked among the ruins, but what he had to say could not be told to anybody. Yet he desperately needed to be heard. 'I should never have got married,' he said. He looked at Walter. 'I made your mother very unhappy,' he said. Then he giggled, with exactly that cry of pain and shame that Hugh and Peter had inherited.

They did not speak again until they reached the cemetery. There was more life in that place than they had sensed in the streets of central London. It was *busy*, busy in the trade of Death. For nowadays there was a lot of it about. People walked through the graves with flowers.

73

Some knelt at gravesides, and others seemed to have lost their way. Neither Walter nor his father knew which way to turn. Mrs Berry had gone to her resting-place some seven years before and had never received a single visitor. Mr Berry only had a vague idea of where she lay and Walter had no memory of it at all. If it had been a Jewish cemetery, he would have known where to find her. She would be lying against the wall, where suicides are buried, out of reach of blessing. Miss Freeman had told him that. But Christians buried them all as one.

It was a very large cemetery and they walked between the graves, scanning each headstone for their kin. They had been walking, and in silence, for about an hour. But neither of them was tired. When one walks through a burial-ground, even for hours, there can be no fatigue, because, with one's steps, one is crossing not space, but time. And time does not tire.

The sun was lowering in the sky when they found it, and deciphered the name of Priscilla Berry through the verdigris on the stone.

The grave was overgrown with grass and weed, and husband and son stood before it and both were ashamed. Walter moved away. He wanted privacy for his moments with his mother and he assumed that his father wished the same. He watched him kneel by the grave then he turned away.

Mr Berry stroked the weeds that covered her. 'I'm sorry,' he whispered. Over and over again, crushing his lips against the grass as he begged her pardon. He knelt there for a long time, as if he could never be sorry enough. Walter watched his heaving shoulders, his hands clawing the earth the while, and for his sake he was relieved, for God knows how long his guilt had charred within him. Neither of them could entirely purge themselves, but they would come again, both of them, to honour her grave.

After a while, Mr Berry rose, stood for a while, then kissed the stone at her head. Then he turned away, away from Walter, leaving his son to his own confession.

Walter knelt by the graveside. Long ago, it seemed, his

tears had been shed on Miss Freeman's bosom. Now he could tell his mother that at last he understood, and that would be the end of his mourning. He started to weed, the first gesture of his remorse. When he had weeded the small square, nothing was left but the earth and a few blades of grass. Now it looked more like a resting-place. He picked up a single white pebble and laid it at the earth's centre. And one too, for his father, so that she would know that she had not been forgotten. In time he would pebble it whole.

He rose and went towards his father. Then taking his arm, they walked slowly out of the cemetery.

It was growing dark, and they hurried to the bus-stop, anxious to get home before nightfall. Driving through the centre of the city, they noticed how the streets thronged with people. For despite the lull, the doubting Londoners were making for the undergrounds for the night's shelter. Whole families, with their sleeping-bags and suppers, waited patiently at the mouth of the tubes. One of the men amongst them carried a squeeze-box, an Orpheus of the underworld, whose music would drown the sirens and lull the children asleep.

By the time Walter and his father reached the suburbs, it had grown dark, and they had to use their torches to guide their way through the blacked-out streets. As they alighted from the bus, they heard the distant din of the anti-aircraft guns.

'Poor old London,' Mr Berry said. 'They're in for it again.'

They had a good way to walk from the bus-stop. The sky was starless. Mr Berry thought it had never been so dark. For some reason his stomach heaved, and he quickened his steps. As they reached the corner of their street, a sudden light lit their passage, and a hubbub of noise broke the silence.

'We must get home,' Mr Berry shouted. There was panic in his voice, and he ran, scanning the street for his home. But where it had once stood was fire. He stopped, his one foot suspended in the air, paralysed by fear. Walter held him steady.

'Come,' he said. 'We have to see what's left.'

'Is Terry left?' his father whispered. For that was the only 'left' that mattered.

'Come,' Walter urged him again, and he dragged him as gently as he was able to where his home once stood.

'This yours?' one of the firemen said. 'You were lucky to be out. Damned lucky. A doodle-bug. Direct hit.'

'Was there anybody inside?' another fireman asked.

Anybody? Mr Berry thought. Everybody was inside. His whole world was inside, and his whole world had turned inside out. He made a rush to go into the flames, bent on his own suttee. Walter held him back. They could do nothing but wait for the fire to be extinguished.

A neighbour came to comfort them, offering tea and shelter. But Mr Berry would not move from where he stood. Quite swiftly the flames were reduced to a flicker, and behind the grey curling smoke, what was left of the house, offendedly offered its silhouetted armature. Walter gripped his father's arm, and together they trod the ash-strewn spaces of what was left.

They made for what was once the kitchen, for Mr Berry knew he would find Terry there. And there he lay, the charred beauty of him. A saucepan was soldered to his one hand, and one leg was poised, petrified, mid-air. He was probably doing his vaudeville turn as the doodle-bug droned in the skies when the sudden silence froze his mincing entrechat. On what was left of his face, was one eyebrow, raised in disgust at his curtailed cabaret.

Mr Berry turned away, weeping. He wailed like a woman who had lost her child. Walter led him through the hollow house into the garden. There he sat him on a stone wall. Strung up on a line, astonishingly intact, the torn net curtains hung like shredded shrouds.

Chapter 6

I felt like doing a little wood-carving, and I went downstairs to my work-room and prepared my tools. I thought I might make a small wooden toy for Simon. A wagon perhaps, or an animal of some kind. I had just settled myself when I heard the phone ring.

How did I know, and with absolute certainty, that it was my mother? The phone bell tolls in the same pitch for all. Yet I knew it was my mother and perhaps it was the sudden curling in my stomach that told me. I wished I had turned on my answering machine. My mother is thrown by that device. She thinks there's a ghost on the line. Only once she had risked a message. It was a précis, told in telegraphese. She even articulated the commas and stops. Had it been anybody else I would have laughed and possibly been moved by the attempt, but since it was my mother, I attributed it to her stupidity. I thought I might let the phone ring, but if it *were* my mother, it would ring for ever. After some minutes the noise began to get on my nerves. And I knew it was she. It was a long time since I had seen or even spoken to her. I rose wearily from my bench. I wandered into the living-room, and just as I reached the telephone, the ringing stopped. It was just like my mother. I was angry and quickly I dialled her number.

'Did you just phone me?' I said when I heard her voice.

'No,' she said.

I didn't know whether or not to believe her. My mother is not a natural liar. She doesn't have the cunning, nor a memory good enough. I was obliged to accept that she was telling the truth, and obliged too, to wonder who it was who had phoned me so urgently. And I blamed my mother for putting this

77

obligation upon me. My poor mother. She was the target of all my blame, whether or not it was from her provenance.

'How are you Mother?' I said, wondering what else one could say to one's mother. The past was undiscussable. The future full of threat. Only the present was reasonably safe. So, 'how are you mother?'

'I'm well as can be expected, thank you,' she said. 'I haven't heard from you for a long time.'

'I've been busy,' I said. Which was true. 'And in any case,' I added, 'I'm also on the phone. I haven't heard from you either.' It was an underhand blow. I knew how she had to overcome her fears to call me.

'When are you coming to see me?' she said.

'I'll come at the end of the week. Saturday, maybe. I'll ring you.'

I was anxious to get off the phone.

'Well come if you can spare the time,' she said.

'Oh Mother,' I said, because there was no other way to express my exasperation.

'Is there nothing else you want to say?' she said.

'No. Should there be?'

There was a long pause. 'You forgot it was my birthday yesterday,' she said.

And she swiftly put the phone down before I could shout at her for reminding me, and at myself for forgetting.

I needed to get back to my carving, but before doing so, I switched on my answering machine just in case it crossed my mother's mind to send me a reproachful telegram. Then I went and cradled a piece of wood in my hand and in a while, my spirits were soothed. I heard the telephone ring. I was not even curious as to the caller, for I was already well absorbed in my work. It was not until lunch-time that I left my bench and switched on the message tape. There was a nervous cough as a preamble to whatever there was to say. A man's cough, and it sounded like a prelude to ill tidings.

'This is Stephen,' the voice said in plaintive fashion. Then I knew that Florence was gone. I sat down and listened.

'I've been trying to get you but there was no reply. Florence died during the night.'

It seemed to me that such a message was right and proper for an answering machine, and I suspected that Stephen welcomed this means of communication. He didn't want immediate come-back. He wanted a measured response. I thought of phoning him but a non-visual condolence means little. I would have told him how devastated I was with the news, but meanwhile I could have been laughing my head off. I would visit him, I decided, but first I would phone to tell him I was coming.

He answered immediately.

'I'm sorry Stephen,' I said. 'Can I come and see you?'

'Thank you for phoning,' he said.

Stephen had always been meticulous. First things first. 'Could you leave it till after the funeral,' he said. 'It'll be just a family affair. After that I shall need friends.'

'Of course,' I said, and then repeated, 'I'm really very sorry.' I recalled Florence's visit and her unnerving behaviour. Yes, she had certainly made an impression. Stained as it was, I would never forget her.

I felt a depression creeping over me. You know how it is. It takes a death . . . So I dialled my mother's number. I would make it up to her. I would take her to the theatre for her birthday.

She was surprised at my call and even more surprised at my offer. She accepted it so graciously that I threw in supper afterwards. She would leave the choice of play to me, she said. I scanned the theatre columns of the newspapers. I was an experienced enough theatre-goer to give the miss to modern plays. In that area it is many years since I have seen a second act, the interval allowing a blessed escape from an ailing piece that one knows with absolute certainty will never get any better. So I plumbed for a classic. A Shakespeare. Reliable. There was a *Hamlet* at the Lyric, with a lead player my mother would respect. It couldn't fail. Though I did see a *Hamlet* once, an amateur production it's true, in which the Prince forgot to kill Polonius, which buggered up the plot somewhat. I can't remember how they muddled through, but muddle through they did, and the text, ill-delivered as it was, still managed to make my ears water. I rang the theatre and booked two seats in the stalls for the following Saturday. I almost began to look forward to it. I prepared the outing with great care. I arranged for a car to take us to the theatre, and I booked a window-table in a good walking-distance restaurant. I even planned in advance the cross-table conversation, choosing topics that had absolutely nothing to do with my mother's past.

She was theatre-dressed when I picked her up and, I have to admit, she looked wonderful. Had she not been my mother, I would have been happy to take her on my arm. But I did, nonetheless, and I was glad that I had brought her a single rose that I pinned on her coat. She was childlike in her delight. The evening augured well.

There are about thirty theatres in London, not counting the fringe. There are six evening performances a week, and besides those, two matinées. On an average, there are five hundred seats in each theatre. There are about forty-five in each row. There are stalls, dress-circles, upper circles and galleries.

My mother and I were in the stalls Row D. Seats 23 and 24. In seat numbers 25 and 26, sat my father and his Mrs Yellow.

My mother thought I had done it on purpose. She fumed beside me, and I thanked God when the curtain rose. I felt her rage at my side, and her constant irritation. It was the first time in my life, and I sincerely hope the last, that I missed out on the final act of a Shakespeare play, but my mother insisted on leaving at the first opportunity, and I didn't have the strength to deny her. I had lost all appetite for dinner, but my mother's was voracious, fed, I suppose, by her fury. I saw my pre-planned dinner conversation go up in smoke and I prepared myself for the rest of a miserable evening.

We were early at the restaurant, and as I expected, our reserved table was still occupied, and we were shunted to the back of the establishment, close to the lavatories. I insisted my mother have a large aperitif and ordered her a double Martini. I whispered to the waiter that he should go easy on everything except the gin. My only hope was to get my mother well and truly sozzled, thus rendering her insensible to previous events. And I ordered a bottle of wine at the same time. I was quite prepared to carry her home, as long as she kept her mouth shut. But she started even before the Martini had arrived. I remained silent, waiting for the waiter to bring her glass. And when it came, she gulped it in the most uncharacteristic and unladylike fashion, but alas, far from subduing her, the gin seemed to feed her fury. It crossed my mind to cancel the bottle of wine. She insisted that I had deliberately arranged the seating. Despite my denials, she could not accept that it was an unhappy coincidence. And frankly I don't blame her. If I had been in her position, I would have thought the same. Out of sheer fatigue, I ceased denying it, and she took my silence as one of admission, which gave her licence to admonish me. No doubt she would come to my father later. And no doubt she did, for I had ceased listening. I consumed glass after glass of wine, and she ranted to herself between undainty mouthfuls, and it was only when I heard the silence across the table that I knew she was spent. I could have wept for her, and for myself too, and for the whole wretched evening. But there was nothing on earth that I could do.

She refused dessert, having no words left to punctuate the fare. I paid the bill and went out into the street to hail a taxi. The fresh air did me no good at all, and I promptly threw up on the pavement. Taxi after taxi passed me by, but I didn't have the strength to lift my arm. In any case it was doubtful whether any cabbie would have stopped for such a wretched fare. My mother would be waiting in the restaurant and perhaps suspicious that I had left her. She was disposed to rejection. But I didn't give a damn. I hated her. I hated her for no reason at all, and for every reason under the sun.

It took me a little while to compose myself, and then of course, not a taxi was to be seen. It was the time when theatres were turning out, and those die-hard second-acters thronged the streets. It would just be my luck to run into my father. When someone tapped me on the shoulder, I guessed that it was he. In the coincidences of the evening it would have figured nicely. And turning, I saw with relief that it was the waiter in the restaurant, who informed me with little concern, that while waiting, my mother had passed out. I suggested he call an ambulance. It was one way of getting home. I returned to the restaurant, unworried, convinced that my mother had had too much to drink. But when I saw her face I feared another cause. I knew that heart attacks are often due to stress, and God knows she'd had enough of that for one evening. I went to her side and held her hand, praying that she would respond in some way. I noticed that the red rose in her buttonhole was still in full and splendid bloom, and I took heart in it. I pinched her cheek to give it an equal colour and she opened her eyes and muttered that she was alright. I was relieved when two first-aid men entered the restaurant and laid her gently on a stretcher. I followed them out, and into the ambulance, and we were away with the bells clanging. I could not suppress a boyhood excitement at my mode of travel.

When we arrived at the hospital, my mother was whipped away and I was told to wait outside. I spent that waiting time in a paroxysm of hate against my father. It was the first time in a long while that I had experienced such feelings in that quarter, and there was some relief in it, as well as my mind a certain logic. But I took no pleasure in it. I was beginning to hate hate. I was beginning to loathe blame. Whatsoever and whomsoever the target. I knew that it stunted my own growth, and I had a life to get on with. Walter's life, if nothing else. I longed to get back to my freezer.

After a while, a doctor emerged and came towards me. I studied his face for clues. It was not smiling, neither was it severe. His expression could have meant anything. Then, when he reached me, he smiled at last.

'There's nothing to worry about. Your mother has had too much to drink. That's about it. Her heart's as strong as an ox. We'll keep her in overnight. She's dead asleep anyway. You can pick her up in the morning.'

'Are you sure, Doctor?' I said. 'Are you sure that there's nothing else?'

'Nothing,' he said. 'She's as fit as a fiddle. Not used to drink, obviously.'

Then I smiled at him and with such gratitude, as if he had saved my mother's life.

I left the hospital and decided to walk home. It would tire

82

me and I could sleep without dreaming. The whole evening had been a fiasco, but its ending had not been dire. I heard myself laughing.

In the morning I drove to the hospital. My mother was waiting for me outside the ward. She looked acutely shame-faced and I decided to make a joke of it. This she accepted with gratitude. I noticed that the rose had wilted, but it did not disturb me. Its purpose was now outgrown.

'What will you do today?' I asked as I dropped her off at her house.

'I'll rest, I think,' she said, 'and write a few letters.' She turned to me and smiled. 'I'm sorry,' she said.

I was stunned. Never in my life had I heard an apology escape her lips. I had to acknowledge that revolutionary change. So I kissed her. Not on the forehead, my usual target, which is but a token and no kiss at all, but on her cheek, which signals the beginning of affection. Then I took her arm and delivered her to her door.

After that whole episode I was more than ready to return to my freezer. I had missed Walter and it had seemed a very long time since he had given me a thought. I recalled his latest, a thought that had directed me to Terry's death, and I hoped that his next would presage a brighter future. I syphoned.

> *His ignorance was encyclopaedic. He knew*
> *absolutely nothing about absolutely*
> *everything.*

I smiled. I would have given a great deal to know to whom that thought referred, but I had no notion of the circle in which Walter moved at the time. If that thought had occurred later on in my syphoning, I would have known that it referred to a book reviewer. But at that time, I couldn't be sure. Perhaps my fiction would reveal a suitable candidate for such an assessment. Next came a more positive clue.

I have found a family at last.

I was satisfied with that one. I felt it had certain possibilities. I put Walter back in the freezer with my usual caress of gratitude. Then I went through my postponement routine; the coffee, the Scarlatti, and the coffee again. Then I took up my pen once more.

. . . the torn net curtains hung like shredded shrouds.

Mr Berry died shortly after the fire. Nobody ever knew exactly why. He took to his bed, or rather, one in a neighbour's house, and he never rose again. He probably had too much death on his hands. The loss affected Walter deeply. Now, fully orphaned, he smelt his own mortality, and the urge to live and to live intensely governed his every move. He prayed for his brothers' safe return. The Berrys had given enough. And if not to England, it served. The boys had been apprised of their father's death, and this news initiated a correspondence between them, in which Walter shared with them his recollections of their childhood. He hoped his letters would form the basis of a future togetherness.

When his call-up papers came, he welcomed them. For the first time in his life, he longed for company. Any kind of company. He would not discriminate. A rowdy barracks would suit him nicely. He was given a choice as to which service he would join. He had never in his life travelled, short of train journeys to and from school. He had heard of the horrors of air and sea-sickness, and short of an overseas posting, he felt he would be more at home in the army. And safer too. It was the winter of 1944 and victory in Europe was in sight. There was a chance of course, of shipment to the Far East, where the war was still raging in its final course. Walter kept his fingers crossed and for three months he enjoyed a rowdy barrack company somewhere in the south of England. During this time he enjoyed the comradeship of many men, but only one could he consider as a possible post-war friend.

Thomas Greenfield, a student like himself, but one who had managed to graduate before his call-up. Tom was some three years older than Walter, but that difference did not affect their friendship. In his last year at university Tom had married a fellow student. Many of his contemporaries had done likewise. Threatened with the call-up, and its possible fatal consequences, they felt they ought to qualify for mortality. Wedlock was a statement of adulthood. To be married was to be grown-up, and to be grown-up entitled one to a licence to die. Only once had the notion of marriage crossed Walter's mind. That was in the Miss Freeman days when he couldn't imagine any other woman on earth as a Mrs Berry. There had been do doubt in his mind that he would marry her soon after he left school, and now when he recalled her end-of-term rejection, he felt a great debt of gratitude. He wondered what new Walter she was teaching, and even now a small pang of jealousy assailed him. Miss Freeman was his sole excursion into the marriage stakes, and he was quite convinced that he would never make such a trip again. Yet the concept of marriage fascinated him, and this curiousity no doubt initiated his friendship with Tom. He plied him with questions as to a husband's status, and Tom, so newly-wed, was more than willing to spell out its delights. He never tired of talking about his wife whom he still referred to as his bride. He kept her photograph in his breast-pocket. He looked at it often and sometimes shared it with Walter, and when he wasn't looking at it, he fingered it in its khaki fold, as a touchstone of sorts. If battle there would be, it would protect him.

Over the next few months, the friendship between the two men deepened, and on Walter's part came close to a sibling love. With Tom, he could enjoy that closeness he had longed for with his own brothers, an intimacy that in his childhood both Hugh and Peter had rejected.

Towards Christmas of that year, the barracks received

its marching-orders. The regiment would sail for India on New Year's Day. On the whole the news was greeted with joy. India was still Empire, and its name conjured up promise of endless exotic delight. Of beauties unknown and unguessed at. Men who had only dreamed of travel were now going abroad, and about as abroad as one could get. Most of them looked upon it as a chance of a life-time. Walter was one of these. There was nothing now to keep him in England, and he considered he might even stay in India and find a new way of life there. But Tom was desolate. He was assailed by all manner of fears. Dying was the least of them. It was the thought of how his marriage would endure his long absence. And even whether it would endure at all. Walter did his best to comfort him, though in no way could he give any assurance.

When the men were promised a Christmas leave before sailing, Tom was greatly cheered, and then once more despondent, when he thought of his leave-taking. Not all the men were allowed leave, and many volunteered to stay in camp. Christmas celebrations were promised them, already a bonus and more than most of them would have received back home. For indeed, many of the men had no homes to return to. Nor families. For them, the barracks were home and their comrades their family. Walter had made no such swift transference. He stayed in barracks because he simply had no home to return to. Nor family. Tom had offered him Christmas hospitality, but Walter had refused, sensing that on his last home leave, Tom's wife would not welcome intrusion. So he stayed with the other orphaned men and it was like no Christmas he'd ever had before. He recalled his child-hood Christmases and his present-less and wretched outsiderness. Then he remembered the Christmas dinner at the hotel, the year when Mrs Yellow was too drunk to stuff a turkey. And his last Christmas of all, when Terry had cooked and his father wore a paper hat and threw streamers across the table. But now, sitting around the barracks table, with Christmas fare and Christmas cheer,

Walter felt very much part of a community. He would not confuse it with family, but for the first time in his life, he felt that he *belonged*. That if he were to leave that table, he would be missed. And that was a feeling that was entirely new. And matchless. He wondered if Peter and Hugh were celebrating. Often at Christmas, there would be a wartime truce and each side would aim only carols at each other. Across the divide, 'Away in the Manger' would be exchanged for 'Heilige Nacht', and on both sides the men would wonder what they were doing there, and all of them longing for home. Whatever that home was made of.

There was little work to do over the holiday period. The men played football in the fields, or darts in the mess-room. Some of them wrote their last letters from England, and Walter wondered whom they were writing to. He wished he could do the same but he had nobody to communicate with. No home address. But he would write anyway. To himself. A diary. He bought a large note-book from the stores, and with some excitement he viewed its first page, white and unmarked. It seemed a shame to deface it. Nonetheless he put the current date in the top right-hand corner, but even as he wrote it, he realised its irrelevance, for one day was very much like another. So he crossed out the date, and decided to use such a label only when it was pertinent to what he had to say. For the book would be less of a diary than a note-book, a receptacle for all his thoughts, and, in small writing, illegible to all but himself, his feelings. At first his pen stuttered a little. He was embarrassed, aware of the personal nature of his pursuit. So he wrote in general terms about Christmas. It was a theme that could apply to anybody. Only later, by the light of a torch, did he particularise his thoughts, and he wrote about the first real Christmas he had ever spent. He relished the speed of his pen and the joy of hearing his own secrets. Translated onto the page, they seemed less burdensome. He was delighted at his new discovery and he resolved to treat himself to a page of revelations every day.

Those who had been on Christmas leave dribbled back to the barracks. Tom was one of the last to return. Walter would have expected a general depression amongst them. But they were unexpectedly elated, excited at the thought of an overseas posting. They had made their farewells and they were ready to go. Walter and Tom greeted each other like long-lost friends though only a few days had separated them. Tom was elated and depressed, both at the same time. Elated because he was about to become a father, and depressed that he would not be in England at the time the child would be born. Walter insisted on celebrating the former, and reminded him of what happiness would be awaiting him on his return, and as he did so, he felt a touch of envy. After his father's death and the time of mourning, he had felt a sense of freedom. He was no longer responsible for anybody. His visit to his mother's grave had finally absolved him from the burden of memorial. He had shown her that he had not forgotten. But now that he was cleared of all duties, he no longer viewed it as a freedom. He *wanted* someone to protect, someone to love. But at the same time, he wondered whether he was capable of either. That night he comforted himself in writing out his feelings in his note-book, and though afterwards he felt relieved, he feared that the note-book, and all that it contained would, over the years, become a substitute for the living of which he was not capable.

They sailed from Liverpool on the 1st of January, 1945. There was little to do on the crossing apart from keeping the ship scrupulously clean, and by the time they docked at Bombay, some three weeks later, Walter's note-book was almost full. He was not tempted to read through what he had written. He was almost frightened to read through his feelings. It was enough that he had written them down. That way, he thought he had accommodated them. He realised he would have to expand his canvas a little. Perhaps he should centre it less on himself, and write about those with whom he came into contact. But that was a challenge of another kind.

Their posting was in Lahore in a barracks that overlooked the Old Fort. Walter and Tom were assigned to
store-keeping. They were responsible for the distribution
and handling of clothing and general equipment. It was a
comfortable job, undisturbed by the rigours of army
discipline. The nearest theatre of war was many miles
away in Burma, and but for the uniformed men and the
arms they carried, the notion of hostilities seemed a pipe-
dream. Evenings were spent wandering around the
market places, or going to the cinema, but much of their
free time the men passed in the cantonment amongst
those whom they knew and could tell apart, for the
foreignness of it all frightened them. They stayed indoors,
little tempted to excursions into the city. They made the
war their excuse. War was no time for tourism. In any
case, there was unrest in the town. Sectarian violence.
The Sikhs walked around with unsheathed daggers, and
there were many mysterious fires. There was no point in
running into trouble. Besides, the humidity was relentless. At least in the barracks, they could occasionally cool
off in the showers. But Walter and Tom were eager for
adventure. And without scruples. If the war didn't
require their combatant services, there was no reason at
all why they shouldn't take a tourist advantage of their
posting. And one day, on a Sunday, when both were free,
Tom suggested a shopping expedition to the open market.
He wanted to buy a silk sari for his wife.

There were myriad little shops around the market
square, and each one displayed a rainbow of silks. Once
Tom had shown a certain interest in some of the wares,
word spread along the market grapevine and he was
surrounded by hopeful shopkeepers each enticing him to
view his display. The friends decided to make a general
production of the event, and they visited each shop in
turn, as a gesture of courtesy to their owners. The silks
were so tender and their colours so radiant, that Walter
wished he had someone in England to whom he could
bring such a present. So he took a vicarious pleasure in

helping Tom with his selection. The swathes of silk were strewn in their turn across the carpeted floors.

'Is it real silk?' Tom asked.

'If it's real,' the storekeeper said, 'it will be passing through your gold wedding ring. That is the test. Let me show you. Are you married Sir?' he asked.

Tom nodded.

'Then let me have your ring.'

'We don't wear wedding rings in England,' Walter said. It sounded like an apology.

'Then we'll use mine,' the shopkeeper said. He laughed as he struggled to withdraw the ring from the fatty nest that was its home. He sucked at his finger, then gently withdrew it, laughing all the time. At last it was free, and he took a silk sari from the rack and threaded it smoothly and swiftly through the ring's centre. The sari glided like a ship in full sail.

'Silk,' he pronounced when its passage was complete. 'Pure silk.' He replaced the ring on his finger. He could do no more to authenticate his wares.

'I'll have that one,' Tom said suddenly. He pointed to a yellow silk with a Paisley design.

Walter held his tongue on the yellow, but he applauded the Paisley design because he knew of Tom's Scottish parentage and the pattern reflected his sickness for home.

The shopkeeper once again wrestled with his ring. When Tom told him it wasn't necessary, he nevertheless insisted, and once again, the silk slithered through its golden cage.

'Shall I show you how to wear it?' a woman asked. She was perhaps the storekeeper's wife.

'No,' Tom said quickly. He wanted no-one to try it on. His wife would be the first.

They wrapped the sari very gently in many tissues and they wished his wife luck and joy from it, adding a scented greetings card to the package.

When they left the shop, Tom expressed his wish to return to the barracks. He wanted to put the sari in a safe place. Walter agreed. He was tired. The heat and humidity was enervating. They turned in the direction of the Fort. As they reached the outskirts of the market, those little narrow streets that housed the fringe pedlars and their pavement wares, they heard screams and the roar of fire. And as they turned the corner, they saw the tongues of flame licking the sky. It seemed that a whole row of food stores had caught fire, and from the screams it was clear people were trapped within. A crowd had gathered on the street, and they watched, horrified, for there was nothing that they could do. There was no sign of a fire-engine, though a few pathetic buckets of water appeared from nowhere and were frantically thrown on the flames. Then from one of the open windows, a child's hand appeared. It waved limply, up and down, and the gold bangles on the wrist struck the rotting window-sill. Walter noticed that the little finger-nails were painted red.

'Here,' Tom said suddenly, turning to Walter. 'Hold this for me.' He handed him the packaged sari and he rushed towards the burning store.

That was the last that Walter saw of him. Not counting the charred remains of his friend which, some time later, when the flames were spent, the tardy fireman brought out on a stretcher. The body had been covered with a sheet and its sandalled feet hung over the edge of the canvas.

'It's my friend,' Walter said to one of the firemen.

'Come in the ambulance, sonny,' the man said. 'We'll need his name and particulars. A hero, your friend,' he said.

Walter followed him, and when the ambulance door closed, the fireman raised the sheet. Walter stared at his friend. He thought of Terry and he reckoned that in his own life he had supp'd full enough of fire.

'Thomas Greenfield,' he said. '45th battalion.' His voice broke on his friend's identity and he made no attempt to hold back his tears. He felt a dragging pain in his wrist and looking down, he noticed how his hand gripped the sari package as if it were a life-line. He must get it back to the barracks, he thought. For safe keeping as Tom had wished.

'Cry it out, sonny,' the fireman said.

Walter noticed that there were tears in the man's eyes as well. In India men were allowed to weep without seeming to lose their virility. He put his hand on Walter's arm. 'A hero, your friend,' he said again.

'More than that,' Walter said. 'He was my brother.'

Although Tom had not died in combat, he was buried with full military honours. And the dignitaries of Lahore, informed of his heroic act, turned out in full to pay their respects. Around the fringe of the cemetery, the market people had gathered, many themselves in mourning. And children too, their kohl eyes wide with wonder. When it was over, the mourners turned away, but Walter lingered there, kneeling by the grave. He did not hear the child's footsteps running on the gravel behind him. But he saw her as she stopped by the graveside. Around her neck hung a garland of flower petals. She lowered her head and slipped the necklace onto the grave. Walter noticed the gold bangles on her little wrist and the chipped red nail-polish on her baby nails. The gesture heartened him. Somehow it made Tom's death less futile. He decided he would call on Tom's wife if ever he returned to England and give her the sari that his friend had bought with such love.

The repatriation came sooner than expected. On the 2nd September, 1945, Japan surrendered to the allies and the Second World War was over. At the end of that year, Walter sailed home to his first Christmas of the peace. And he had nowhere to go. He wondered whether his brothers had come home, and how he could contact them. The thought crossed his mind to visit Mrs Greenfield. It had been over six months since Tom's death. Time to recover perhaps. And the baby must have arrived and eased her sorrow. But perhaps a reminder of Tom's death would be ill-timed. Too early or too late, perhaps. He would wait until the new year. Meanwhile he had to find somewhere to live.

He found student digs near the university. He had been given a choice of addresses and he chose one in Doughty Street because it boasted one of the many London-strewn Dickens blue plaques. The house was run by a Mrs Waterson. There were six lodgers in all, and all of them men. For some reason, unknown even to Mrs Waterson herself, women lodgers were not welcome. She lived alone in her basement quarters. There had been a Mr Waterson, but he had died in the early stages of the war. He was a chronic asthmatic, and he had suffered an attack during a heavy air-raid over London. Deep in the underground shelter, having forgotten his medication, he had expired, already, as Mrs Waterson reported, half way to burial. He was only thirty-five, and it seemed to Walter that in war time, it was an illegal way to die. Much like Tom's death. Unauthorised.

His room overlooked the street and echoed the traffic. He was glad of the noise. It was company of a kind. He found it hard to settle. After a week, his kit-bag still lay packed at the foot of his bed. He had many things to do. Bureaucratic things. His demob papers to be put in order. His university grant. His search for the whereabouts of his brothers. This latter nudged him most, but every day he put it off till the morrow. Until one day, Mrs Waterson took him in hand. She asked him into her sitting-room and with a cup of tea and a digestive biscuit, she encouraged him to talk. To her sympathetic ear he revealed his orphanhood, Tom's death and his present lack of anchorage, and when it was all out, he felt relieved and unburdened.

The following day he went to the appropriate quarters in search of his brothers. He paid sundry visits to different offices and on the fourth, Hugh and Peter were located. They had only recently been demobbed and were now registered at a hostel in the Old Kent Road.

For the first time since his home-coming Walter was excited. He ran to the bus-stop laughing aloud. He was impatient to reach the hostel and from his front seat on the top of the bus, he urged the bus driver through the traffic. He had difficulty in recalling his brothers' faces, but that did not disturb him. They shared the same mother and father, and though their description of their childhood would be radically different from his own, they were still blood, and the only kin he had.

The address that the army officer had given him was in a quiet street well hidden from the main road. It was part of a terrace of houses, three of which had been united for the purpose of temporary accommodation. The main door swung open and the caretaker sat in a booth in the hall.

'Peter and Hugh Berry?' Walter enquired.

The caretaker consulted his book. 'Oh,' he said looking at Walter, 'the smilers.'

Suddenly Walter recalled his brothers' faces, feature by separate feature, and he heard the giggles that shaded each one.

'Room 27,' the caretaker said. 'Top floor.'

Walter sprinted up the four flights and knocked on the door of number 27.

'Who is it?' he heard from inside.

He didn't know whether it was Hugh's or Peter's voice.

'Walter,' he called. He heard the hesitation in his voice, and he realised how unsure he was of his welcome. But the door was answered immediately, and Peter stood there with Hugh behind him, sharing a wide grin between them with the giggle not far behind. And without any forethought, because thought would have stifled the gesture, they fell into a trio of embrace and held it for a while until the giggles broke and Walter was able to convert them into laughter.

The three of them sat on one of the bunks. 'Where shall we begin?' Walter said. He suddenly felt older than both his brothers, and the one who had to orchestrate their recall. The one to direct proceedings, as it were, or organise an agenda of events that would cover the years of their separation.

'You first,' Hugh and Peter said together. They were happy to be guided by their younger sibling.

'Where did we leave off?' Walter asked.

94

''39,' Peter said. 'Almost six years. Dad was living with Terry.'

Then the cover-up laughter in which Hugh joined.

'You were still at school,' Hugh said.

So Walter told them of his last years at Haydon Lodge. But he held his tongue on Miss Freeman. That baptism was not for sharing. He told them about their father's last years of happiness and about their joint visit to their mother's grave. Then their return to the house that was no longer there, and what was left of poor Terry in what was left of the kitchen. And finally their father's death. Inexplicable. Except by way of metaphor. He dwelt long on these stories reliving them as he spoke. And in contrast, he dealt swiftly with his Indian experience. All that remained of it was the silk sari in his kit-bag, and that and its provenance was another event that was his and his alone.

'Now you,' he said. 'Your turn.'

The two older brothers looked at each other. Both knew they could not match Walter's narrative. Although they had been in the front line and taken their share of risk and danger, it seemed to them that Walter's war, non-combatant as it was, had been more violent and perilous than theirs. In any case, they were men of few words. Always had been, and the war had not loosened their tongues. At most they could only itemise their experience. They had seen little action until the summer of 1943, when they were part of a contingent that entered Sicily.

'But that was over in two months,' Hugh said. 'The Italians surrendered.'

'What was it like, the fighting?' Walter asked.

And in answer he had to make do with giggles but that laughter told him all that he needed to know.

The brothers were more expansive about their non-combatant times.

They talked with a certain nostalgia about their billets on various Italian farms. Then Hugh said that they had decided to go into farming. That with their gratuity money they could buy a smallholding, in Yorkshire perhaps, where they had friends they had met in the army.

'That's our story,' Hugh said, and Peter gave the giggle coda.

'What about you?' Peter said. 'What will you do?'

'I've got a place at university. And a grant. I won't have to worry for a few years.'

Then there was a silence. It seemed that all had been said, and once again Walter felt himself the younger brother. The outsider. Once their news was exhausted, he had little to say to them, and they to him, yet he felt a deep affection for them both and he knew that they felt likewise towards himself. But for all of them it was inexpressible.

'I'm going to visit Mum's grave next week,' Walter said. 'Want to come?'

Although they had nothing in common except for their parentage, he didn't want to let his brothers go.

'Yes,' Hugh said, 'let's go together.'

He could leave now, Walter thought, in the sure knowledge that they would meet again. Perhaps together at their mother's grave, they could register for the first time, as a family.

The visit heartened him and when he returned to Doughty Street, he felt ready to declare himself out of limbo. To acknowledge the status of civilian, and to unpack his kit-bag. Of all its contents only two items held any significance. His diary, or rather his note-book as it had become, and Tom's last purchase. He put both items on the table. Both of them represented unfinished business. The note-book would have to be read and appended. And the sari must be delivered.

On New Year's Day Walter made his way to Mrs Greenfield's house. He did not rehearse what he would say to her. He would play it by ear. He hoped that he would not be a total stranger to her, and that perhaps Tom had referred to him in his letters home.

Mrs Greenfield lived in Camden Town, within walking distance of his lodgings. He felt buoyant. The day was clear, that first day of the year, and the chill air was bracing. He found the house with ease. It lay in a close off the High Street. There were about a dozen houses in the alley, all sporting dustbins at their front doors. The area was rather more up-market than Walter had expected. It was distinctly middle-class, a social standing he would have least surmised in his friend. No doubt he had married above his station. Walter rang the bell of number 5. From such a front door, he expected chimes, so he was relieved to hear the echo of a low buzz, a sound without pretension. The door was opened by a woman, a baby on her arm. Walter presumed that she was Tom's wife. Again he was surprised. She was clearly older than his friend, and in other ways, seemed an unlikely partner. She was flamboyantly dressed, which indicted a temperament far removed from Tom's quiet reticence.

'Mrs Greenfield?' he asked.

She nodded. 'Can I help you?'

'I was a friend of Tom's,' Walter said. 'I was with him in Lahore.'

He saw a smile quickly cross her face. 'I was with him when he died,' he said.

Mrs Greenfield touched his arm with a tenderness that was sublime. A resigned gesture of her widowhood. 'Come inside,' she said.

He followed her into the living-room. A framed photograph of Tom first caught his eye, and a sadness overcame him and a deep sense of loss.

'I'm glad you came,' she said. 'Let me make you some tea.'

'That would be kind, Mrs Greenfield,' Walter said.

'Since you are a friend of Tom's, you must call me Christina,' she said.

The baby started to whimper on her arm, as if asking for introduction.

'And this is Amanda,' Christina said.

Walter felt like a trespasser. This was the child whom Tom had never seen, whom Tom had talked about almost daily before his death. He cursed the fire that had taken

97

his life, and his wanton heroism. And he himself had stood by and helplessly watched. How Christina must resent him for surviving. He would tell her everything, he decided. So over tea, he told her about the fire, and of Tom's funeral, and of the little girl who had laid her necklace of petals on his grave.

Then he handed over the sari.

She cried quite openly as he told his tale, but managed a smile when she opened the gift.

'He knew my colour,' she said softly.

Walter hoped that she would not try it on. It would be another sight that he had stolen. But she smoothed its silk with her hand and put it aside.

'You are good to have come to see me,' she said. 'I hope you will come again.'

Walter was hoping for another visit. Christina reminded him a little of Miss Freeman. He would be more than happy to know her better.

When he was leaving, she repeated her invitation. 'You're a link with Tom,' she said.

Walter was happy to accept that as a basis for their friendship. It was an honest enough beginning, and that initial honesty gave it a licence to lead wherever it would.

Chapter 7

I could almost hear my late mentor's snort of disapproval. Alright Walter, I said to myself, I know I've cheated a bit. But don't be hard on me. I have reached a point in my story where fact and fiction must inevitably overlap. For in another chapter or two, we move towards the period of our first meeting. I know about Christina and Amanda. I know their names, that is. But I didn't know how you met and you never told me. So I made it up, but as things seem to turn out, it might not be fiction after all.

I don't know why I felt this need to explain myself to Walter. Writers on the whole do not acknowledge their sources, leave alone apologise to them. I am grateful to Walter for having enabled me. But there it must end. As a writer, I am now free to cheat, to steal and to distort at my will. What a cunning trade we ply. Now, as I went once more to my freezer, I felt like a safe-breaker, and faintly scrupled, I resorted to my Scarlatti and coffee routine. And prolonged it, and for some reason, I felt a growing Walter-resentment. A borrower of money will eventually come to dislike his lender. To hate him almost. I suppose it's the same with ideas, and I knew I had to refrain from biting the hand that fed me. A rest perhaps. A break from my freezer.

I had renewed appetite to see Amanda again. But I was wary. She could not help but be a source for my fiction, and I wanted nobody else's facts. I simply wanted my own invention. I recalled the last time we had met. My dinner party, and possibly poor old Florence's last public appearance. I had been so engrossed in Walter's passage to India, that the thought of Stephen's bereavement had entirely slipped my mind. I would go and see him as I had promised. I dialled his number. His answering machine gave out a number to contact him in Canada. I knew that Stephen had a brother there and I surmised that he had gone abroad to put some distance between himself and his sorrow. I would wait for his return. In some desperation, I then dialled Amanda's number. But that call was no more promising than the one to Stephen. For Amanda's housekeeper informed me that she had gone on holiday and would return in three weeks. I was relieved in a way, but somehow I felt deeply rejected by everybody. I was about to throw in the sponge and make my way to the freezer when the phone rang and I have never been happier to hear its bell. The fact that it was my mother on the other end of the line only slightly reduced my pleasure. At least there was somebody who was available, and moreover, willing to make contact. But her voice unnerved me. I realised suddenly that I had not been in contact with her since our eventful evening at the theatre, and I could rightly expect some tone of reproof in her voice. But there was no hint of that. Her tone was one of a plea, and moreover, a plea in panic.

'What is it, Mother?' I said.

'Your father's had a heart attack. They phoned me from the hospital.'

'Where is he?'

'St Martin's,' she said. 'Would you come with me?' she pleaded.

'Of course,' I said. 'I'll be over in ten minutes.'

Of course she was afraid. Not only for my father's life, but of the sure possibility of running into her replacement at his bedside. She clearly needed my support. On the way to her house I wondered why she had been contacted at all. Although my father had never married his Mrs Yellow, he'd lived with her for well over fifteen years. I wondered too what I ought to be feeling myself. I drove quickly, careless of the traffic.

She was waiting for me at the end of the drive, clearly in as much haste as I. We drove in silence to the hospital, as if any words that passed between us would delay our arrival. I parked illegally in a doctor's space, considering my visit an emergency one, and we hurried into the foyer. My father's room was quickly located and a nurse asked us to wait outside. Shortly we were told that we could enter.

'You can see your husband now, Mrs Peabody,' the nurse said.

My mother noted the status she'd been offered but she was too anxious to reflect on it. She pushed me forward into the room as some kind of advance protection. Mercifully there was no-one else present and my mother's relief was plainly visible. I walked across to the bed and she followed me, placing herself on the other side. It was an intensive care ward and two other patients were fighting for dear life. My father was attached to numerous tubes and to sundry batteries that registered his body's functions in a kaleidoscope of colours. I thought that if I put a penny in one of the slots, it would speak my weight or perhaps turn out a tune. And I realised then what I was feeling. A sense of total ridiculousness. I took my father's hand in mine. On his wrist was attached his identity. Idly I read the details through the plastic. My father's name with which I fully agreed. No mistake about that. But I had trouble with what followed. His address. Loud and clear it spelt out my mother's house and I realised then, that at death's door, he had accepted that he had never left her. No doubt he had registered her as his next-of-kin, which explained the absence of Mrs Yellow and the phone call from the hospital. I covered his wrist with my hand. I did not want my mother to see it. In fifteen years she had never given up hope of his return. That label would feed those hopes, that label that pronounced only a coffined return.

'How are you dear?' my mother said.

I was glad that that question was her first priority. For myself, I was anxious to know where it had happened, who had brought him to this place, and above all, where was Mrs Yellow? And did she indeed *know*? But those questions would have to wait, or maybe forever remain unanswered.

'I'm alright,' I heard my father say, and again, 'I'm alright.'

He was telling himself to recover. I hoped fervently he was not going to apologise to her, to say he was sorry about the way he had treated her, for such an apology would surely

101

have signalled his death. And I didn't want him to die. He had given me little cause to love him, but all that ill-treating past was now irrelevant. He might well have been a monstrous father but I still didn't want him to die. His death would be no-one's loss except my very own. I squeezed his hand. He turned to me and smiled. We stood there for a while, my mother and I, smiling at him. We knew that conversation, even if we had any on our tongue-tips, would tire him, and it was a relief when the nurse approached the bed and suggested we should leave.

'Come back this evening if you like, and bring his toiletries and fresh pyjamas.'

'But . . .' my mother started to say. His pyjama'd days were well in her past, together with his toiletries.

'We'll do that,' I said quickly. I could easily furnish my father with night-clothes, but I was terrified that they might serve as a shroud. My mother bent over and kissed my father on his forehead, and I followed suit.

'We'll come back later,' I said.

Once outside the door, I asked to see the doctor. I needed answers to questions, questions that I could only address to a stranger. Where did it happen? How and why? And who brought him in? And who filled in his particulars? But most important of all, was he going to die? I asked that last question first. My mother hovered at my elbow. 'Of course not,' the doctor said. 'It was only a slight attack. The next twenty-four hours are crucial of course. He'll stay in intensive care. You can phone or come in at any time.'

Suddenly all the other questions that had crowded my tongue seemed to be irrelevant. The who, the where and the why no longer mattered. My father stood a good chance of survival and that was satisfying enough, for I was nowhere near ready for him to die. I took my mother's arm. I was suddenly terribly hungry. It was almost six o'clock and I suggested an early supper and then we could return to the hospital.

'I'm starving,' my mother said. 'I don't know why.' She sounded ashamed.

I was relieved that she shared my sudden appetite. I suppose it was for life as much as it was for food.

I found a restaurant near the hospital but when I discovered that it was Indian cuisine I demurred, for my mother was in no way adventurous in her eating habits. But she insisted that she try something new. There was a sudden light in her eye, and I had the feeling that, whether my father lived or died, my mother had recovered from his betrayal.

We took time with our meal. My mother insisted on sampling almost everything on offer.

'I like this food,' she said. 'I must tell Violet. We'll buy a recipe book.'

She was loathe to leave the restaurant, fearful perhaps of a hospital return. But when we arrived, there was still no other visitor and my father had undergone no change. He was sleeping and the nurse showed us into a small annexe waiting-room.

'There's an electric kettle if you want to make yourselves coffee,' she said. 'The milk's in the fridge, and the bed is quite comfortable.' She clearly thought we would stay the night and because of that, we both felt obliged to satisfy her. My mother made no objection. Indeed, I think she wanted to be there to be on hand for the latest bulletins. She said she was thirsty, but that coffee would unsettle her stomach. I went downstairs to the hospital shop and bought some cold drinks. When I returned I found her settled cosily in the bed. She looked as if she were on holiday. I checked on my father and he was still sleeping. I urged my mother to sleep too. I promised to wake her if there were any bulletins. I settled myself in the armchair with a magazine on flying. It was the only reading matter available. It was a subject about which I knew absolutely nothing and in which I had not the slightest interest. I gave it a dutiful try, but tired of it soon enough. I was aware of a sudden quiet in the room, and looked up to find my mother in a quiet doze, a small smile lingering on her lips. And immediately I thought of Mrs Yellow. And felt sorry for her. I assumed she could not possibly be aware of what had happened, and she must by now be deeply anxious as to my father's absence. I thought I ought to phone her, but I knew that her intelligence of my father's condition would quickly wipe that small smile from my mother's lips. It hovered there simply because it was she and no other who'd been made privy to my father's condition, and I felt it would be an act of supreme disloyalty were I to inform Mrs Yellow. It wasn't my business anyway. I watched my mother sleeping. I think it was the first time in my life that I had caught her napping. It was a form of eavesdropping without fear of discovery, and as I watched her, I felt a little ashamed, because I knew she was not in control of her looks and gestures. I think she must have fallen into a deep sleep and the smile had deepened too. It no longer hovered. It had planted itself firmly from ear to ear. Despite the smile, I'm sure that she did not relish my father's condition. She was smiling because it had enabled her to forgive him, and she could now, with some reliance, look forward to a future unsoured by her bitterness and rage. It was a smile of infinite relief, and I wished her well of it.

I left the room to check on my father. He was still sleeping. I told the nurse that I was going to collect his night things and that she should tell my mother if she woke. I hurried to my car and was grateful that my anti-social parking had gone unnoticed. Once in my bedroom, I went to my pyjama drawer. I am very fussy with my clothing. I buy only the best materials. The money from my father allows me to indulge myself. No doubt he would deeply disapprove of the silk pyjamas I was about to lend him and possibly he would consider them his right to keep, for he never tires of reminding me of how well I am endowed. But that didn't bother me. In fact, I rather relished this act of role-reversal, in which I had been called upon to look after my parents. Not that my father had ever looked after me. But all that didn't matter any more. I went into my bathroom for toiletries. I gave him packets of my best soaps. I had a spare electric razor and I packed that too, though I was none too sure he'd given up the strop he'd used in my childhood. Then I threw in a bottle of very expensive after-shave for good measure. The thought crossed my mind to add a bar of chocolate to the package. My father had really become a child for me and in this mood I could think of him kindly.

I rushed back to the hospital and there was no change on any front. My mother was still asleep, and probably enjoying her most restful night for years. My father too was sleeping, and as I watched him, I saw his eyelids quiver in dreams and I wondered whether in the morning they would bear the telling. I spent most of the night commuting between my two sleeping begetters, and it was a salutary experience. Any residual anger I felt towards either of them was quickly diluted as I watched them sleeping. For in such a state, even the foulest villain assumes a look of innocence, and can thus be forgiven. When I looked at my father, I could in no way connect him with the belt-buckle scars on my back, and my mother's drowsy face gave off not a hint of her voracious expectations. It did me a power of good to watch them both. That nocturnal viewing offered me a respite from the ragged rage that had dogged my childhood and growing-up years.

My father was the first to waken. I waited outside the ward while the doctor was inside. I was nervous of his verdict. I did not think that my father could die. He had too much unfinished business on his hands. I knew that to be a fatuous thought, but a man in the state of anxiety can be forgiven a lapse of intelligence. I did not have to wait long. The doctor emerged and came straight towards me.

'Your father's condition is satisfactory,' he said. 'If he continues in the same way, he should be out of intensive care and in his own ward by this evening.' Then he was gone, before I could question him, even though I had no questions to ask. He had delivered his verdict like a written bulletin and I wondered whether he was capable of ordinary conversation. I went in. My father was still attached to numerable machines but he was sitting up and looking cheerful. A nurse followed me in with his breakfast and asked if I would like some coffee. I accepted gladly. She asked me if she should wake my mother, but I told her to let her sleep.

'Your mother still here?' my father said.

My mother had a name, I thought. Priscilla. Prissy, as he used to call her in my childhood days. Now the name had slipped his tongue, and 'mother' was the distance that he chose.

'She stayed the night. She was worried,' I said.

'There was no need,' was his graceless response.

My old feelings towards him slipped comfortably back into gear. I had not been easy with my erstwhile forgiving nature. My father was awake, and he was on the mend and I no longer had to pardon him. I took his hand, not out of any affection but to draw his attention to the lie on his wrist. I feigned surprise as I read the label.

'You've given Mother's address,' I said. 'Why?'

'It was all rather difficult,' he said. I was surprised at the strength in his voice. My father always shouted when he was in the wrong.

'Anne's away, you see.' Anne is the name of his Mrs Yellow. 'She's in Australia. Her mother's ill in Sydney.'

It seemed to me that the location of Anne's mother's illness was totally irrelevant, but my father was elaborating, postponing the point he wished to make.

'She's not likely to survive.' More ornament. 'Anne's very upset.'

Yet more.

'Get to the point, Father,' I said.

'There was no point in giving my address,' he said.

'But why Mother's?' I insisted.

'They wanted to know how to get in touch with my wife.'

'Wife?' I said.

'Oh it's all so difficult.' He put some toast in his mouth, hoping I'd have the decency to engage him no further in explanation.

'She was just convenient,' I said. I left it at that. 'I'll tell her you're awake,' I said. I would leave them both to it. I noticed when I left, how he hid his labelled wrist beneath the bedclothes and I felt a surge of that blessed indifference that I had worked for so long to acquire, and I was at ease with myself. I went to the annexe to give my mother the latest bulletin.

She was awake and drinking coffee. I noticed that she had applied make-up to her face and I felt vaguely sorry for her.

'How is he?' she said.

'He's on the mend. He should be out of intensive care by this evening.'

'Is anyone with him?' she asked.

I smiled at her. 'The coast is clear,' I said.

'Then I'll go and see him.' She rose and smoothed down her dress.

'I'll wait for you. Then I'll run you home.'

'I won't stay long with him,' she said.

I watched her leave. I wasn't fearful for her. She was a much stronger character than my father. Whatever shit he chose to shovel her, and intensive care would not stop him, she would take in her stride. Her newly-acquired stride of confidence. I hoped she wouldn't be long. I was anxious to get home. Anxious to get back to my freezer, that oasis of sanity. I was deeply confused. My experience in the last twenty-four hours had questioned in my mind the need for fiction. Was not reality crazy enough? And what was I doing with my mentor's thoughts? Was I turning fiction into fact? Or vice versa? I realised that it was futile to speculate on my motives. I just had to sit down and do it, and leave its motivation and its genre to other people to assess. I heartily wished my mother would make it short, whatever the 'it' was, and as if in answer to my prayer, she suddenly appeared in the doorway and said that she was ready to leave. She did not seem to be in any way upset. Indeed that small smile of victory still played on her lips. She had little to report on the way home and I took care not to pump her. She talked about buying an Indian cookery book and I knew that she had taken my father's illness in her stride. She asked me into her house for breakfast, but I declined. She showed no resentment and she urged me to get some sleep. But sleep was the last thing I wanted. I could not wait to get back to my freezer. Yet when I arrived home, a sudden fatigue overcame me and I knew that I was in no state to go a-syphoning. I had a shower and went straight to bed, and almost at once fell into an untroubled and dreamless sleep. I think I must have been faintly conscious at the time, for I remember relishing that sleep, knowing that I was in it. When I awoke, I dressed and went straight to the freezer. No coffee, no Scarlatti, no woodwork. I caressed Walter, as was my wont, as I set him on the kitchen table and reverently went to work.

The first decipherable thought to emerge was as follows.

*Old age is not a blessing. It is simply a
reward for having looked both ways before
crossing the road.*

Now that was a signpost indeed. Remember, I was steeped in
Walter's work. The thought that I had just syphoned was the
theme of his very first novel. Although he was a mere twenty-
five at the time, he had written a book about old age. I myself
was only fifteen then, but already immersed in contemporary
fiction, and even I, novice as I was, knew that a prodigious
talent had surfaced. The book was called *Autumn*. Not the best
of titles, a little obvious, a little lacking in self-confidence, but
the novel itself had such authority, it was astonishing that it
had come from such a young pen. So that latest idea that I had
syphoned was a signpost indeed, for I knew that it marked
the beginning of Walter's career as a professional writer.
Having thus been guided in the course my autobiopsy should
now take, I made myself some coffee. And I could not resist
another Scarlatti. I still had over five hundred sonatas to go,
more than enough to see me through even the most desperate
of procrastinations. In fact, I indulged in two sonatas, because
I was wary and a little nervous of picking up my pen once
more. Because a mere thought as a signpost is much more
difficult to validate than an out-and-out event, such as those
specific happenings that I had relied upon hitherto. I was
tempted to syphon further, to locate an actual incident, but
the simple idea of old age as a signpost was a challenge, and
my Scarlatti was a means of 'screwing my courage to the
sticking-place'. In so doing, I found it helpful to sing the
melody as I played. And continued to do so even after I had
left the piano. And even as I took up my pen. I don't know
when I stopped singing, but I was well into my first paragraph
before I was conscious of the silence.

. . . and that initial honesty gave it a licence to lead where
it would. Soon after that first meeting, Walter started his
course at university. He had chosen to read English, a

course he was later to regret. He had steeped himself in the great nineteenth century English novel tradition and at the same time he started to write. Short stories at first, culled from those notes he had assembled in India. But he regarded these as five-finger-exercises, for he knew instinctively that the novel was his form. So he made a start on *Autumn*. In the beginning, it stuttered along. Every sentence was a hurdle. His mind was buzzing with the great English novel and he found it singularly inconvenient to write with Trollope at his elbow and Dickens breathing down his neck. So he gave up on his English literature course and switched to Language. He had no fear that Beowulf and Gawain would disturb him stylistically. He was grateful simply to achieve a translation of the Old and Middle English and that understanding was all he needed to win a degree. And he stopped reading fiction of any kind.

But he made time to visit Christina occasionally and soon in their meetings, they no longer felt the need to talk about Tom. He warmed too, to little Amanda. He had never forgotten his vow as a child that he would avoid the siring of children. He felt that Amanda was a neat compromise. One day she asked him if she could call him 'Daddy'. Christina was embarrassed. She feared that Walter might view the child's request as a form of blackmail, and though she would dearly have wished to settle down with Walter, she wanted that status on her own account and not on her daughter's behalf. Walter sensed her awkwardness.

'That depends on your mother,' he said. When he heard his words, he realised that they were a proposal of sorts. He didn't regret them. Indeed he was glad that Amanda had occasioned them, because he knew he would never have the courage to state his simple wish to marry her mother.

'Can I, Mummy?' Amanda asked.

'If you like,' Christina said.

Thus Walter proposed and Christina accepted, both

through the agency of a third party and the method suited all of them.

'Daddy, Daddy, Daddy,' Amanda shouted, skipping across the room. The marriage was a fait accompli. All it needed was a certificate.

Christina suggested that first he should finish his novel. Then they would have a double celebration. Walter was grateful for her understanding. That night, when he returned to his lodgings, he sensed that his future had been planned, and though he had participated little in its organisation, he felt a great sense of security. Thereafter, in the knowledge of having secured her, he saw less of Christina, confining his visits to weekends. And he worked feverishly on his novel.

He finished it as he neared the end of his degree course and he realised that he had done precious little academic revision. A few weeks before his final exams, he shut himself up in his lodgings and worked for his degree. He didn't even visit Christina. He was not after academic glory. He would be satisfied with a simple pass. He had given up on any notion of a career. He was a writer, and by that means, and only by that means, would he earn his bread.

He borrowed a typewriter from the college, and prepared his manuscript for presentation. Then he went to the reference library and studied the *Writers' & Artists' Yearbook*. He copied out a list of literary agents and, not trusting the post, he carried his completed manuscript to the agent nearest his lodgings.

Richard Baron was an accessible man, and very friendly. He had only recently started his own agency and he was hungry. He promised to read the manuscript within the week. Walter went home and waited for the phone to ring. He hadn't seen Christina for almost two months though he had telephoned her regularly. Their conversations were loving and gentle, but devoid of fire or urgency. Christina was no Miss Freeman, and Walter wondered whether ever again he would feel that passion that his English teacher had engendered. Yet he would marry Christina. He was bespoke. Amanda had been the marriage-broker. He was happy enough to fulfil his obligation. Marriage was perhaps a necessary factor in life, but already, even before it had happened, it had assumed less importance than his writing. He was confident that Christina would understand. She too after all, had had her passion. She had, in her time, loved in Tom's fire. She too would now settle for the warm embers of companionship and mutual caring. He told her about his novel and promised to visit as soon as he had news.

Meanwhile he waited. He left his door open so that he could hear the communal phone ringing in the hall, and at each ring, he darted to his door, and waited for the landlady's call. On his third day of waiting, a small seed of anger sprouted in his heart. He took down his handwritten manuscript and started to read. He decided to read it slowly and carefully, as an agent should. It did not occur to him that Richard Baron had anything else in the world to do apart from reading Walter Berry's first novel. He would allow him the first three days' grace, more than enough he thought to prepare himself for the reading. But now he would time him. He looked at his watch. Half past eleven. He turned to the first page. After the first chapter, he gave his agent time to make himself some coffee. He was entitled to that. And Walter made coffee for himself, to keep him distant company. Half way through the novel, he allowed his agent yet another break. A half an hour to be exact, which he thought was more than generous. Then back to the novel. Slowly and carefully. By about chapter fifteen, Walter was too engrossed to allow himself a break and he was damned if he was going to grant his agent one, so he persisted to the very end. Then he looked at his watch. A quarter to three. He allowed that he was a quick reader, so perhaps he should give his agent leeway of an hour or so. This he did, and at four o'clock he took up his stand at the door of his room. And waited. For two hours a screaming silence echoed down the hall, and Walter had to accept that, by that time, Richard Baron had left his office.

The next morning, Walter awoke with a single thought in his mind. He was going to kill his agent. But first he needed breakfast. He left his room for the first time in almost a week. And he went shopping. He took his time. Killing could wait. He had no fear of losing his appetite for the deed. And why indeed go home at all? He might even buy a newspaper and read it over breakfast in a café, a rare treat. Let Richard Baron stew his last hours away.

He lingered over his breakfast and he read the newspaper from cover to cover. It was eleven o'clock before he returned to his lodgings and the good Mrs Waterson was waiting for him.

'There was a call for you,' she said. 'A Mr Baron. He said you should call him. I left his number on the telephone pad.'

'Thank you Mrs Waterson,' Walter said. He tried to appear cool. He walked slowly upstairs to his room. He would take his time with his return call. It was Richard Baron's turn to wait. But he grew impatient and before even reaching his room, he turned sharply and beetled down the stairs to the telephone. But he dialled the number very slowly, for his own sake, in order to control his itching anticipation.

Richard Baron was a one-man business and he answered the phone himself. 'Baron speaking,' he said.

'It's Walter. Walter Berry.'

'I've read it Walter. And I think it's wonderful.'

Walter almost dropped the receiver in his excitement. 'Really?' was all he managed to whisper.

'Really. I think it's very funny. Very moving. And profound too. I'm really excited about it. I'll get working on it right away. I'll be in touch as soon as I have news. Then I'll take you out to lunch.'

Walter wondered whether his agent could afford it, and he resolved that he would pay his own way. For already he was developing that desperate gift of many writers. That excruciating talent for gratitude. Richard Baron, whom only that morning he had vowed to kill, had now become the object of his idolatry. In view of what he had said about his novel, Walter Berry would have laid down his life for him. He decided to visit Christina. She was entitled to share the good news. He could not expect another phone call in the immediate future, so he could afford to leave his room for a while.

Christina was delighted to see him, but Amanda surpassed her in her welcome. She clung to his legs as he came in through the door calling him 'Daddy' as if reminding him of his promised role, after such a long absence. He took her in his arms. As he cuddled her, he suddenly felt at home, and the thought crossed his mind that were it not for the child, he would not consider marriage to Christina. It was through his daughter rather than his wife he would honour Tom's memory.

He told Christina the news from his agent. She was overjoyed for him, and she opened a bottle of wine for a celebration. She sparkled with pride in him, and Walter was deeply affected by her obvious pleasure in his success. So he began to talk of marriage plans. Christina suggested they wait until the novel was published. She was absolutely confident of its success, though she'd never read a word of it.

'Would you like to read it?' Walter asked.

She nodded shyly.

'You shall,' Walter said. He envisaged their future together, when Christina would read his work in progress. Writing was a lonely pursuit and her presence and her reading participation would lighten his solitude. He began to look forward to his married status.

Within less than two weeks, Richard Baron had found a publisher for Walter's novel. His agent was so excited that Walter suspected this was the first sale of his business 'I hope this is the beginning of a life-long partnership,' he said when they met for lunch the following day. He outlined the details of the contract. The publishing house was one of the oldest establishments in London, with the best fiction list of them all. They were willing to pay £100 advance, which Richard thought was very generous for a first novel. They were excited about it, he said, and intended to publish it in their autumn list in about six months time.

Walter was elated with the news and he went straightway to Christina to share it with her. And to make plans for their wedding. They would live in Christina's house. She did not suggest he leave his lodgings. That move would not be appropriate until the wedding. 'It would not be suitable for Amanda,' Christina said.

Walter was undisturbed by her decision. There was nothing urgent in his physical need for her. Indeed, in their year-long relationship, they had not once made love. Nor had either of them been tempted. Each of them had been before to that place, and it is possible that both would remain satisfied with that one journey. They were young of course, and that very youth might prompt further excursion. Time would tell, and so would the status of marriage. For the moment, both delighted in the security of their future together.

In the meantime Christina arranged for a certain refurbishing of the house. Her father had died some years earlier, and had left her a small bequest. With that money, she built an annexe onto the back of the house, and earmarked it for Walter's study. In her mind, she settled to be married to a writer.

Walter, for his part, spent the waiting time in working on his second novel. They saw each other regularly, and apart from their celibacy and separate domiciles, they behaved to all intents and purposes like an old married couple. And it bothered neither of them. It simply cemented their sense of security. But it was Amanda who was the first and last bolt of their bonding, she who had been provided with a target for the 'Daddy' word that had lain dormant in her mouth since her birth.

In the autumn of that year, six months after its virgin submission, the novel *Autumn* by Walter Berry hit the bookstands and the headlines. It was an immediate success. Critics hailed a new and exciting talent. Walter made several appearances in bookshops to autograph his work for eager buyers. In all the celebrations, he included

Christina, and wherever possible, Amanda. With *Autumn* Walter Berry achieved overnight fame, a fame which he was to maintain till the end of his days. But it did not go to his head. He could have been forgiven a little arrogance, a little conceit, but that he left to Christina who translated it all into pride.

They were married on New Year's Day in 1949.

The wedding was attended by the literati of London, and the Paris honeymoon by Amanda. The innocent little ménage à trois was set for a happy future.

PART TWO

Chapter 8

At this stage of the autobiopsy I decided to take a break and try a little living instead. Walter had always said that writing was a substitute for living and I was beginning to understand what he meant. But there was another reason why I needed to lay the book aside for a while. I have to confess that I've been to the freezer quite often on the quiet. And all I have extracted have been notes for novels. Ideas that have already found their place between hard covers. It had never been my intention to write a criticism of Walter's work. That was already in the capable hands of Frank Watson. No. I was after his life-story and the latest idea that I had syphoned related to that very novel which had been the occasion of our first meeting. From this point I knew that the autobiopsy would take on a different hue. So I needed time to distance myself from it and to see myself simply as an extra character in the tale, to write about myself honestly as Walter might have seen me. No mean assignment that. To see oneself in the third person demands a great degree of honesty, and perhaps even a measure of self-diminishment, and I wasn't quite ready for that. Besides, I had other things to do. I had to check on my mother's new-found beatitude, and to see if it still held. I had to enquire into my father's health. I had had no phone calls in that respect so I presumed he was on the mend. And I had to see Amanda. But first things first. And because that phrase has nothing to do with priority, I dialled my mother's number. It was Violet who answered the phone. My mother was out, she told me. She'd gone out to lunch and she would tell her I'd called. My mother had certainly undergone a change. It was the first time that I could remember that she'd been out when I called. So I dialled my father's number. Mrs Yellow answered the phone, clearly returned from the Sydney sickbed. It crossed my mind to ask after her mother, but I couldn't be bothered. She told me that my father was well and had gone out to lunch, and I wondered whether the two lunches of my phone calls were one and the same. With these two calls, I felt I had done my filial duty. So I dialled Stephen's number. His voice gave no indication of recovery.

'How was Canada?' I asked.

'It was a help being with family. I'm thinking of emigrating. I could teach there.'

'Can we meet?' I asked.

'Of course,' Stephen said. 'But let me ring you. I've so much to do in the next couple of weeks. I'll ring when I've surfaced.'

'I'll leave it to you then,' I said.

I have to admit that I put the phone down with some relief. Stephen as a husband was hard enough to take. As a widower he was likely to be impossible.

I paused before dialling Amanda. I was aware that to initiate some kind of relationship with Walter's step-daughter entailed a certain risk. Having introduced her into my autobiopsy, she was, in a sense, already mine and I could mould her to my will. The flesh of her, her reality, could possibly be at odds with my fictional portrayal, and could well put me off course. But I could not deny the pull she had for me and I found it difficult to define the cause of that attraction. Was it simply for her own sake, or did I not see her as an extra conduit to the events of Walter's life? If the latter, that would be a deception of sorts, and even I, thief that I already was, had scruples about that. Yet the two possible reasons for my attraction towards her could not help but overlap and it was up to me and what was left of my conscience to sift the one from the other, and to acknowledge what was real and what was fiction. Having made that decision in principle, I felt free to admit that I was not to be trusted. So it was a highly cunning finger that dialled Amanda's number.

She answered straight away and seemed glad to hear my voice. Foolishly I had not prepared what I would say to her so I had only a short interval to decide on a lunch or dinner invitation. It seemed to me that dinner was more serious. Dinner was the deep end and should not be entered without sufficient preamble. On the other hand, lunch was not exactly paddling, for it suggested an even greater intimacy than dinner. The thought crossed my mind to invite her to tea, but there was a suggestion of 'deep end' on my own home ground. While I was thus wrestling with myself as to my best move, it was Amanda who solved my unspoken problem. She invited me to lunch the following day. On her own head be it, I thought. If she chose to be *metteur en scène*, it was up to her to call the shots. I was nervous of the rendez-vous and I was tempted to go to my freezer as some kind of sedative. But I was aware that Walter's subsequent thought, whatever it might be, could well plunge me once more into my autobiopsy and render me more confused than ever. So I spent my waiting time sensibly. I played and practised three Scarlatti sonatas, then exchanged ivory for wood. I had started on a model of a horse, a Pegasus, that I intended to present to little Simon at a propitious moment. And that opportune time depended very much on whatever stage I had reached in my relationship with Amanda. Thus little Simon's birthday, a legal occasion for such a present, might well go unnoticed. I am not a very nice man.

While I was working at my bench, my phone rang. I had deliberately switched off my answering machine, a token perhaps of my own contentment and self-confidence. I was available to everybody. Even to my mother, as it turned out to be. Her chirpy voice echoed my own. Even if it had jarred at her normal martyred pitch, it would not have fazed me.

'You rang me?' she said.

'I wanted to say hello. And also to find out how Father was doing.' I could not mention that I had rung Anne.

'I spoke to him yesterday. He's fully recovered.'

So my notion of their lunch together had proved false. 'Violet said you'd gone out to lunch,' I said. 'Who with?' I tried not to sound like her mother. She was not yet old enough or dependent enough for role-reversal.

'A friend of mine,' my mother said. 'You don't know him.'

That pronoun knocked unannounced at my heart, and for some reason I felt sorry for my father. I had the sense not to enquire further, both for her sake and mine. I switched the conversation back to my father. 'Is he fully recovered?' I said. 'Doesn't he have to convalesce or something?'

'I think he's doing that,' my mother said.

'I'd better give him a ring,' I said.

There was a pause. A noticeable one, as my mother had intended it to be.

'What's the matter?' I asked.

'He's moved,' my mother said. 'He told me on the phone. I don't know where he is, but he told me he would be in touch.'

'Does Anne know where he is?' It was the first time I'd actually pronounced her name in my mother's ear, but I felt that if my father had left her, her name was now free and could have belonged to anybody.

My mother gave a girlish giggle and it riled me a little.

'I think she will be the last person to know,' she said.

I didn't know how to answer that one. I couldn't understand it at all, and I was wary of asking my mother for her interpretation. Besides, I did not want to disturb her new-found happiness. When I put the phone down I realised that she hadn't asked me to visit. For my mother's part, that was a good sign. But it was not all that good for me. Children complain that their parents will not let them go. God knows, novelists write about it all the time. But the reverse is often true too, and I was not yet ready to give my mother her freedom. I thought about Anne. Poor Anne. How much longer could she claim an out-to-lunch partner? But my father's move puzzled me. Walter had once spoken to me of post-heart-attack patients. It was à propos a friend of his. His accountant in fact. A straight uncomplicated, untroubled man. Twenty-six years of good marriage behind him, and two grown-up unaccusable children. Yet after his attack, he had left the marital home and struck out on his own. Walter's reading of the event was that, having tasted mortality, his friend now had a greater urge to cling to life, and moreover to a life that was very different from that life he had led hitherto. For now he viewed that old life as frightfully dull and predictable. He was enrolling in the pursuit of excitement, and all the risks that that entailed. Such a reaction was understandable. But

122

my father had left my mother without the spur of a heart attack. Perhaps Anne had turned out as unadventurous as my mother. I was glad I had no means of contacting him. I would have been at a loss as to what to say. And at an equal loss as to what to say to my mother.

That nonchalant, thrown-off 'him', still echoed in my ear. That anonymous lunch companion. Was it possible that my mother had been infected by my father's frisson of mortality, so that she too felt obliged to seek fields and pastures new? I felt totally out of my depth and I fled back to my work-bench and a piece of work that I could control.

Between the Scarlatti and the Pegasus, pursuits laced with my troubled filial thoughts, the day passed quickly enough. On waking the following morning, I switched on my answering machine, an act that was testimony to my waning self-confidence, and did nothing to lift my spirits. Even the anticipation of my impending lunch-date was threatening to evaporate. But when I stood at her front door listening to the echo of the bell, excitement supplanted my filial cares and a little nervousness too. But Amanda put me at my ease immediately. She welcomed me in an open-hearted manner which could in no way have been assumed. I have a good nose for affectation, and Amanda's welcome was no doubt genuine. There was no sign of Simon. When I asked for him Amanda told me he was spending the day with a friend. It had been arranged for him to spend the night, she said, but she had no doubt that by tea-time he would have cold feet and ring to be taken home.

'In a way, I hope so,' she added. 'I miss him when he's not here.'

I wanted to ask her about Simon's father and whether he had any contact at all with his son. But I felt that that was too intimate a question, and no doubt in the course of the afternoon, she might volunteer the answer herself.

As we settled down to lunch I asked her how Frank Watson's biography was going. I suppose I was just making conversation, for in truth I had absolutely no interest in Watson's estimate of Walter's work. I doubted whether I would read the book when it was published. I had my own opinion of Walter's oeuvre and was entitled to it, having read every word that he had written.

She told me that she had heard from her mother that it was almost finished. She had completed her research, and now had little contact with him. But her mother saw him from time to time, she said. She would not allow any of Walter's papers to leave the house, she said, so that Frank was sometimes obliged to work there. But not in Walter's old study. Her mother had insisted on that.

'Papers?' I asked nervously, sensing that Watson might be trespassing.

'Just his reviews and contracts,' Amanda said. 'That's all he's entitled to.'

I breathed a sigh of relief. I was so wary of my theme being inadvertently stolen. I know that for novelists there is nothing new under the sun. That everything has been written about in one form or another. I knew too that if *I* hadn't written it, it was new. It was uncharted territory. I knew all that in principle, but as yet, did not have the confidence to apply it to myself.

'Did you have a good holiday?' I asked. Safe enough ground, I thought, and nothing to do with Walter or his biographer.

'Quite terrible,' Amanda laughed. 'We went to Djerba. Only because I didn't know where it was.'

'Where in fact is it?' I asked.

'Tunisia. A peninsula.'

'Why was it so terrible?'

She laid down her fork and looked straight at me. 'There are more Germans in Djerba than there are in Germany,' she said, 'and all of them were staying at my hotel.'

I laughed with her. 'You inherited Walter's teutonic phobia, I see.'

She laughed. 'Well, he had reason,' she said.

I sensed that if I questioned that reason I would be in troubled waters. But Amanda was elucidating.

'He was in a detachment of American soldiers. The first of the allies to enter Belsen. He never forgot it, and he never forgave. Yes, I have indeed inherited his loathing. Whenever occasionally I meet a pleasant German, I find it very inconvenient.'

I toyed with the fish on my plate. I had got it wrong. I had called him up into service much later than his real time. And moreover I had sent him to a different station. But at least I'd put him in the right service. The army. I had to tell myself that all that was irrelevant. That the autobiopsy was *my* invention, guided only by the occasional reality of Walter's ideas. And that if sometimes I got it right, I should not even look upon it as a bonus. Or even a piece of luck. Magic, that's all it was. And no writer on earth had the recipe for that. I brought Amanda back to Djerba. 'So what did you and Simon do all day?' I asked.

'Not much,' she said. 'The hotel was in the middle of nowhere. The nearest town was ten miles away. And I wouldn't risk a taxi. They drive like maniacs over there.'

'What about swimming?' I tried.

'The sea was full of seaweed, and the pool was full of Germans. We opted for the seaweed. They say it's good for the skin,' she laughed, 'but Djerba's a long way to go for skin-cream.'

I was beginning to feel more at ease. Djerba was a long way from Walter and I was anxious to keep her there. But Amanda was equally anxious to forget about it, and to write it off as an expensive mistake. So I allowed it, and asked after Christina.

'She's coping well,' Amanda said. 'She's gone back to painting. It's what she used to do before she met Walter. She gave it up shortly after they were married. Walter took up all her time. She paints rather well. You should ask her to show you her work sometime.'

'Of course I will,' I said. 'I'd like that very much.'

'Keep in touch with her,' Amanda said. 'You're her link with Walter. You were the closest to him.'

'Does she have many visitors?' I asked. 'Walter's old friends?'

'Not any more. They came for a while after he died but their visits are pretty infrequent now. My mother lived always in Walter's shadow, but take it from me, she's as good a value as my stepfather was.'

'I don't doubt it,' I said, as I recalled the house I had fashioned for her and its tasteful décor. Yet keeping in touch with Christina was as risky as my contact with Amanda. And moreover it would be devoid of any personal attraction. Yet I would visit her, I decided. And often, if only for Walter's sake.

When we had finished lunch we moved into the drawing-room. Amanda lived pretty well. I gathered that this had been her marriage home and I presumed that she was well supplied with alimony. And no doubt she had benefited financially from Walter's death. I wondered why she hadn't remarried. But that too was a question of premature intimacy. I looked around for some vestige of Simon's father. A picture I thought, on the mantelpiece, but there was no hint that he had ever been. I knew from Walter that the marriage had been an unhappy one and it was possible that Amanda wanted no reminder of it. But I couldn't help thinking that Simon was entitled to a token of his father, however small. It was none of my business, but in time, I hoped, I would make it so. Amanda poured the coffee and when it was done, she put her hand on my arm. A friendly gesture, I thought, and very welcome, and I would accept it just for what it was.

'I want to ask you something,' she said.

I noted that her voice had fallen to a whisper. 'It's a favour.'

'Anything,' I said, rather foolishly, as I think about it now in hindsight, but at the time I was overcome by the feeling of trust she had placed in me. It was the whisper that did it, that sense of conspiracy.

'You know that when Walter died, he was in the middle of a novel. In fact it may even be almost finished.'

Then I realised what was coming. What favour she was about to ask of me, and my heart sank with fear.

'Mother would like it finished,' she said. 'I don't entirely agree with her, but it's her wish. It's she who suggested that I ask you.'

'Ask me what?' I whispered back, temporising.

'To finish it,' she said. 'You would be acknowledged of course.'

'But why me? I've had a block for years.' I was not about to tell her that that block had been breached, or by what terrible means.

'What about his other friends?'

'He was closest to you,' Amanda said. 'You followed every word he wrote. You knew his style, his feelings. No-one could do it better than you.'

'But I don't think I could do it,' I pleaded, and truly believed so. 'I'm afraid I feel like you, Amanda, that it shouldn't be done at all.' It would be a form of cheating I thought, and I was already up to my neck in that business. 'I'll try and persuade Christina to let it be,' I said.

Amanda took her hand from my arm and the whispering was over. I felt flattered that I had been asked to perform such a task and I could not help wondering whether Walter would have approved. In his kindly way he would have hoped such a task would have broken my block and I was beset with scruples at the thought that he had already unwittingly done so. When the coffee was finished, I made to take my leave. Amanda did nothing to detain me, and I felt sadly that the purpose of the lunch invitation had been solely to pass on to me her mother's request. But she asked me to come again. And soon. Simon had taken a liking to me, she said. 'He will be sorry to have missed you.'

When I left, I was not as elated as I had hoped, but I was satisfied. Flattered too. On the whole, I could count it as a successful meeting.

When I reached home, my answering machine was flashing. A single call. It was from my father. He left his new telephone number and asked me to ring back. No explanation. But that I understood. An answering machine is no channel to convey a major event. I studied the number. Its location was Mayfair. A large step up in the world. Whatever he was doing, my father was doing it splendidly. With a certain excitement, I dialled his number. The phone rang for quite a while. I thought that he might be sleeping, and as I was about to hang up, he answered.

'Father?' I said. Although I had adopted that word myself, I was never at ease with it. When I was a child, I called him 'Dad'. But that 'Dad' gave me such a hard time with his buckle-belt and his pointed finger, that I thought that for me at least, 'Dad' was an unlucky word. I tried 'Daddy' for a while. It sounded like a plea, and that perhaps was what I meant by it. But that didn't work either. In my teens, I began to call him 'you'. It was a word that slipped quite naturally from my lips. And though it made no difference to his cruel indifference towards me, I sensed that 'you' was the only title that was appropriate. As far as I was concerned, I had put him in his rightful place and that gave me a measure of relief. I hung stubbornly onto the 'you' until he left my mother, and then he automatically became 'him'. When I first saw him after their separation, 'him' was no longer appropriate, to say nothing of its crass lack of grammar, so I called him 'Father'. It was a term that could have been equally addressed to God in whom I didn't believe. Besides, the word was graced with two syllables, and that allowed for a cadence of contempt. 'Father' was simply a more sophisticated way of saying 'you'.

'Were you sleeping?' I asked.

'No,' he said. 'There was someone at the door.'

It was on the tip of my tongue to ask, Who? with that same play at role-reversal that had made me curious about my mother's lunch-time 'him'. But I refrained. 'Are you well?' I asked instead.

'Never felt better,' he protested.

'You've moved,' I said, stating the obvious.

'I've a lovely flat in Mount Street. A service flat. Suits me down to the ground.'

He was so intent on proclaiming his satisfaction that it was clear I could not argue with it.

'What about Anne?' I dared to ask. If he was as well as he claimed, he could stomach that question.

'Oh she's fine,' he said. 'She understands.'

I saw no point in further discussion. If Anne's 'understanding' consisted in lunch-date inventions, my father was showing an acute lack of sensitivity. But that did not surprise me. He had played the righteous know-it-all with my mother.

'Well as long as you're feeling well.' I said. 'Take care of yourself.' It was something to say, something to signal the end of the call.

I poured myself a drink, not a habit of mine, especially during the daytime, but I needed to take stock of my situation. All my life, guilt has been my companion. I don't count myself unique in this respect. Guilt is almost everybody's friend. Indeed, to be without such an ally would lead to a pretty sterile life I'm afraid. So when I sit down to take stock, it usually entails a little board-meeting with my shadowy friend. Well I had dealt with my family, my friend's most constant and perennial demand. Unfinished business. Another friendly nudge at the elbow. Pegasus lay unfinished, it's true, and Scarlatti hardly begun. But both could wait and my friend would tolerate that. He would even bear with me as far as my freezer was concerned. But despite all the tolerance, I felt him breathing down my neck. And I knew on what account. Christina. I had no intention of attempting to finish Walter's last novel, but I had to think of an excuse that would be acceptable to his widow. I had tried my inability on Amanda but she had brushed it aside. I could plead an excess of humility, but that wouldn't wash either for it was an attitude never displayed, since it is totally foreign to me. I could say I was too busy and I thought I might use my father's heart attack as a reason for keeping me on my toes with his care. But despite my agnosticism, I am superstitious and I did not want to tempt fate. So it was as I was wrestling with alternatives, all of them unworkable, that the phone rang and afforded me some relief. But it was Christina and I had no excuse to the ready. She had spoken to Amanda, she said, and my refusal was a great disappointment to her. My friend at my elbow swelled with pride.

'But I couldn't do him justice,' I said.

'He would have wanted you to try,' she said coldly.

So now I owed not only to Christina, but to my mentor as well and my elbow friend fairly burst with satisfaction.

'Just do one thing for me,' Christina was saying. 'Just read it. Then whatever you have to say, I'll take more seriously.'

It was a fair enough request and one that I could hardly refuse. So I suggested I pick up the manuscript the following day. She asked me to lunch but that might well have been the hors d'oeuvre to blackmail, so I refused pleading pressure of work, whatever that meant. I said I would pick it up in the early evening on my way to dinner with a friend. That ruled out a possible invitation to supper. I felt my friend deflate a little at my elbow, but I knew there was plenty of breath in him still.

So that evening I went to collect Walter's unfinished novel. Christina tried to detain me with the offer of a drink, but I pleaded lateness. I was anxious to avoid conversation. The manuscript was loose-leafed and lay in a transparent holder. There was no title. I knew that Walter always left that until after the book was finished. In this instance I resented that habit of his for it might have given a clue as to its ending. But it is likely that Walter didn't know the ending himself. One sentence generated the next, he often told me, and that maxim applied to the very last. In any case I had no intention of granting Christina's favour. I would read the manuscript only as a gesture of courtesy.

I went straight home and opened the book at once. I tried to play down my enthusiasm and curiosity in fear of where they might lead me. But that was difficult. Walter's work had always excited me and always aroused my curiosity. He was, above all, a story-teller. In his novels he would peel off layer after layer of narrative as if his tale were an onion, and the reader was held in its peeling spell, breathless to reach the core. In this respect, this last manuscript of his was no different. I read it with my true Berry addiction and took my time, savouring each word. It was neatly typed yet there was the occasional blank in a sentence. They were reminders of his death. Christina, in her loyal copying, had been unable to decipher the odd word and no-one was there to enlighten her. Walter always wrote in long-hand. He scorned the word-processor. He told me he regarded writing as a kind of confession, and that he needed the pen close to the page. Silent, without third party interference. There are writers and there are typists, he would say, and the difference showed in their work. I must confess that I myself use a word-processor. Having suffered such a long and painful block, I like to think that my machine postpones the loss of faith.

As I read through Walter's manuscript, I found myself filling in the blanks. Then I stopped myself because I had to stick to my decision not to grant Christina her favour. I read through the night, pausing from time to time to relish its ingenuity. I was loathe to come to the end, especially since I already knew that there *was* no end. But towards morning I read Walter's last sentence. 'She saw only its shadow as it streaked the kitchen wall. It proclaimed no gender and she . . .'

'And she WHAT?' I shouted aloud. It was clear to me that at this stage Walter was very close to the end of the book, and the thought crossed my mind that he'd done it on purpose as if he thought that the reader might do bit of work for a change. It was just the sort of tease he would bequeath. And a great tease it was. For the key to the whole novel lay in the identity of that genderless shadow on the kitchen wall. It could have belonged to one of at least six major characters and it was clear that only one would do. I made myself some breakfast. That shadow haunted me. Its identity was a challenge. I tried out all possibilities, even to the extent of making notes. I knew that there was a way of solving the problem. The only way, and moreover, the way to which I alone was privy. It would be cheating of course, but was I not cheating enough already? I could turn Walter upside down again, and hope that amongst his last thoughts, lay a clue to the novel's ending. But I was wary of that ploy. And for two reasons. Firstly it would be the beginning of granting Christina's favour, which I had sworn never to do, and secondly, it would throw my own autobiopsy out of gear. I swiftly dismissed the idea and concentrated on eating my breakfast. I had done what Christina had asked. I was entitled now to stick to my decision.

I finished my coffee, switched on my answering machine and went to bed. But I couldn't sleep. It was that bloody mate of mine at my elbow. I decided to ignore him, but before doing so, I thought it wise to speak my guilt aloud. It's a technique they use in some types of therapy. 'Imaging', they call it, and it's about as cock-eyed as most of their theories. But I thought I might give it a try. I sat up in bed and I placed my guilt-companion in the chair facing me, that chair that held my discarded trousers. I tried to give him a face. I don't know why I thought of guilt as masculine, for women can be naggers par excellence. I suppose I thought that because it was *my* guilt, *my* companion, it would automatically take on my gender. So I worked on his face. He had a beard – God being the dubious reason for that I suppose – and a moustache. The former gave him a look of authority, and the latter one of menace. I suppose that more or less summed him up for me. But for form's sake, I gave him eyes, ears and a nose. I was about to conjure up a mouth for him. But forbore. Guilt does not have a mouth. It doesn't need one. It does very well thank you with everything else. It sees for you, hears for you, smells for you, and touches. But it never speaks. Its silence is its supreme menace, its ultimate blackmail. So no mouth. I was pleased with my image of him and I contemplated it for a while. Then I spoke.

'Now listen,' I said, glad that I'd given him pretty good ears. 'I don't expect to come to an agreement with you, but out of courtesy I want to let you know where I stand. Well maybe not courtesy. I *need* to tell you. Let's leave it at that. I want you to know that you don't get on my nerves, that you don't disturb me, and that never in my life have I wished to rid myself of you. I *need* you, you see. I need you by my side, down my neck, or at my elbow. Wherever you choose. Why? Because you're my prime source of creative energy. That's why. So I don't care how much you inflate yourself, or how sometimes you shrink. But for God's sake don't shrivel away to nothing.' I looked at his face, then let it fade, and then I did the most extraordinary thing. I started to cry. I don't know whether they were tears of sorrow, or simple relief, but whatever they were, I knew that I was weeping for my mother, my father, and even for all the Mrs Yellows of the universe. I felt purged. Maybe there was something in this image therapy after all.

I gave up on sleeping, had a shower and dressed. And went straightway to my phone to dial Christina's number. I had to get it over with.

'I've read it,' I said, and I hoped my voice sounded decisive.

'Already?' Christina said.

'I sat up all night. It's wonderful. But I cannot finish it, Christina.' I used her name to soften the blow I was about to

132

land and I left no pause for her dismay or argument. 'I don't think it should be finished. An unfinished legacy is what Walter would have wanted to leave. He would have wanted to leave people guessing. That way he will be remembered. With a little irritation perhaps, but always with affection.' I paused. I really had no more to say, and I hoped that Christina could hear the finality of my decision.

There was a silence for a while. A charged silence. A mother-silence if ever I heard one. The mother of all mother-silences. But I would not be fazed. I waited. It was undeniably her turn. I would sit out that silence as part of my new-found self-esteem. My guilt was silent too, having swollen to offended proportions. I smiled. At last Christina spoke.

'I'm very disappointed in you,' she said.

'I'm sorry about that,' I said quickly. But really I wasn't sorry at all. Bemused rather, for in that silence, she had taught me more about Amanda and her problems than I could ever have hoped to learn. I promised to go and see Christina shortly. It was the only way I could get off the phone. Afterwards I sensed a quiet relief. For the first time since I had started my autobiopsy, I felt at peace with myself. I was no longer nudged by any scruple. I owed it all to Walter and it was with that gratitude that I went once more to my freezer.

Chapter 9

I noticed that Walter had shrunk considerably. I reckoned that I had less than half way to go. Each time I opened that freezer, I was reminded of one of the first thoughts that I had syphoned off in the days before I turned him the right way up. *'No more fear. No more fear. Free for ever now of accusation.'* That thought haunted me, and at each syphoning I wondered what gross sin Walter had committed to merit such fear. And such shame. Each time I went to my freezer I hoped for a clue. Perhaps now, more than half way through his fiery vision, I would cull a hint. I spent more time than was my wont caressing that shrunken globe, but the habitual apology did not fall from my lips. I syphoned gently and a number of thoughts, which I knew pertained to novels, emerged.

A marriage based on mutual inferiority.

I reckoned that that was a thought relating to his novel *Closer and Closer Apart*, a story of a desperate marriage.

Is nothing cubed, better than nothing?

I couldn't pin that thought onto any particular novel, and I deduced that it was one that Walter might have dropped in any of the sundry drawing-rooms he frequented. But novels were not my province. They were Watson's. So I ignored them. Then I uncovered a thought that was germane to my own work. And a signal indeed.

> *Amanda started High School today. Why*
> *does she frighten me so?*

I caressed the globe once more and put it back in the freezer. No Scarlatti, no Pegasus, not even coffee. I went straight to my desk and set to work.

... the innocent little ménage à trois was set for a happy future. Walter settled easily into married life, and Christina, who had done it before, albeit for such a short time, gently initiated him, and in doing so, unwittingly instilled in him a deep sense of gratitude. In later years this sense was to plague him. It is not good to owe anybody anything. With Walter's growing success, Christina compounded that debt by devoting herself entirely to his work and all that that entailed. At night she read the words he had written that day. But she made no comment. That was not what Walter sought. He simply needed her acknowledgement. At the end of each chapter she would start typing, occasionally referring to him for a word she could not decipher. When it was finished, she attended to Walter's small revisions. She dealt with his agent and his publisher. As his output grew, so did his fan-mail. Christina dealt with that too. She checked his contracts and sensibly invested his growing fortune. She prepared him for his many tours, in England and abroad. Walter knew, and so did Christina, that he would be lost without her. He was content. Christina was a fine cook and they entertained frequently. In their fourth year of marriage, and after Walter's fourth best-selling novel, they moved from the little cottage in Camden Town to a large apartment in Hampstead. If Christina wanted more children, she kept that wish to herself, because she knew that Walter had no wish for a child of his own. He was devoted to Amanda and probably as much a father to her as his erstwhile friend would have been. He took time off from his writing to teach her to read. In the very beginning, when they had first married, all that he did for Amanda, he did for the sake of his friend. But as she grew older, he grew to love her for himself and that love confirmed his need for no further children. And so Walter wrote and Christina typed and Amanda grew.

Only very occasionally did Walter take stock of his life. He avoided such confrontation because he was beset by nagging doubts that his life was faintly unsatisfactory. Despite his success, his wealth, his fame and his friends, the endless round of dinner and publishing parties, he was aware of a painful lack in his life, an ulcerous gap that his work only partially filled. He could not identify its cause, but it nagged at him. In despair, he would count his blessings. Christina, Amanda, their beautiful home, their many friends. But as he did so, the stock-taking appalled him. For he knew that to count one's blessings was to abdicate. It was to resign oneself to what one had, and to be thankful for it. Counting one's bless-ings was a pursuit which smelt of God, and that holy odour was in itself enough to dismiss it. So Walter avoided the blessing routine and immersed himself in his work, knowing full well that that work had already become a substitute for living.

It was in this awareness that he started on his eighth novel, and without any conscious deliberation on his part, he found himself writing a love-story. He surprised himself. He had never attempted the genre before and he didn't understand what had happened to him that he should risk it now. As he wrote it, he grew excited. With his pen he entered the passion of the words on the page. But he noted that on completion of each day's work, he was overcome by such a deep depression that, without fatigue, he took early to his bed, the single couch in his study. Christina, as always, understood. And sometimes Walter could have hit her for her decency. But once he was back again at his desk, his depression quickly lifted and he warmed himself by the fire of his words. Christina, as always, typed the work in progress and tried not to notice the rare subject-matter and the passion that singed each page. She had not failed to notice that while he was writing this novel, he had not once slept in their marriage bed. She tried not to be over-concerned. When the novel was finished, she had no doubt he would return.

But Walter was fearful of finishing the work. Once the book was done, he would not know what to use to lift his depression. There would come a time when the book had inevitably to write its end, but he kept his final chapter by him, withholding it from Christina and going each day to his study to stare at the blank wall.

It was during those days of tormented idleness that Walter had to acknowledge the nature of that nagging cavity. Quite simply, he was living a life without passion. He had known passion in his time. Just once. But it was unmistakable. He recalled his evenings with Miss Freeman, and as he relived those times, he felt those same tremors that had stirred his young limbs so many years ago. And inside himself he raged against that loss. He had never felt such passion with Christina. He had not expected it so he had not been disappointed. But now he saw what folly it had been to cut himself off from that extra heart-beat, that waking each morning as the loved name trembled on one's sleepy lips. That mood in which one viewed the sunrise as a daily miracle and noted each season with each sharpened sense. Nowadays, the sun rose almost because it had no alternative; the waking lips were dry and empty of sound, and the seasons changed sadly unremarked. But there was nothing he could do about it. That is, nothing he intended to do about it. He knew about the Mrs Yellows. His mother had died of one. There was no other colour except the final pink of his father, the Terry-pink that could never be his colour. Yet he felt a certain relief. Having pinpointed the cause of his malaise, it was as if a great weight had been lifted. He felt at ease, yet without pleasure. But he would not count his blessings. Not again. He would simply settle for what he had and give them no more value than that which they were intrinsically worth. Now he could give the last chapter to Christina. He knew that he had changed. He knew too that Christina had noticed it. He realised that in some ways Christina was no different from himself. Tom had been her Miss Freeman, and after him the sun set only because night had to follow day. They were both set in the paralysis of acceptance. It was about the only thing they had in common.

Walter called the novel *The Flower*. The title had no direct relevance to the contents of the book and if asked to explain it, he would mumble something about the impermanence of beauty. It was the only way he could explain it to himself.

The novel was a great success. Film rights had been bought at its proof stage. Reviewers noted the radical change of subject-matter. Walter would have preferred the novel to have been less remarked upon, for he knew that it was the first time in his work that he had so openly revealed Walter Berry. At school Amanda bathed in her stepfather's reflected glory. Her friends had heard of *The Flower* and its contents and they couldn't believe that anyone as old as fathers could know about love. Some of them privately considered Walter Berry a dirty old man, but others marvelled at his retained youth. Whatever they thought, Amanda's friendship was eagerly sought as an avenue to celebrity.

That summer, Christina and Walter would celebrate their twelfth wedding anniversary. Apart from their honeymoon and some trips to the sea with Amanda, they had never had a real holiday together. Walter decided that that summer, when Amanda's school term finished, he would take them both away for a serious holiday. He asked Christina where she would like to go. She did not hesitate.

'I'd like to visit Tom's grave,' she said. She did not speak in the manner of a request. Her statement was so decisive that Walter could not help hearing it as a veiled

138

rejection. In the last few years, Tom had rarely been spoken of. Now his name was a sudden and fearful intrusion.

'I'd like Amanda to see where her father lies.'

Despite the gentleness in her voice, her request was like a stab in Walter's heart. He had grown so close to Amanda, he had almost come to think he had sired her. He knew he had to respond quickly else his hurt would show. And moreover, he had to respond with enthusiasm.

'That's a wonderful idea,' he said. 'I'll take you to all the places I went with Tom. You're right Christina. It would be good for Amanda too.' That was enough, he said to himself. He didn't want to overdo it. Besides, he was sick at heart. He would happily have spent the rest of his life without seeing Lahore again. In his own mind he had wished for a trip to Africa, a safari perhaps, but to suggest that now would have sounded like a slur on Tom's memory. Christina's sudden Tom enthusiasm worried him. He would never want to see Miss Freeman again. He knew that she belonged to another time. And so did Tom in Christina's time.

'I've never really believed he was dead,' Christina was saying. 'If I could see his grave, it would remove all my doubts.'

Walter put his arm around her. Sometimes she had the power to move him unutterably. But never, alas, to the extent of that extra heart-beat.

He booked three first-class flights to Pakistan and the best hotel in Lahore. Amanda was excited. She whispered to Walter that she was indifferent to seeing her father's grave. She would do it for her mother's sake, but she assured Walter that in her eyes, he had always been her father. She gave him a kiss to confirm it. Walter understood. It was a long time since she had kissed him. She was almost sixteen and had never been one to show outward affection. In that respect she took after her mother. He remembered Tom as an outgoing man who showed his enthusiasm without restraint. As he thought of him, he missed him suddenly, and mourned him for the youth that they had lost together and the manhood that he had never reached. He put his arm around her shoulder. He was careful with her, knowing her age and her nudging womanhood.

'You'll love it there,' he said. 'It's so different from anything you've ever seen before.'

And he was right. From the very beginning Amanda thrilled to each moment. At first the flight excited her. The endless champagne, the seats that reclined almost into beds, her private television, the meals served directly from a trolley with white napery and silver plate. She was used by now to luxury, but to experience it in the air, with a wonder as to where it all came from and how it was all produced, was a luxury tinged with magic. Alongside her, across the gangway, Walter and Christina were reading. Walter's book was in manuscript form. The leaves were loose and as he read each one, he passed it over to Christina. They read at equal speed and Christina echoed the laughs and sighs that Walter had transmitted before handover. Their reading would be over almost simultaneously.

'What are you reading?' Amanda said.

'One of Daddy's fans. A writer. This is his first novel.'

'Any good?'

'Not bad at all,' Walter said, and went on reading.

Among Walter's many virtues was his generosity towards younger writers. He considered he had been very lucky in his career and he was deeply aware of the struggles of other writers. This generosity of his was bruited abroad and as a result, he was besieged with requests for advice, agents and even publishers. Although he never asked to see a sample of their work, from time to time an unsolicited manuscript was found amongst his post. Christina was in favour of sending them right back. She knew how carefully and conscientiously Walter would read them and how time-consuming it all was. But Walter insisted on reading them, and in a move to placate her, he asked if she would share them with him. He would value her criticism. This put a new complexion on the problem. For Christina, those readings would be as much a task as typing Walter's novels and generally looking after his affairs. So she had agreed. And had grown to like that form of sharing. She even looked forward to the next unsolicited script. This latest one had arrived the morning of their departure.

'We'll take it with us and read it on the plane,' Walter had said.

So it was that Walter first heard of Martin Peabody. In his letter that accompanied the manuscript, Mr Peabody announced that he had read every word that Walter had written, that he was a devoted fan and that he knew that it was presumptuous to send his work. But he didn't want help of any kind. The book had already been accepted for publication and he mentioned the name of a highly respected House, and all that he wanted, though he knew that it was much to ask, was his valued opinion. 'If this is too much of an imposition on your time,' he added in a postscript, 'please return the manuscript in the enclosed stamped addressed envelope.'

Usually manuscripts arrived with no return postage and it was this rarity that urged Walter to read it right away. They were touching down in Teheran when Walter handed Christina the last sheet. There was very little on the last page, and Christina finished quickly. 'We can talk about it in the transit lounge,' Walter said.

They were first off the plane in Karachi. Amanda and Christina were nervous. Each took Walter's arm as if in need of protection. This move pleased him. His fear of being de trop in Lahore was slowly evaporating. He began to think he might even enjoy himself. In the transit lounge, Amanda browsed among the many duty free shops while Christina and Walter sat on the sidelines and talked about Martin Peabody's novel.

'I'm really impressed by it,' Walter said. 'It has remarkable insight. And it's well-crafted too. Pretty good for a first novel. How old would you say he was?'

'I would suspect he's young,' Christina said. 'Not that the writing is immature. Far from it. But it has the audacity of youth. The fearlessness. Most first novels have that. There's nothing to lose. Lots of writers never improve after the first. You're an exception,' Christina said.

'Thank you my dear.'

'Will you write to him?' she asked.

'I think I'd rather talk to him. Remind me when we get home. We can ask him for tea.'

They slept most of the way on the last lap of their journey to Lahore. It was early evening when they arrived and Walter suggested a preliminary stroll before dinner, and an early night. 'We have a big day tomorrow,' he said. He didn't know what to expect. There would be tears no doubt, wonder, perhaps even a little joy. Whatever kind of day, it would be a 'big' one. He felt tender towards Christina, and wished to offer her a premature consolation. She, for her part, was grateful for his support and understanding. That night, they made love with a passion – yes, that was the word, Walter thought – a passion that had never surfaced in all their married years. Walter began to have hopes for that extra heart-beat. He held her closely as she slept. He was not to know that he would never make love to her again.

In the morning Christina expressed her wish to go directly to the cemetery. Walter would have wished it otherwise. He would have wanted to have set the scene long before Tom's death and burial. He had it in mind to show them the barracks where they were first stationed, then to take them on their frequent walks about the city and to see the sights meanwhile. He had intended to reserve his last walk with Tom for the last day of their sojourn in Lahore. He had planned it meticulously. He would retrace their last walk together. Step by step. They would start at the barracks, and take exactly the same route to the market place. They would visit the sari stalls and linger in that very shop where Tom had made his last purchase. With luck it would still be there, with the

142

same husband and wife sewing team. He had even fantasised buying a sari for Amanda and using Christina's wedding ring as a proof of its pure silk. Then they would pause. A little lunch perhaps, to fortify them against the trauma of the site of the fire. Then and only then, would he take them both to the small cemetery where lay the English dead. He doubted whether he or even they, would have the stomach to make that journey backwards, but Christina had made her decision and in the glowing aftermath of their loving night together, Walter could not deny her. He hoped that at the cemetery she would find the relief that she sought, the erasure of all her doubts and uncertainties.

He noticed with some alarm that Christina was wearing a black dress for the occasion. He had never seen it before. Indeed he had never known her to wear black. Yet it was not a new dress. Her figure had not changed in the years that he had known her. Perhaps she had bought it on hearing the news of Tom's death and had put it aside when beset with doubts as to her genuine widowhood. Now she was going to make absolutely sure, and she had dressed herself for the occasion.

Amanda, on the other hand, in line with her indifference, wore a light linen trouser-suit, severely cut, but offset by a frilly cotton blouse. He admired her turn-out, but he could not bring himself to comment on Christina's. It frightened him. He himself had not considered a sober dress for the occasion. Tom was gone and he had mourned him in his time. A youthful mourning from which he had quickly recovered. And he had taken over his wife to seal their friendship. He felt more like a tourist guide than a mourner, and he had dressed accordingly. But a tourist guide who was going backwards, backwards from death, and he knew that no good would come of it.

They picked up a taxi outside the hotel. Walter couldn't remember where the cemetery was, but he hoped it would be a short ride. He harboured a distaste for the excursion and he wanted it quickly over and done with. He hoped that Tom's grave had been well-tended.

143

He felt that if it were overgrown with weeds, Christina would place the blame on his shoulders.

When they reached the cemetery he took her arm. But she loosened it gently. This was her own and personal pilgrimage and she wanted to share it with nobody. Except perhaps Amanda. But Amanda clung to Walter's arm underwriting her indifference. Christina walked alone but a little behind them. She needed Walter to lead the way. Then Walter panicked. He had absolutely no memory of where Tom was buried. There were not many graves, but they were wide-spread and many tortuous paths led to them. He was glad to see at least, that they were all well-kept and tended. They walked around until it was clear to Christina that Walter had no idea where he was going.

'Where is it?' she said and she could not disguise the irritation in her voice. The heat was relentless, and the humidity appalling, a climate not conducive to a treasure-hunt.

'I don't know,' Walter said simply. 'I just don't know where it is.' He only vaguely remembered coming to this place. He remembered holding back his tears. But he was in no way inclined to remember the path the cortège had taken. He had never expected to come here again.

'He could be anywhere,' he said. 'We'll just have to look. Perhaps they were buried chronologically,' he offered feebly.

He recalled the year of Tom's death, and almost whooped with delight when he came across the grave of one who had shared Tom's death-day. But alongside it was an illegal American, one Joe McLevsky, who had given up the ghost more than three years earlier. Walter looked at his watch. It was ten o'clock. The sun could only get higher. They wandered through the many paths as the sun rose. After about an hour of fruitless search, Amanda pulled Walter aside and whispered in his ear.

'For Christ's sake, won't any old grave do?'

It was then that Walter decided that they should formulate a plan.

'There are three of us,' he said. 'Let's separate. I shall look due north, Amanda south and Christina east.' Too bad if Tom lay in the west. He saw Christina open her tired and irritated mouth and he forestalled her. 'Then if we don't find him, we'll all try the west.' He regretted not having thought of that plan much earlier. He directed the women, then set off himself. He was glad to be alone. He found Christina's black display oppressive, and there was something faintly offensive about Amanda's indifference. He didn't care who found the grave first. He rather hoped it would be Christina, else she would feel in some sense robbed. He looked around and saw Amanda weaving down the paths. She didn't appear to be looking at the headstones. She was clearly fed up with the whole business. He looked in the other direction towards Christina. She was walking slowly, scanning each tomb pausing at every one of them, mourning them all. She looked like a newly-minted widow, fresh in her weeds.

He continued in his northerly direction. After a while, he heard a shout. He could not recognise the voice. It was a wail of sorts. Cries of grief come from the stomach, and all have the identical print. Such a cry is genderless, ageless, beyond language or faith. Its commonness approaches vulgarity. He turned. He saw Amanda first. She was still strolling. Nothing could disturb her nonchalance. Then he pinpointed Christina. She was kneeling and keening and he was glad that she had been the finder. He decided to leave her alone for a while, and to join her when she rose to leave the graveside. He saw Amanda dawdle towards her mother. He could have slapped her. Yet he knew he was being unfair. Amanda had never known her father. Why now should she show an interest in her siring? He realised what an intrusion this visit was on her life and her assumptions. She didn't want to be confused by a phantom father. She didn't want to be embroiled in her mother's mourning. And mourning it certainly was. Christina's keening echoed across the cemetery. From where he stood, Walter could see how she raised her hand to clasp the headstone for support, and how her body shook with her sorrow. He thought he ought to go to her, but she might well see him as an intruder. He recalled their last night together. Their night of loving. And it was hard indeed to equate that tender voice with the furious wail that echoed across the stones, and to believe that they came from the same heart. He watched her for a while, waiting for Amanda to join her. He saw Amanda kneel, but carefully, mindful of the creases in her suit, but she made not a sound. But Walter was glad to see her put an arm around her mother and press her weeping head to her shoulder. Then Walter walked towards them. Suddenly the path became familiar and his steps echoed his fifteen-year absence, knowing them by heart. He had marched then, slowly, and in step with others from Tom's unit. He couldn't remember a single one of their faces, for they were all in the uniform of mourning. He remembered that Tom's death had affected them all, had frightened them, for it suggested that they could die without fighting. He could almost hear the mournful drum-beat that had conducted their marching steps, and as he neared the grave, he heard the gun-fire salute and the sad bugle of farewell.

When he reached the tomb he stood before it. A separate mourner. Christina's wailing was now muted into sobs, silent for the most part, but punctuated occasionally by a twisted and breathless moan. He tried to understand her. He tried not to think that fifteen years was long enough to get over anything, except perhaps the loss of one's child. That was a grief from which one never recovered. He tried not to be impatient with her.

After a while, Christina lapsed into silence. She made to rise, and Walter dared to put his hand under her elbow. He tried not to notice how she shivered at his touch. But when she turned her face towards him, she could not hide her revulsion. He dreaded the rest of their stay.

'Shall we go somewhere for lunch?' he asked.

'I couldn't eat,' Christina said. 'I want to go back to the hotel right away.'

Walter did not argue. It would be better if she were alone for a while. 'I'll take you back,' he said. 'You won't mind will you, if I take Amanda to lunch and show her a bit of the city?'

'You must do as you please,' she said. She was talking to him as if he were a total stranger.

Walter was disturbed. He had never seen her like this. Something had happened to her at that graveside. It was as if a new soul had entered her, one that had waylaid her in the cemetery. He hoped that she was simply in shock, and that in time she would get over it. He insisted she have some lunch sent up to her room. She shrugged her shoulders with an indifference that was sublime. He took her to the hotel lift where she insisted he leave her. He turned, took Amanda's arm and steered her out of the hotel.

He found the market place very easily. It was but a short walk from the hotel. A sense of familiarity slowly overtook him, rather like his exact recall at the graveside. They entered the way that he and Tom had emerged, or rather, as only he had emerged, with Tom on a covered stretcher, immune to exits or entrances. On his left he saw the building that had replaced the fire. It looked exactly the same, overcrowded, with but one access, and as much a fire-hazard as it had ever been. But no children peered out of the windows. All he saw in their frames were old men and women, discarded ones, for whom it was hardly worth building for safety. He decided not to point it out to Amanda. If she had been indifferent to her father's grave, she was unlikely to be interested in the location of his dying. But he himself nodded at the building in acknowledgement. But he refrained from prayer.

They entered the market place proper. Amanda giggled with pleasure. She stopped at every stall, examining jewellery and trinkets.

'These rings are beautiful,' she said to Walter.

'Choose one,' he said.

'Really?' She laughed with happiness.

'Any one you like.'

'You help me,' she said.

Walter had never played such a role before. Christina had never asked his advice as to her wardrobe or accessories. He was totally inexperienced in such a role. And it excited him. He loved beautiful things if they were put in front of him, but he couldn't have chosen one.

'Which one do you like?' Amanda was saying.

He was nervous. He did not trust his own judgement. He risked a silver filigree with a single turquoise stone.

'That's exactly the one I wanted,' she marvelled. 'I like the lacing when the skin shows through.'

She was extraordinarily sensuous for a sixteen year-old, Walter thought, but then realised that age made no difference. She was probably born with that taste.

'Can I wear it?' she said.

'Of course.'

'Then you put it on for me.'

Her flirtatiousness disturbed him. 'Put it on yourself,' he said. He tried to hide his unease, so he laughed and hoped that that would pass.

'Don't worry about Mummy,' she said, as she fitted the ring on her finger. 'She'll get over it. She only knew him for a year, and you've been together so much longer.'

'I'm not worried,' Walter said, irritated by the girl's insight.

He paid for the ring. 'Let's go,' he said.

She kissed him on the cheek. 'You're a great Daddy,' she said.

They walked through the market place, jostling with the crowds, and as they did so, Walter's temper improved. All the sari shops looked exactly the same and Walter despaired that he would find the one that Tom had chosen. Then suddenly he saw it. He knew it was the same, because the owner was standing outside and it was the face of fifteen years ago. Aged a little, but immediately recognisable. He hoped that the man would not remember him. It would make things awkward for Amanda. He wondered whether he ought to try another shop, but it

148

seemed to him right and proper that Tom's daughter should be fitted out with a sari from that same shop that had supplied her mother so long ago.

They paused outside the shop and were immediately ushered inside. And there against the bolts of silk stood the shopkeeper's wife, and when she saw him, a flash of puzzled recognition streaked her face. She came straight towards him.

'I've seen you before,' she said. 'A long time ago. With your friend. In the army.' Then she turned to her husband and let out a stream of excited Urdu. Her husband studied Walter's face, and after some hesitation, nodded his head.

'Your friend bought a silk sari,' he suddenly remembered. 'A yellow one, yes? I put it through my ring.'

'Was that my father?' Amanda asked.

'Yes. He bought a sari for your mother.' Walter said, 'though I don't think she has ever worn it.'

'Thank you for bringing me here,' she said suddenly. She was indeed a creature of moods, Walter thought.

'Now *I* want one,' he said. 'One for my daughter here.'

'Oh Daddy,' she cried again. 'Are they real silk?'

'You choose one,' he said, 'and this good man here will prove it to you.'

'How?'

'Wait and see.'

But the proprietor saw no point in her waiting. He pulled a bolt of silk from the rack and asked his wife for her wedding ring. Walter remembered how last time he had used his own which he had prised off with some difficulty. Now he noticed that that ring was deeply embedded in his finger and that the passing years had nested it for ever.

'Pure gold,' he said to Amanda, holding his wife's ring aloft. 'If this is pure silk, it will pass through the ring without stopping.'

Amanda was goggle-eyed with wonder as he placed the silk into the hoop and threaded a little of it through to get a sufficient hold.

'Are you ready?' he said.

Amanda smiled. He pulled swiftly and in seconds the entire silk was through.

'I believe you,' Amanda said.

'Now you choose,' Walter told her, 'and don't ask my advice. It's you who has to wear it.'

He watched her as she moved along the rolls of silk. Occasionally she paused. Inwardly he prayed that she would not choose yellow. But she seemed to have no interest in that colour. She hovered amongst the reds and the greens. Finally she settled on a pale green one with a bird motif. She draped it across her body and turned to Walter for his approval. There were sighs of admiration all round. She had chosen well. Again there was a kiss for Walter and she jumped up and down with glee. Amanda's sudden shifts from childishness to adult sophistication unnerved him. He wondered whether that ambivalence was the normal pattern of sixteen year-old girls. He had no-one with whom to compare her. All his friends seemed to have sons. He was not sure whether he should treat her as a child or a grown-up. He would have been happier to deal with the latter role, though he had learned precious little about either.

He took her to a grown-up restaurant for lunch, and lingered over it, postponing their return to the hotel. He was wary of seeing his black Christina, perhaps still in a mood to match her clothes.

When they returned to the hotel, Christina was still in bed. She hadn't even taken off her clothes. The black crumpled cotton lay on the white sheet and its sharp contrast seemed a declaration of sorts. A forbidding statement. Her eyes were open. She wasn't even pretending to be asleep.

'Did you have lunch?' Walter asked.

'I'm not hungry.'

'But you must eat something,' he protested.

'Just leave me alone,' she said.

He stroked her forehead and he noticed how, in a reflex, she cringed. And he knew at that moment that their marriage, such as it had been, was over. That they

150

would probably stay together, but for form's sake, and because divorce would be inconvenient. That both of them would live without love for the rest of their lives. It was a sour realisation. And for a moment he hated her. And even Tom, and his wretched memory that had wrought such change. He left the room. He and Amanda would go sight-seeing as he had planned.

As soon as Walter had left the room, Christina turned her face into her pillow. She didn't want to sleep. She simply wanted the dark. She wanted blackness which amply translated her mood of desolation and her sense of loss. At the graveside, she had learned once and for all that Tom was dead. She had felt suddenly young. Bride-young, and the heart-break that assailed her now was that acrid pain of youthful loss. That bewildered pain. Unjust. Tom was dead. Hitherto, all had been hearsay and rumour. Walter had simply stood in until Tom would return. Now she saw her marriage to Walter as a fifteen-year-old exercise in adultery. She accepted that she was Tom's widow. Her weeds would proclaim that status, until her year's mourning was over.

They were scheduled to remain in Lahore for another day, and then go to New Delhi and Agra and the Taj Mahal. Nepal would follow and a close sight of Everest. From there they would fly to Calcutta, and afterwards to Madras. Altogether their journey would take a little over three weeks. In all that time, Christina never moved out of the hotel bedroom she happened to find herself in, and forever draped its white sheets with her black reparation. No persuasion from Walter or Amanda could rouse her from her mourning. At first, Walter was angry. By Nepal, he had grown indifferent, and when they reached Calcutta, he took himself a separate suite.

The first real words that Christina spoke to him, she delivered on the return plane home.

'I'm sorry this has happened,' she said. 'You haven't deserved it.'

He was silent. He could not tell her he understood for although he did, he was fearful of the consequences. He didn't want her to tell him to go away. If for no other reason, he would miss Amanda. In the last few weeks, they had grown close to each other. He had learned to adapt to her ever-changing moods, to the sudden swings from child to woman. Sometimes he had even been able to be angry with her, to scold her for her behaviour, something that he would not have done hitherto. He had become a real father to her, and all thoughts of replacing Tom in the paternal role had vanished. He *was* her father, as much as if he had sired her. He looked at her across the gangway. She was a child again. Her feet were tucked under her body and she was reading a comic book that she'd bought at the airport. And giggling to herself.

Christina spoke again at his side. 'I want you to stay with me Walter,' she said. 'That is, if you wish. For myself, I would be lost without you. But things will be different,' she said. 'You have to understand that.'

Again he understood, and his understanding was beginning to get on his nerves. But he did not confirm it. He was relieved that she wanted him to stay. He put his hand on her arm. 'We'll stay together,' he whispered.

The steward came down the aisle to replenish their champagne. Walter looked across at Amanda, and noticed how, at his approach, she took her feet from under her and quickly stuffed the comic behind her back. She then put on her woman's smile and gave it to the steward. Walter felt a positive pang of jealousy. Yet there was pleasure in it too, for was not this feeling a rightful entitlement to all fathers of growing daughters? Yet it unnerved him, and he looked away. He took Christina's hand which she gave gladly. She took it as his agreement to their new mode of life together. For his part, he needed her hand for protection, but from what, he dared not question.

Chapter 10

It occurred to me after I had finished that chapter, that my mother had not phoned for some while. I wasn't worried that she was ill. Violet would have phoned me immediately. I could only conclude that the 'him' of her lunch-date was still lunch-dating her and perhaps, with luck, had even moved towards dinner. I was curious and I rather resented that she should keep me in the dark. It was a way *I* would behave, as any son was entitled to, but I could not accept that a mother was allowed to have secrets. I could not conquer my curiosity and I dialled her number. There was a cheer in her voice which maintained its pitch even on hearing my own. She'd always kept a special tone for me, one of disappointment, but this was now absent and I took heart from it. I was not worried about asking her how she was. She was well, she said, and sounded it.

'Why haven't you phoned me?' I asked. I was aware of the new role I was playing, and so was she it seemed, for she giggled.

'I've been busy,' she said.

'Busy doing what?' I was quite cross with her.

'Oh things,' she said, and the laughter was still in her voice.

'Have you got a lover or something?' I heard myself shouting.

'Martin,' she said. 'You actually sound jealous.'

I paused. I felt suddenly unanchored. The mother I had known, the mother who I thought, would never let me go, had loosened her grip without as much as a moment's notice. I should have felt free. I should have rejoiced in the shedding of those gross maternal chains, but I felt myself floundering in a new role, a role for which I hadn't had time to learn the words.

'I spoke to Father,' I said. I was aware that she hadn't mentioned him, another sign of her new-found freedom. I was waiting for her to ask me if I'd seen him, but that question wasn't forthcoming either.

'I haven't seen him though,' I said.

'I saw him,' she said. 'He invited me to his flat. It's very luxurious. I think he's happy there,' she said.

'D'you see him often?' I asked. I made no attempt to veil the sarcasm. I was angry that I had not been invited to inspect his new quarters. I felt doubly rejected though the paternal aspect pained me less.

'Only once,' she said. 'But I keep in touch.'

She gave me the impression that the ball was now clearly in her court and that my father, for a change, was on the receiving end. I should have felt happy for her. For so long I had wished for this very change, but I'd not rehearsed for it. I kept what cool I could. She had not yet asked me to visit her.

'D'you want to see me?' I said. I heard it as a new line. Brand new. The first new line of my new role.

'You know I'm always pleased to see you,' she said. 'Violet too. She was asking after you the other day.'

'Then I shall come and see Violet,' I said. I managed a laugh after that one. I had to learn my new part slowly, but my mother must forgive me the occasional lapses into the chained child that I had always been. She did not force a specific arrangement, and I did not press for one. She told me to keep well and to stay in touch. She might have been talking to a stranger.

After that phone call, it took a little while to settle myself. The thought crossed my mind to ring my father, but I dismissed it. It was not difficult to refrain. I was concerned only for his health. No more, and my mother had assured me that all was well. I noticed that I was beginning to lose appetite for anything except the continuance of my autobiopsy. And certainly Amanda would have been a disturbance at this time. In my book she was developing as a piece of fiction, and I would have been confused if confronted with the reality. I suspect, in any case, that I could not have believed in that reality. So I gave up on all thoughts of living, and I decided to make once again for my freezer. But now in the business of writing, I was also in the business of procrastination and I treated myself to a little Scarlatti. Then coffee. And coffee again. At last I went to my freezer and leaned against the door for a while.

It was then that I suffered the black and terrible moment that strikes at the heart of every writer during the course of a novel. That terrible question that has for so long been stifled, and suddenly claims audience. 'What is all this *for*?' That question is a writer's low, and to attempt to answer it can only lead to a greater depression. I remember asking Walter how he dealt with it.

'I don't try to answer that question,' he would say. 'Instead I ask myself another. What is *anything* for? and then it's easier to get on with it.'

I tried the same trick on myself. If it worked for Walter, it had to work for me. It must have, I suppose, because I was able to open the freezer door, if not with enthusiasm, then with a little less uncertainty.

As was my wont, I laid Walter on the kitchen table. The caress followed, and the offering of thanks, and then, very gently, I pressed my thumb. I had noticed that as Walter grew older, there was less waffle to extract. Not that every idea was profound. There was banality in plenty. But the ideas, trite or meaningful, were unmuddled. The first that emerged was as follows.

If you are born without a birthmark, there is nothing to show that you have been born at all.

I smiled. Not so much at the thought itself, but that I recognised its placing. Just half way through Walter's oeuvre, he had published a novel about a reluctant foetus, so I knew

155

exactly how far I had progressed with his life. The next thought confirmed its chronology.

> *The style of the best writers I am told, is a mixture of the perfect and the downright shoddy.*

That had been a self-mocking line from the same novel and I was pleased with its symmetry. Poor old Frank Watson. What would he have given to be in my kitchen at the time? There followed a number of thoughts which I could identify with the same work. Then a random thought that seemed to be pertinent to no novel that I could identify. Therefore I saw it as a signpost all of my own.

> *The Catherine Wheel has come full circle.*

An intriguing thought. *King Lear* had been one of Walter's favourite plays. But for some reason he had adapted that great penultimate line. I saw it as my duty almost, to discover why. And that discovery would be my clue to the next stage of the autobiopsy. I refrained from more coffee, and went straight to my desk.

> . . . For his part he needed her hand for protection, but from what he dared not question.
>
> Christina continued to wear black. When they dined out, or entertained at home, friends remarked on how well the colour became her. Had they known its provenance, they would have remained silent. Walter winced at each compliment, but Christina did not hide her pleasure. She

preferred to think that it was widowhood that became her, rather than its colour.

Walter invited Martin Peabody to dinner. He had been impressed by his novel and its memory still lingered. He invited a number of writers at the same time, all well known, but none so grand that they would inhibit his first-time guest.

When Martin Peabody received the invitation, he read it many times over, hardly believing his luck. Absolutely informal, the invitation said. Which was a relief, for he was not a suit man, and in any case, at that time, he could not afford one. Walter Berry's letter so delighted him that he was anxious to share it with somebody. But none of his friends had literary interests, and though all of them had heard of Walter Berry, they would be seduced by his celebrity rather than his literary value. And he didn't have a girlfriend. Nothing but a few casual one-night stands whose names he couldn't remember, and who certainly would not know Walter Berry from a soft fruit drink. The person he most wanted to tell was his father, not so much to share his pleasure, but as a veiled 'I told you so'. For his father had always scorned his literary ambitions. Once he had even told him, 'You'll never make a Walter Berry.' It would have been an extra pleasure to have shared the news with him. But his parents were separated and at the time, Martin's relationship with his father was very cool. Cool enough to forbid a phone call. That left his mother, who would probably, like his friends, bask in his reflected glory for all the wrong reasons. But it would certainly be a pleasure for her and that he would not deny her.

He dialled her number. Her answering voice was cheerful enough, but it dropped a few decibels on hearing her son's. He let it pass.

'How are you Mother?' he said, and he himself mouthed the reply.

'As well as can be expected,' she said. 'How are you?'

'I had a lovely invitation today,' he said.

'What was that?' Her voice was more cheerful now. Despite her own misery, she would not deny her son's happiness.

'I had an invitation to dinner from Walter Berry,' Martin said. He waited for her delighted reaction. A sigh would have done. He would have been satisfied with a monosyllabic 'Ah'. Martin Peabody did not ask much of his parents. As far as they were concerned, he had set his sights reasonably low. But she said nothing. She just paused to gather together what she thought her most appropriate response.

'Whatever are you going to do for a suit?'

Martin swallowed. 'He said it's informal,' he told her tonelessly.

'Well you can't be too sure,' she said. 'What the likes of Walter Berry call informal may only be a dinner-jacket.'

Well, he had tried, Martin thought. She meant well, he knew. It was just that her own misery coloured all.

'Well I thought I'd just tell you,' he said. 'I thought you might be happy for me.'

'But I *am*,' she protested. 'It's the best thing that could have happened. It's a great honour. Walter Berry, for heaven's sake.' Now she was going totally overboard. 'I'm really happy for you Martin,' she said.

It sounded as if it really came from her heart. As if for a moment, she had broken through that wall of personal misery and had seen somebody else's light.

'I'll let you know all about it,' Martin said, and he put the phone down with unexpected satisfaction.

Yet for the occasion, and for his own sake, he splashed out on a new suit. He looked in the mirror before leaving for the Berry house and smiled. Even his mother would have been pleased with him.

All of the guests were assembled by the time Martin arrived. He had brought Christina a bunch of flowers. He noted her black dress, and for some intuitive reason he took it not for fashion, but for mourning, and the flowers suddenly curled like a wreath in his hand. But she welcomed him profusely, mentioning that she had liked his novel as she ushered him inside to meet Walter and the others.

In Walter's eye, Martin Peabody bore no relation to the man he had imagined from the novel. This one was puny, timid and clearly ill-at-ease. His brand new suit pathetically proclaimed it all. Yet the novel hinted at an author of consummate strength, older certainly, and with a self-confidence that was almost overbearing. And because of this, this paradox of a man, Walter was very moved by him. In the light of his newly discovered feelings of fatherhood for Amanda, those feelings that had flowered on their Indian tour, he felt he could embrace this Martin Peabody as a son. He welcomed him warmly.

Martin had heard of most of the writers present. He had even read some of their books. He did not think highly of any of them, and measured against their host, they were pygmies. But they were pleasant enough, he thought, if a little condescending.

Christina had seated him next to Walter at dinner. Martin had prepared some dinner conversation. He would talk about Walter Berry's books. He would itemise each one, for he had read them all. He would be careful to offer no criticism and he hoped that in return, the great man would compliment him on his own first foray into the field. But nothing discussed at that literary table had anything to do with fiction, or indeed with literature in general. Around the table was a babble of sheer gossip and salivating malice. Literary agent after literary agent was used to wipe the floor. Publishers fared even worse. Their meanness, their greed, their illiteracy. But at the nadir of that parasitic heap lay the judges and juries of literary prizes. None of them knew anything about anything. They had taste in their mouths and nowhere else. Thus the insults were thrown across the table, with a great deal of laughter, each guest vying to top the story of another. And Walter Berry orchestrated it all.

'You must forgive us,' he turned to Martin, 'but we all have to let off steam once in a while.'

It was growing late, and most of the guests were well into their cups. Yet the dessert course had not yet been reached. The cheese was still doing its round when Amanda joined them. She was wearing a very short dancing dress and looked radiant. A tired curl hung over one eye, and marked her as a mere teenager.

'My daughter,' Walter said to Martin, and then to Amanda, 'Did you have a good time?'

'Smashing,' she said.

'Her first dance,' Walter explained to the table.

Amanda kissed her mother. 'Any pudding left?' she said.

'We haven't started on it yet. You can get out the plates,' her mother said.

Amanda looked around the table. Then fixing her eyes on Martin, she said, 'You're new.'

'This is Martin Peabody, Amanda,' Walter said. 'He's certainly new. But from now on, he'll be a regular, like all of them.'

Martin blushed, and mostly with pleasure at his host's promise of invitations to come.

'Tell us about the dance. I'm getting tired of all this gossip,' Walter said good-naturedly.

Amanda served the pudding, then sat next to her mother.

'She looks like you,' Martin said to his host.

'Better looking I would hope,' Walter said. His heart was joyous. It was the first time any stranger had noticed a resemblance and it was the first time he realised, that he had not used the word 'step-daughter' in his introduction. He could have blessed Martin for his comment. It was sincere, he knew. Perhaps there *was* a resemblance, he thought, available only to a stranger's eye, one who assumed his siring. He stared at Amanda and tried to see some vestige of himself. But there was nothing. He could not even see Tom in her. She was all Christina.

The dinner party broke up soon afterwards.

Walter shook Martin's hand warmly. 'You'll come again. And often, I hope,' he said.

When all the guests had left and Amanda had gone to bed, Walter and Christina had a companionable brandy in the kitchen.

'What did you think of Martin Peabody?' Walter asked.

'A bit weedy, I thought,' Christina said. 'Not a bit like I had imagined. In fact, I found him rather dull.'

'I think I'm rather fond of him,' Walter said. 'Don't forget, he was slightly overwhelmed. I don't think he's met many writers.'

'I hope he didn't expect any serious talk about fiction,' Christina said. 'Your friends get more and more spiteful.'

'They're funny though, aren't they?' Walter said. 'And what they say about agents and publishers is more or less true. You can't blame them. Some of them have had a rough deal.'

'Well, at least tonight you didn't get round to talking advances. That really *is* the pits.'

'I like that part the best,' Walter laughed. 'Because on that subject all writers are liars.'

'Not you,' Christina said.

'Only because I can afford not to be.'

Thereafter Martin Peabody was a regular guest at the Berry household. Within six months it became his second home. He had earnestly accepted the filial role which Walter seemed to expect of him, but Christina in no way played a complementary part. She was always polite to him, but he found her cool and distant. He did not take it as a personal affront, for she behaved in the same way to all Walter's friends and indeed to Walter himself. Towards the end of the year that they had met, Martin became a daily caller. Occasionally he took Walter to lunch or dinner, for by that time he had money to spend. His book had been published to much acclaim, and although he made little money on it, there were promises of foreign rights and even a film on offer. Besides, his father's conscience had at last overcome his meanness, and had offered itself to easy assuagement by the payment of a generous allowance. In their many meetings together, Walter encouraged Martin to talk, because he knew that he was stuck on his second novel.

'The second novel is the hardest,' he said. 'Especially if the first, like yours, has been successful. One is suddenly aware of reputation, of minding your grammar and style. I sometimes think that one's first novel is in many ways, one's best. Because nothing is expected of it. It is free, and full of abandoned audacity. In a way, one never writes as well again.' He wanted Martin to understand the nature of his difficulty. But he did not ask about the plot or subject-matter. 'If you tell me,' he said, 'it will lose its interest for you.' Instead he talked to him in general about the development of ideas. He urged him to keep a note-book always by him. The two men were very close, but their intimacy was confined strictly to their literary exchange. Walter never talked about himself, about his personal life, and he never probed Martin about his. Walter Berry was a very private person, so private indeed, that he gave the impression that he had much of interest to hide. Only once they came close to another kind of intimacy when Walter owned to Martin that Amanda was not his daughter.

'She's my step-daughter,' he said. 'When you remarked on a resemblance, the first time we met, I was very flattered. But genetically you have to be wrong. She was a baby when I married Christina.'

He said nothing more. He did not offer Christina as a widow, a divorcee, or even an unmarried mother, and he quickly changed the subject to prevent any further questioning.

Yet Martin knew that Christina was in mourning. Even when occasionally he called at their house for breakfast, Christina was in iron-clad black. She was a mystery to him, and he knew she would remain so.

It was almost a year after their first meeting that Walter was invited to a P.E.N. conference in Paris. He suggested to Martin that he should accompany him.

'Lots of writers,' he said. 'From all over. Some good,

most bad and many writers who don't write at all. I have to give a paper there,' he said, 'on contemporary English fiction. I shall mention you.'

'No-one will have heard of me,' Martin laughed.

'But they *will*,' Walter said. 'I shall make sure of it. Will you come? We'll have time to see a bit of Paris while we're there.'

'How could I possibly refuse?' Martin said.

Christina arranged a little supper party for their return. 'Then you can tell us all about the conference,' she said. 'It'll be a change from the usual back-biting.'

Despite Martin's protests, Walter insisted on paying for everything.

'Paris is my treat,' he said. He was excited. He felt he was taking his own son to see the sights. Martin was only a few years older than Amanda, after all. He was sorry he could not take Amanda, but she was in the middle of her final exams. On the plane, Martin talked about her, knowing the pleasure it gave Walter.

'What will she do when she leaves school?' he asked.

'I hope she'll make it to Oxford,' Walter said. 'She's bright enough.'

'You'll miss her,' Martin said. 'She's a presence in the house.'

Walter was the star of the conference. Martin held back but Walter insisted on his being part of it all. The first night they attended a reception given by the host French P.E.N. There were writers from most of the European countries and English seemed to be the language common to all. Many of them were poets, and a party from Belgium announced themselves as essayists.

'What exactly do essayists do?' Martin asked.

'Nothing,' Walter said. 'Absolutely nothing. The nearest they get to an essay is the production of a laundry list, but the label is sufficient to get them admission to a P.E.N. conference. But don't be disheartened. There are still enough serious writers in P.E.N. to merit recognition for the organisation. In time it will improve, and the chaff will be separated from the bran.'

And plenty of chaff there turned out to be. During the reception, Martin circulated amongst the delegates. Nobody seemed to be interested in exchanging literary ideas. It was rather like one of Walter's dinner parties, Martin thought, though less scintillating. Most seemed to have come to the conference for the partying and the chance to pick up a partner for the weekend. In this pursuit, the opening reception was the time to score, so nobody had much time or inclination to exchange ideas. The number of one's hotel room was a far more marketable commodity than an opinion on British fiction. Martin wandered off alone and felt very superior.

In the morning session, Walter opened the conference proper. He was a presence there. Everybody had heard of him, and possibly read him too, since he was translated into several European tongues. He spoke of the state of English fiction, but he realised soon enough that his audience was wary. They were conscious of being in Paris, and it seemed to them a criminal waste of time to be sitting in a stuffy hall listening to the state of a fiction in which they had not the slightest interest, and to British fiction at that, to which their indifference was sublime.

Half way through his speech, which he had already severely truncated, Walter, miffed at their lack of response, shouted: 'Bear with me, ladies and gentlemen. I have a few more pearls to cast.'

The hall was suddenly attentive. And silent. It was unlikely that the audience caught the full insult of Walter's remark, but it smacked of authority and they shamefacedly obeyed. For the rest of the speech they were silent and were as relieved when the end came as Walter himself.

It took a lot to disturb Walter's equilibrium, but that opening session was more than enough for him. He told Martin that they need not attend any longer, since the remainder of the meetings were concerned with P.E.N. business. Politely, he took his leave, and he and Martin began their Paris tour. As did many of the others, even those concerned in the committees, leaving behind, in more conscientious hands, all those motions, eagerly proposed and seconded by their individual branch members. On the last day of the conference, only a few die-hards remained and declared to the hollow and echoing hall the rights and demands of writers all over the world. Few were there to listen, and less were there to care. But the evening farewell reception was as crowded as the opening greeting, with everybody congratulating each other on what a success the conference had been.

But Walter and Martin gave it a miss. They were dining at the Four Seasons and watching a cabaret that would have appalled Christina. Walter knew the city well. His French publisher brought him over at each publication. But for Martin it was the first time, and he drank in its glories like a bookish and astonished schoolboy. Walter found him a joy to guide, and over the next two days, he offered him a tourist's Paris, as well as some of the quarters and sights known only to Parisians themselves.

'I'll be grateful all my life,' Martin said on the flight back home.

'I don't want gratitude,' Walter said. 'Gratitude is banal. Besides, it's been a great pleasure for *me*. Give me thanks with progress with your work. Finish your novel. The third is easier, believe me. Other fences, but surmountable.'

Martin could not wait to get home. He owed it to Walter, to say nothing of himself, to finish his current novel, and when he returned, he started on it right away.

Walter had to call in on his publishers on the way home from the airport, and after this delay, he reached home early in the evening. He let himself in to his apartment and called Christina from the door. She was waiting for him in the drawing-room. He tuned his eyes to the accusing black of her habitual garb but was astonished to find her almost unrecognisable. He realised that it had been a whole year since their disastrous visit to Lahore. The black was gone at last. But of all the colours that she could have chosen to break her black and terrible fast, she had chosen yellow. Why, she was actually wearing the yellow sari that Tom had bought her so many years ago. He should have been relieved. He should have embraced her for her black survival. But this yellow screamed in his face. It seemed to him, that while black was the legal colour of mourning, yellow was the colour of revenge. The Catherine Wheel had come full circle.

Chapter 11

At the end of that last chapter, it struck me that the reader might think that I was cheating. But I have, in all honesty, kept strictly to my fiction. Walter was not responsible for my Paris baptism, for there never was a P.E.N. conference. I don't think Walter ever belonged to P.E.N. By nature, he was not a joiner. He was as disaffiliated as a hermit. He did tell me though, that Amanda was his step-daughter, but that was much later, shortly before she got married. No, I have kept to my self-chosen brief. My autobiopsy is fiction, and if at times it occasionally overlaps with fact that is only because the truth of reality is as unreliable as the lie of fiction.

I decided to take a break for a while. I had been so engrossed in that last chapter that my post had accumulated. None of it had been attended to and much of it was unopened. So I made myself coffee and reached for my letter-opener. The only communication of interest was an invitation from a publishing house. It invited 'Martin Peabody and Partner' to celebrate the publication of Frank Watson's biography of Walter Berry. The invitation to my 'partner' intrigued me. I didn't have one to hand, but I suppose I could have found one for the evening. But Amanda would be there and I considered her my partner even if she had no notion of it herself. I looked forward to the evening. Christina would be there of course and I was unsure of how she would receive me since my refusal of her request. But on that score I still retained my lack of scruple, so for my part, I could face her with ease. I was glad to have a future plan.

My phone rang as I was wondering what to do next. Surprisingly, it was my father.

'I said I would phone,' he said.

I had not expected his call. My father had never been one to keep his word.

'I thought you might like to come around and see the flat,' he said.

'When?'

'Now. Why not come for lunch?'

It crossed my mind to refuse. I like to be given decent notice of an appointment. But my father is one who assumes that people will drop everything to rally to his call. He diminished me by supposing that I had nothing else to do. Nevertheless I accepted, but more out of curiosity than pleasure. I wondered whether I should put on a suit. I was aware that if one entered the heart of Mayfair, one wiped one's feet and minded one's manners. But I'd be buggered if I'd dress to please my father, so I dressed in my elegant but casual attire.

He certainly lived in the grand manner. Though a service flat, it was huge, and housed servants' quarters, where my father lodged his new housekeeper. No Yellow this one. He was a man and a good deal older than my father. He was a gentleman's gentleman, and had been all his working life. In his own terms my father had undoubtedly arrived, and I was moved by how pathetically low were his sights. I noticed that Johnson – that was his name – had spread a delectable lunch in the dining-room. There was smoked salmon for hors d'oeuvre and a dish of choice cold cuts with many varieties of salads. An excellent cheese-board was prepared on the side-board, together with a bowl of non-European fruits.

'You live well,' I said.

'I should have done it years ago,' my father said.

There were so many 'its' that my father should have done years ago, that it was difficult to specify which particular 'it' he was referring to. But I didn't ask him to narrow the field. I sensed it would only lead to argument. And then I noticed something. On the side-table in the living-room there stood a Meissen figurine. A shepherdess. It was my mother's, bequeathed to her from her own mother's collection. It was a standard item in her cabinet and I noted its beauty every time I visited her. I looked around the room and saw other indications of her touch. The flower arrangements could have been Johnson's of course, but the vases came positively from my mother's home. And when we went into lunch, I noted the table-mats. My mother's precious set of framed original English prints. It would not have surprised me to see my mother sitting at the head of the table. But on all these *aperçus*, I held my tongue. But I think I understood at last who was my mother's 'him', and why her voice no longer sank when she heard my own.

We sat down to lunch. Johnson tip-toed silently around the table. He even managed to pour the wine silently. Then he tip-toed out again leaving us to a conversation which neither of us knew how to begin. I took the plunge.

'Has Mother seen this flat?' I asked.

'Yes. She's been here often. You must have noticed some of her things.'

'Has she given them to you?'

'No. Not exactly.' He sipped his wine and squeezed the lemon onto his salmon. I knew he was going to stuff his mouth to put an end to further questioning. But I wasn't going to let him off so lightly. If he was not prepared to talk about my mother, I would try another tack.

'How's Anne?' I asked.

He almost choked on his fish. It was as if the name had rung a cacophonous bell and the noise had deafened him. He swallowed.

'She's alright,' he said. 'She understands everything.'

I wondered whether Anne was still telling callers that my father was out to lunch, or dinner or even breakfast, depending on what time of the day they called. Although I took a dim view of my father's behaviour, I had little sympathy for Anne. The world is full of Mrs Yellows, battening like parasites off married backs, God knows. My best friend Walter had known some in his time. Or was that my fiction? I bit into my salmon to swallow my confusion.

It was a relief when Johnson crept in once more to remove the plates. My father insisted on serving me with the meats and salads. It obviated the need for conversation for the silence was noticeable and oppressive. He made an inordinate noise with the forks and servers, but when all was done, the silence once more invaded. And then my father did an extraordinary thing. He asked me how I was. He asked it me to my face as if he eagerly awaited my reply. And more. As if he were prepared to listen. I was flummoxed. I had to consider my reply. 'Fine' would not do. 'Fine' was an unserious answer to an unserious question. I began to wonder exactly how I was.

'I'm working,' I said. 'I'm over half way through a novel.' It was the truth. I couldn't imagine what he'd make of it.

He put down his fork, a serious gesture for my father, who rarely allowed a disturbance in his food consumption, and certainly not one that he imposed upon himself.

'What's it about?' he asked.

I remembered Walter's instruction never to talk about work in progress. Especially plots. But how could I explain that to my father whose interest was genuine enough. His heart attack had certainly done him a lot of good. So off the top of my head, I concocted a plot that surprised even myself with its machinations. My father listened, fascinated.

'And how does it end?' he asked.

'I'm not going to tell you that,' I said, having absolutely no idea myself. 'You'll have to read it when it's finished.'

'I read your last, you know,' he said.

Another surprise.

'I'm glad it did well. It deserved to.'

Now the ice was truly broken. I was beginning to think my father had had a heart transplant rather than an attack. It was as if a totally different organ had replaced that rigid ungiving beat that used to deafen my childhood with its loud indifference.

'Would you like some more meat?' he asked. He rang a silver bell on the table and even before its echo subsided, Johnson was creeping into the room.

'Sir?' he said.

'Is there more meat, Johnson? We have developed an appetite.'

Johnson smiled for the first time as he removed the meat platter.

'And the salads are delicious,' my father said.

The smile broadened as Johnson withdrew.

My father astonished me. He was now displaying kindness, a trait unpractised and possibly unlearned hitherto. Thereafter conversation flowed easily, though we talked about general issues, skirting all personal matters. After lunch he asked if I would like to see round the rest of the apartment. He was obviously proud of his little castle.

· 'I'd love to,' I said. I was genuinely happy for him. If a man can change at that age, and change so radically, he deserved some little applause.

The flat was larger than I supposed. Apart from the servants' quarters of four rooms, which Johnson allowed me to inspect, the flat itself boasted three bedroom suites. I could not help asking my father why he needed such a large establishment.

In answer, he smiled. 'I've persuaded your mother to sell the house,' he said.

'She's moving in?' I whispered.

'Why not?' he said. 'She loves the flat.'

There had to be a better reason for moving in, I thought, but I knew that my father could not go as far as saying that he wanted her back. A hundred heart attacks would do nothing to diminish his pride.

'I'm glad about that,' I said. 'And I'm glad you asked me to lunch.'

He took me to the door. 'We must see more of you, Martin,' he said. And by 'we', I knew he was not including Johnson. He was asking me back into the family to which he himself had returned.

On leaving him, I went straight to see my mother. I did not bother to phone. I just hoped she'd be at home. When I arrived, I noticed a strange car in the driveway. Violet let me in and I could see at once that her mood was sullen.

'Your mother's somewhere in the house Master Martin,' she said, offering to take the coat and hat I wasn't wearing.

'Whose car is that outside?' I asked.

'Strangers,' she said. She would have spat the word, had she been less genteel.

I heard people walking upstairs, and my mother's cheerful voice.

'This room gets the sun all day,' I heard. Then I knew that

171

the strangers were prospective buyers and I understood Violet's sullenness.

I went out into the garden and sat on the bench under the mulberry tree. The site of my first nursery rhyme. I had sat there on Violet's lap as she carefully intoned each syllable. Then, as soon as I could walk, we danced to the words. As I sat there, I realised I was making myself available to all manner of happy childhood recall. Hitherto, I had only been able to remember my father's beatings and my mother's silent collusion. Now I saw that silence as fear of my father. She didn't want him to think ill of her, and to that purpose she was prepared to turn a blind eye to my misery. As I sat under the mulberry tree, I was able to forgive her. I thought of my father, and was astonished that, with that thought I felt no buttock-twinge of his belt buckle. It was the first time that that almost Pavlovian reflex had been missing. I was growing up, I thought. I was moving into a forgiveness phase which could only be explained by the tentative growth of my own self-esteem. But it was Violet who moved me most, and to whom I was now so tardily grateful. For without her, my childhood would have been unmanageable. I had never liked this house. As a child I was aware of all its fineries, its many hallmarks of civilised living, yet, instinctively, I knew it for a sham. For in my young eyes, it was a cruel and barbaric prison. But I hadn't recalled the garden, that site of my occasional freedom. And now as I looked around me, I was sorry that my mother was selling the house, and it crossed my astonished mind to ask her if she would let me live in it once she had moved.

I heard the strangers' car drive out of the driveway. I rose to join my mother in the drawing-room. She was surprised and delighted to see me.

'Martin,' she said, 'I wasn't expecting you.'

'Are they going to buy it?' I asked.

'How do you know I'm selling?'

'I went to see Father,' I said.

'So you know.' She smiled.

'Yes. I know. And I'm glad. But are they going to buy it?' I insisted.

'I don't think so,' she said. 'They want a bigger garden.'

I thanked God for their refusal. That garden was more than big enough for me. Just the square around the mulberry tree would have sufficed for my comfort.

'Please don't mention it to Violet,' she was saying. 'I haven't told her yet.'

'I think she knows,' I said. Then after a pause, 'Father has a lovely flat. You'd look well in it. I'm rather impressed by Johnson.'

'Oh Virginia,' she laughed.

'Why Virginia?'

'Because he's a creeper,' she said.

Where had my mother's sense of humour suddenly come from? I remembered not a vestige of it in my youth. Perhaps her present happiness had released it. I felt it a propitious moment to offer my proposal. 'Don't sell it Mother,' I said. 'Let's keep it in the family. I'd like it. I could sell mine, and somehow make up the rest of the money.'

'Are you serious?' she said.

'Of course.'

'I think it's a lovely idea,' she said. 'I'll talk to your father about it.'

At that remark, I found it hard to keep my temper, for in my mind it represented a total backsliding into her past serfdom. 'No you *don't* have to talk to Father about it. This is *your* house. It was your *mother's* house. It's *your* decision.'

She smiled. 'It's habit I'm afraid,' she said. 'A bad habit.'

'And you have to grow out of it,' I said. 'In any case, I'm sure Father would agree,' I assured her. 'There's one condition,' I added.

'What's that?'

'I want to keep Violet. You can have Virginia.'

'You'll have to discuss that with Violet,' my mother said. Then added, 'And I'm sure she'll be over the moon.'

Thus it was settled. At least in principle, and on my drive home, I went through the house of my childhood with the eyes of one who would bequeath that childhood to another. But a happy one. A mulberry tree one. And I peopled the house. With Amanda and Simon. I saw them both fit in superbly. I even heard Violet and Simon singing around the mulberry tree. I don't think that ever in my life I had been happier. And to cap it all, there was a message on my answering machine from Amanda herself. On it she said that she hoped to see me at Frank Watson's publication party. My life had changed, and I wondered how much part I had played in its turning. Walter had initiated it certainly, and his death and his purloined bequest had set in motion a series of changes that had driven my life into new, untried directions. He had broken my writer's block, and in the course of writing, I had learned to forgive my parents. And in writing, I had also learned to love. I felt so grateful to my old friend, that I went to my freezer if only to thank him once more. This I did, and caressed him, and was saddened by his shrunken gaze. I knew that soon I would lose him, and I hoped with fervour that in the course of that loss, he would teach me to live without him.

When the day of the publication party arrived, I woke up in a fever of excitement. I played Scarlatti most of the day to calm my nerves. And when I was soothed, I went to my work-bench and laid Pegasus on the table. He was almost complete. A little minute carving was called for on one wing, and by now my heart and hands were steady. I set to work, and within a couple of hours, the figure was finished to my satisfaction. I placed it on a shelf and viewed it from a distance. It was full of life and movement and, given a finger-tip touch, it looked as if it would take flight. I left it there. It needed only a polish and a veneer perhaps and then it would be ready for presentation. I already imagined it standing on the mantel-piece in the bedroom of my boyhood, on that exact spot where my favourite aeroplane stood, the machine that my father had said was too expensive to play with. I remembered then, how once, after a beating, I had taken the machine and broken it into several pieces to teach my father a lesson. The aeroplane was never referred to, though I did leave all the pieces on the floor, loud and clear. Violet took kindly pains not to clear them away for several days, so he couldn't have missed them. But he said nothing. He did not want to acknowledge his defeat, or perhaps he had a moment of remorse. But whatever it was, it didn't last long for his belt buckle still itched in his hands, I wondered whether he still had that same belt and whether he wore it sometimes to keep his hand in. But I couldn't believe that that belt belonged to my post heart attack father. He would never believe that he could have used it for any other purpose then keeping up his trousers. Once more I saw Pegasus on that mantelpiece in that screaming belt buckle gap. But I knew I must not let myself be carried away. It might after all, be a mere pipe-dream.

I took a shower and prepared myself for the reception. It was not good form to arrive too early. It showed a certain naive eagerness. No well-known writer would put in an appearance till the party was well under way. He would plead attendance at an earlier party, and he would leave soon after his arrival, claiming a dinner to attend. The myth of being famous and in constant demand, even if self-manufactured as it usually was, had to be kept in circulation, bruited about and kept forever green.

The party started at half past six, and officially ended at nine o'clock. I thought a quarter past seven would be a reasonable time to put in an appearance. And at a quarter past seven precisely, I arrived. It was crowded. I am not a tall man and that lack of height can be a distinct disadvantage in a crowd. There was a platform at the end of the hall and I made my way towards it. I grabbed a drink from a passing tray, and eventually I reached the platform and joined the others who, for lack of height, had been unable to spot anyone they knew. Despite the raised platform, I was obliged to stand on my toes, a position not conducive to dignity. So I tip-toed only occasionally and as nonchalantly as I could, so that a casual observer might have taken me for a ballet-dancer who never lost out on an opportunity to limber up. It was during one of these ham-fisted entrechats, that I spotted Amanda amongst the crowd, and straightening, I descended from the platform and made for her spot. She caught sight of me before I could reach her, and she held out her hand.

I stretched my fingers to reach hers, and she gripped them in a gesture of possession. I was flattered. I would gladly be owned by Amanda and once again I saw her reigning supreme in my childhood home. A tray of sausages floated beneath my chin.

'Don't eat anything,' she called over the gap. 'We're going out for dinner afterwards.'

I wondered who the 'we' was, rather as I had mused over my mother's 'him', and I smiled at this recent onset of pronoun curiosity. Had 'we' meant simply Amanda and myself, she would have whispered the invitation, but its public announcement hinted at a larger 'we' and would probably include Christina and the biographer himself. I moved over to a table where a number of copies were on display. Two untouched piles of them in fact, and so clearly there to be stolen, that no-one had yet had the nerve to deplete the pile. But I had no such scruple, and quite openly took away a top copy, so that the neat symmetry was disturbed. There was now an open invitation to a second thief to restore the equilibrium. I thought I should scan the volume, just in case Frank Watson was part of the 'we' for dinner. I looked at the chapter headings. They were the titles of Walter's complete works in chronological order. Nothing terribly original about that. The last chapter of the book was headed 'The Heroes', the title of Walter's last published novel. I turned to the last page. I thought an epilogue might perhaps have made reference to the unfinished work, but there was no mention of it. This omission pleased me for it now seemed that that unfinished novel fell in my domain, in my domain of fiction if I so wished, and if towards the end of my autobiopsy, I should syphon off a thought that pertained to this last work, I could fashion it to my will. I looked up and saw Frank Watson himself standing beside me and I reddened. Not for the theft of his book but for the theft of his omission.

'What d'you think?' he said.

'Looks good,' I answered, like the hypocrite I am, for whatever its matter inside, it certainly didn't *look* good. It was a cheapish production with narrow margins and poor quality paper, and I didn't think the binding would endure too many openings. But I pressed on. 'I'm looking forward to reading it,' I said, without the slightest intention of ever opening it again. I tucked it under my arm. It would make a handy duty

Christmas present. As I walked away, I was overwhelmed by Christina. She seemed to have loomed from nowhere. She fixed me with a steady eye, and though she did not touch me, I felt throttled by her non-embrace.

'You'll dine with us afterwards, I hope,' she said.

It was a statement rather than an invitation and she was clearly still bristling from my refusal of her request.

'Of course,' I said. 'I would love to.' I responded like a grateful invitee, whatever she thought. Amanda's 'we' was expanding. It now embraced Christina and the hoped-for intimacy evaporated.

'By the way,' Christina said. 'Don't worry about Walter's last novel. Frank has been kind and respectful enough to offer to finish it.'

'Good,' I said, feeling as unkind and as disrespectful as she meant me to feel. 'I'm very pleased. I'm sure he'll do it justice.'

She moved away, leaving me to reflect on the wisdom of her choice. Such a choice seemed to me neither kind nor respectful, and if Walter had a brain in his head, which he hadn't, he would surely have turned in his grave. I could only hope that his publishers would reject Frank Watson's completion as a simple sign of their reverence. I avoided Frank thereafter; Christina too and hoped that I would be placed by neither of them at dinner.

But alas, I found myself between them both, and I suspected Christina had arranged it on purpose. I could think of nothing to say to either of them. Fortunately there was a great deal of noise around the table so our silence passed unnoticed.

Frank was the first to speak. 'I'm going to complete Walter's last novel,' he announced.

He said it in a tone of one-upmanship, which rattled me.

'What d'you think of it?' I said.

'I haven't seen it yet. I'm picking it up tomorrow.'

'I read it last week,' I said. I was delighted to infer that he was the second choice. 'It's a difficult one,' I added. I did not look at his face, but I heard him swallowing. 'Personally,' I pressed on, 'I think it should be left alone.'

'I'm doing it for Christina's sake,' he said.

I wondered whether he and Christina were having an affair.

They were both of a similar age, and both were alone. I caught Amanda's eye across the table. She shrugged. It was a gesture that could have meant anything. I took it to mean her helplessness with respect to the seating. I smiled at her.

'See you afterwards,' she mouthed.

With that promise in store, I was happy to remain imprisoned between Frank and Christina, who possibly found me as disappointing a neighbour as I them. I looked around the table and was surprised to see none of Walter's close friends. I assumed the company was Frank's choice, and I had a sad sense that Walter had already been forgotten, and that Frank's book and his threatened completion of Walter's last work would be sufficient to bury my friend once and for all. I felt that Walter's memory now lay solely in my own guardianship and I was suddenly anxious to get back to my freezer. Even at the prospect of spending time with Amanda after dinner, I did not waver. But out of courtesy, I would have to sit it out until at least the end of the meal. I decided to spend the time being pleasant to my neighbours.

'You're looking lovely Christina,' I said, and for the first time I noticed that she was wearing black. This threw me a little for I recalled that in my last sighting, she had broken her black fast and given way to yellow. But I had to remind myself that yellow was my fiction and my confusion disturbed me. Now I needed more than ever to get back to my freezer. When the dessert course arrived, I excused myself. I pleaded a splitting headache. I have never had a headache in my life. But I knew the phrase well. It had fallen often enough from my mother's lips when I was a child. I wondered then what it was and how it felt, and I wonder still. But whatever it was, I knew it was a good enough phrase for an exit line. I crossed over to where Amanda was sitting and offered the same excuse in her ear, saying that I would phone the following day. She looked both sympathetic and disappointed, and both looks pleased me. I pressed my hand to my forehead and stumbled out of the room. Then I ran into the street blessing my escape. As I drove home, I realised how powerfully my work had assumed the upper hand and even the delightful prospect of spending time with Amanda had suddenly become quite secondary. I did not regret my choice. People can be kept waiting. But not words.

There had been no incoming calls in my absence, and I left the machine on, not wishing to be disturbed. I went straight to my kitchen. As a rule, my forays to my freezer took place in broad daylight. But now the light was artificial and the windows framed a black starless night, and as I placed Walter on the table, I sensed that I was touching a ghost. I was frightened, and for a moment I regretted having left that dinner-table where all was light and everyone around was real. And if not real, then at least alive. I caressed Walter's shrivelling brain, but not gently as was my wont. I pressed my fingers into the membrane, as if to confirm its solidity, and to prove to myself that it was not an airy nothing, that I would give it a 'local habitation and a name'. The freezer in Martin Peabody's kitchen. And Walter. Walter Berry, the greatest novelist of our time.

I syphoned. Again there was little waffle. As he grew older, it seemed that Walter had cleared his mind of all jumble. As if every idea that he had harboured, trivial or otherwise, was clear and purposeful.

> *I can hear the sound of crow's feet*
> *marching across my face.*

This was the first thought that I syphoned off that evening. It was a sad thought and an unexpected one. For during my long friendship with Walter, I had never known him conscious of the years that were passing. Indeed he often said that writers, like good wine, usually improve with age. It seemed that of a sudden, vanity had assailed him, and that assumption was confirmed by the next thought that dribbled from his mind. And a strange one it was. Not in its content, but in its style. For Walter had suddenly third-personed himself, and that, to my mind, is the very extreme of vanity. And often of despair.

Good for old Walter. He deserves it mind
you. Usually that prize goes to a writer
whom no-one on earth has ever heard of.
Well at least Walter's famous and that
makes a change. Honoured ladies and
gentlemen. I am indeed delighted to be the
recipient of the Nobel Prize. I would like
to . . .

I heard myself laughing aloud, and with deep affection, for
somehow that day-dream made Walter just like the rest of us.
Though for my part, I have to confess that, even in day-dreams,
my sights are slightly lower than my friend's. I would be very
happy, thank you very much, to settle for the Booker, and from
time to time, usually when the writing goes painfully slow, I
fashion a little speech of acceptance. What writer doesn't? I ask
myself. I syphoned further. And again, the third person.

Such a good man, Walter Berry. So honest.
So decent.

Then there came a sigh that rattled like a ghost.

Ah. How misled they are. How duped by
appearances. They don't know. They don't
know the half of it. Nobody knows. And
nobody shall ever know.

I rested my syphon. I needed a little time to absorb this last
revelation. For I was reminded of the last thought that had
emerged from Walter's brain before I turned him the right way
up. '*No more fear of accusation.*' And I felt that at last, I would
be given a clue to that terrible shame of his that had echoed
his death-rattle. But when I started re-syphoning, there was

silence for a while. I had not believed that a brain could ever be so absolutely devoid of thought, but it seemed that, in his despair, dear Walter had temporarily taken his mind off his mind, and left a screaming silence there.

I withdrew my syphon. I was loathe to interrupt that silence. I had to let it be. For it signalled that Walter would give no clue to his terror, that he could not bear even to think about it, and that his shame, whatever it was, could be swallowed in that terrible silence. I gave it time, then picked up my syphon once more.

> *In old age, the past is always present.*
> *Constantly.*

My friend was truly becoming more and more obsessed with aging, yet at the time, he could have been no more than fifty.

> *I hate God.*

Again I had hopes of a clue.

> *What does a woman do when she hates*
> *God? It's a man's world. A man can fuck a*
> *nun. That way he can cuckold the Saviour.*
> *Whereas a woman who fucks a monk only*
> *succeeds in fucking a monk. The*
> *destruction of faith is not available to a*
> *woman.*

The plot thickened, and the thought that followed did nothing to clear the air.

*In times of crises a man can only resort to
clichés. Every cloud has a silver lining. It's
all part of life's rich tapestry.*

Poor old Walter. He was clearly in the depths of despair. Yet
how closely he had kept his black moods to himself. For
throughout our friendship he never showed signs of sadness.
I admired him more and more. Once again, I rested my
syphon. It was as if I wanted to give Walter's depression time
to lift.

I went to the window. The sky was black without a single
star, and exactly translated the mood I had left on my kitchen
table. I wondered whether I should call it a day, and put my
friend back in the freezer in the hope that the intense cold
would anaesthetise his pain. But I was anxious for clues, if not
to his shame, then at least for my next chapter. I returned to
the table and picked up my syphon once more. Again there
was a long and utter silence. This time I waited, and after a
while a thought emerged. Or rather a cry. For it was laced
with tears.

Dear God. She's breaking my heart.

I put Walter away. I could not bear to syphon further. And in
any case I had direction enough. Though as to the identity of
the 'she' who was breaking Walter's heart, I had no idea.
Again I was set on a pronoun hunt. I went to my desk, but on
the way, my head began to throb and for the first time in my
life, I understood the meaning of headache. That unknown
pain that I had pleaded earlier in the evening, now became an
excruciating reality. I decided to go to bed. In the morning I
would start on my voyage of discovery. The who and the why
of Walter's heart-break.

Chapter 12

... yellow was the colour of revenge. The Catherine Wheel had come full circle.

Christina had dyed her mourning yellow and that was the only change that she allowed. She still kept to her own quarters and Walter to his, but now without question or complaint. For he had settled for a celibate life. His spirit was almost completely containable in his work but his workaholic nature had its side effects. A growing awareness of aging was one of them, and a sudden vanity that that awareness prompted and the self-distaste that followed. Hitherto a mirror or a shop-window reflector never troubled him. Nowadays, he avoided both. He took to using an electric razor to obviate the necessity of a mirror. Instead, he felt along his face for its smoothness or otherwise and he shaved accordingly. In so doing, he developed his sense of touch and applied it to all parts of his body, trusting his hands more than the looking-glass. With his two fingers he registered every aging line and wrinkle, and with his cupped palms he weighed the shrinking growth of his hair. Each morning he saw how its grey reminder lingered on the comb. Then the thought crossed his mind to colour it. He had heard of hair applications which would cover all the grey. Their advertisements made that solemn promise, but he dismissed the idea when, one morning at breakfast, Amanda remarked on how distinguished he looked.

'It's the grey,' she teased. 'It becomes you.'

He could survive on Amanda's occasional compliments, he thought, but soon she would no longer be around to offer them. She had been offered a place at Oxford to read history. Walter had been overjoyed at the news, and only afterwards did he realise that the offer entailed her absence from home. He would miss her. But more than that. Her absence would ground him with Christina and there would be no third presence to offset the silences between them. Not that those silences were hostile, but they might well become embarrassing and lead to a certain questioning as to why they both had to dwell in such ridiculous isolation. He began to dread Amanda's departure. Fortunately he was due to do a book-promotion tour a few days after Amanda would leave, and though he would often forgo such tours, he counted this one as a blessing. He felt that Christina welcomed it too. It would give them both time to adjust to their new circumstances. But on the whole, nothing changed between them, except perhaps that their friendship deepened. It had become almost sibling. And with that change it seemed that Christina felt free to refer more and more often to Tom. 'Tom would have been very proud of Amanda,' she would say, and Walter would resent her constant references to a man who had been dead these eighteen years. And to one who had had nothing to do with Amanda's growing, and who had never even seen her. 'I'm very proud of her too,' Walter would say, feeling that much of her achievement was due to his interest and encouragement.

During the first few weeks of her Oxford residence, Amanda phoned home often. Clearly she was homesick. But after a while the calls were less frequent, until there came a time when a phone call from Amanda was a pleasant surprise. When she came home for Christmas, she appeared restless and moody as if she resented having to leave Oxford. It was not that she was unhappy. On the contrary, at times, Walter heard her singing with joy. Every morning she would rush to collect the post, and her mood that day depended on its delivery. She spent much of her time in her room, appearing only for

184

meals and donating an almost silent presence at table. Walter asked her about her course and her tutors. He was genuinely interested in how she was faring. She answered in monosyllables. He gathered that everything was alright, no more no less than that, and at times he was irritated by her sheer and utter boredom. Once he shouted at her, and she burst into tears and left the table. Christina gave Walter an accusing look.

'There's something the matter with Amanda,' he said. 'I sometimes wonder whether she goes to lectures at all. She seems to know nothing about what's going on in her college and if she does, she's certainly not letting on.'

'It's all very new to her, Walter,' Christina said. 'She's finding it hard to adjust.'

'Why is she so moody, for God's sake?' Walter said.

Christina put a hand on his arm. 'I think she's probably in love,' she said.

Walter felt his stomach curdle, and his reaction appalled him. He knew he had no right to such feelings of rage, and of a sudden he thought of Miss Freeman, and once again he swallowed that monstrous bile of rejection. He took Christina's hand. He was glad that he no longer looked upon her as his wife. After her journey to Lahore, she had offered him nothing more than her hand in friendship and now for the first time, he was able to accept it with relief. For now, at this moment, he desperately needed a friend. He squeezed her hand.

'I suppose I'm behaving like a typical father,' he said. He managed a smile.

'And so you should,' Christina laughed.

Despite this reassurance, Walter was relieved when Christmas was over and Amanda returned to Oxford. Occasionally she phoned and her lively conversation more than made up for her Christmas silences. She was enjoying her course, she said, and working very hard. In her enthusiasm, Walter sensed that she was protesting too much and when he asked her exactly what she was working on, he could not help but hear and almost see her hesitation at the end of the line. She answered that she was doing a bit of everything, and Walter knew that she was doing nothing at all. Once he asked her if she wanted a visit. She refused him gently, pleading pressure of work. The thought crossed his mind to surprise her one day but he was afraid of having his worst fears confirmed. For he doubted whether she was attending classes at all. He tried not to think about it, and he threw himself into his work. But it nagged at him. He didn't know what upset him most. Whether it was his fear that Amanda had found the pressures of Oxford too much for her, or whether he should consider Christina's surmise, and he had to confess that, despite his love and respect for learning, it was the latter that disturbed him most. He tried to concentrate on his work, but every time the phone rang, he eavesdropped at his door as Christina answered the call. But Amanda had not phoned for almost a month. He did his best to keep his fear from Christina, but one night at dinner, she herself broached the subject.

'I'm a little worried,' she said. 'We haven't heard from Amanda since she went back. D'you think we should go and see her? She might be ... well ... who knows? I think one of us should go.'

'I'll go tomorrow,' Walter said quickly. He was grateful that she had given him an opening and had left him to carry the burden, if burden there was, alone.

'I'm sure there's nothing to worry about,' he said. He felt suddenly jovial. 'I'll have a brandy. You too,' he said, 'and stop worrying.' Christina relaxed too. She was relieved that Walter would take the responsibility for enquiry. For she too was concerned with Amanda's welfare. She suspected that it was the pressure of work that disturbed her daughter. She had heard of mental breakdowns amongst students, and even of suicides. She shivered at the thought of it. She took the glass of brandy he offered her. 'Are you going to work tonight?' she said.

It was a question she had never asked before. For years it had been a matter of routine that Walter would go to his study after supper, and Walter understood that tonight she was asking him to stay with her.

'Why don't we watch television for a change?' he said. 'I think there's a good film on one of the channels.'

'That's a very good idea,' Christina said. It would be a way of obviating the need for conversation, yet at the same time, it would ensure togetherness. And this evening, that was what she wanted above all.

'I'll bring our coffee into the drawing-room,' she said.

Soon they were settled, side by side on the chesterfield. On each of their side-tables stood their coffee and cognac. A domestic evening, Walter thought and considered he should allow more of them.

'I'll get an early train tomorrow,' he said. 'It's quicker than driving.' He would sleep well tonight, he thought, having something so positive to look forward to. It was something concrete to do, as opposed to the blank sheet of paper and the words that may or may not happen. He was excited too, more than he cared to admit to himself. He was glad he was going alone. He did not think that he could hide his excitement from even the most unsuspecting eye.

The film was an import from America, a loud western, full of sound and fury. And, as Walter suspected, 'signifying nothing'. But he was glad of the diversion and he noted with pleasure that Christina had slowly relaxed.

'We must do this more often,' he said, and he stretched out his hand towards her. She took it in hers.

The film was moving towards its first hero/villain confrontation and their small conversation was usefully put aside. Together they wallowed in the blood and thunder that throbbed from the screen. And so engrossed were they with this rare and faintly naughty pleasure, that they did not hear the key turn in the front door. Neither did they hear the timid dumping of cases in the hall. Nor even the door of the drawing-room open. If they heard a faint and plaintive 'hullo,' it could well, at the time, have come out of the screen, and it was not until

Amanda placed herself before them that they realised that they had company.

Walter's first reaction was to turn off the set, and the sudden silence that broke into the room demanded some form of explanation. But Walter had the sense to greet her first, to embrace her. He knew that whatever she had to tell, she was afraid of telling. But Christina did not rise from her chair. She moved her body slightly, straightening her back, assuming the attitude of authority.

'What are you doing here?' she said coldly.

And at that reproving greeting, Amanda put her rehearsal aside. Indeed, she forgot it totally. All those words that she had practised in the train, all their various stresses, their permutations, their fine tuning in the taxi on the way from the station. All that rehearsal evaporated in her mother's straight back and accusing stare.

'I've left university,' she said. And without a second's pause, 'I want to get married.'

She had meant to give a detailed preamble to the first bit of news, to give it reasons, and hopefully, some logic. Then she would have assessed their reaction, and only then would she have crept towards her second revelation. But her mother's lack of greeting enraged her, and her declaration was not so much news as punishment. Christina opened her mouth with what looked like the beginnings of a tirade of abuse but Amanda, wittingly or otherwise, cunningly forestalled her. She simply sat down in the chair that Walter had vacated and burst into tears. All they could do now was to stare at her. Walter let her cry a while, then he knelt beside her.

'Why don't you go to bed, Amanda?' he said gently. 'Have a good sleep and then we can all talk about it in the morning.'

'I'm not tired,' Amanda said, 'and there's nothing to talk about. I'm not going back to college and I'm getting married. That's all there is to say.'

'May we ask to whom?' Christina said. She stressed the pronoun with contemptuous grammar.

'Someone I met in Oxford. His name's Ian.'

'Has Ian left college too?' Walter asked.

'He was never there,' Amanda said.

'What does he do then?' This from Christina. Her back was now like a ram-rod.

'He's a waiter. I met him in a restaurant.' In her train-rehearsal, she had given Ian another vocation. He was still a waiter, but she would have added that it was part of his training for hotel-management. She felt it would have softened the blow a little. But now she didn't care.

'Your father would have been very disappointed in you,' Christina said. Then she sank back into her chair. In her terms she could not have delivered greater censure.

Amanda stood up. 'Bugger my father,' she shouted. 'I never even saw him.' Then the tears came again. 'I'm going to bed,' she whimpered.

Walter dared to touch her, and she clasped his hand in gratitude. There was nothing he could usefully say. He walked with her to the door. 'Try to sleep,' he said.

He kissed her goodnight on the forehead, then turned back into the room. He was angry. He thought Christina had behaved stupidly. And her reference to Tom infuriated him. It was unintelligent and hurtful. He wanted to shout at her, but he knew how hurt she was. He decided to make no comment on her behaviour.

'Let's try to have a good night's sleep,' he said. 'And we can talk about it in the morning.'

'I think she's pregnant,' she said. Her tone of disgust was one of accusation and judgement at the same time. Such a thought had not crossed Walter's mind, but now, recalling Amanda's mood, he thought the suggestion feasible. He tried not to think about it and once again he said, 'We'll talk about it in the morning.'

'I don't think I shall sleep at all tonight,' Christina said, rising from her chair. Then, 'Poor Tom,' she whispered.

It was too much for Walter. 'What the hell has it got to do with Tom?' he shouted at her. He was not protesting on his own behalf, though God knows he had cause enough. He was defending Amanda. 'It's not fair to use him as an absent judge. It's blackmail.' He didn't want to hurt her, but of late there had been too many Tom references for his comfort. 'Amanda never knew him,' he said gently. 'In any case, children owe parents nothing.' As he said it, he knew how false was his assumption. He knew from his own sad experience how a child, who is loved least, feels that he owes most. For one cannot legislate for where debt and guilt should lie. He put his arm around her. 'Let's sleep on it,' he said.

They went to their separate quarters, but neither of them slept. Nor did Amanda, tossing and turning in tune with that restless household, and all of them dreading the morning.

Breakfast was late. None of them wanted to be first at table. Nor even last, for all of them would have happily skipped the meal altogether. But in all their minds, breakfast had been designated as judgement time. Each had it in mind to arrive late, and as a result, all of them arrived at the same time. The making of toast took up a little while, the pouring of milk over cereal a little longer. Then there came a time when no more preparation need be made and the munching of toast and the crackling of cereal could in no way disguise the silence that they were so desperately trying not to break. It was Walter who spoke first. Not because he wanted to lead the discussion, but he feared that Christina would open the proceedings and possibly set the wrong tone.

'Tell us about Ian,' he said.

Amanda was taken by surprise. And though faintly relieved, she suspected a certain cunning on Walter's part. He was going to play the 'softie' role. It was her mother who would pass her harsh sentence.

'He's nice,' Amanda said. She aimed her remark at her father. 'You'd like him. He's heard of you.'

'Most people have,' Christina said in an undertone. 'But has he read him? *Can* he read?'

'Christina,' Walter said. 'There's no need for that.' It would not have surprised him if Amanda left the table. He would have understood. But to her credit, she stayed.

'What is it you like about him?' Walter persevered.

'He's kind,' she said, with a pointed look at Christina. 'I'd like you to meet him.'

'Of course we'll meet him,' Walter said. 'But I don't understand what Ian has to do with your leaving college. Are they in any way connected?'

'No,' she said. 'Ian wants me to stay. But I don't like it there. I don't see the point of it all.'

Walter didn't know what to say. The uses of university education was another subject altogether and the mood around the table was not conducive to its discussion. So a silence followed. It was not clear whose turn it was to speak. Walter scratched in his mind for something to say because he feared Christina's interference. He noticed how her back was straightening, filling her lungs with the breath she would need for her attack.

'I suppose you're pregnant,' she hissed.

Amanda stared at her. Then, slowly, she rose from the table. 'I'll be going back to Oxford,' she said, 'and not, as you might think, Mother, to have a baby. I'm in love with Ian,' she said. 'But what would you know about that?'

She went quickly from the room, and when she had gone, Walter turned on his wife.

'I hope you're satisfied,' he said. He didn't care how hurt she was. He cared that she was driving Amanda away, out of his reach and out of his loving. 'Now listen to me,' he said. 'I shall go upstairs and talk to her. I shall ask her to bring Ian home. We are going to welcome him as a guest in our house. We're going to do our best to like him. If he loves our daughter, that's good enough for me and it should be good enough for you. If she insists on marrying him, we must bless their union. Then perhaps we can persuade her to go back to college.' He noticed how her back had crumpled in her chair and he left the room, disliking her a little.

He knocked on Amanda's door. 'It's Daddy,' he called. 'Can I come in?'

He heard her come to the door and turn the key. He reflected sadly that the door was locked against Christina. He went inside and was relieved to see no signs of

191

packing. A dent on the counterpane showed where she had been sitting, a depressed depression on the quilt. She filled it again and he sat by her side.

'You mustn't be angry with your mother,' he said. 'She only wants the best for you.'

'For me? For her? Or for the father I never knew? I'm sick of having him thrown up in my face.'

'You must try and understand her,' he said helplessly. 'It's not easy for me either.'

'Oh Daddy,' she said, and she put her arms round his neck. The tears came again.

'Tell me really why you're upset,' Walter said. 'You're in love. That should make you happy.' He recalled his Miss Freeman bliss and remembered how close it was to tears.

'I want you to like him,' Amanda said. 'Both of you. And I know you won't.'

'Why don't you give us a try?' Walter said. 'Ask him down for the weekend if he can get time off from his work. I'll talk to your mother. She'll come round. Don't you worry.'

She kissed him and he rose from the bed. He felt uncomfortable with himself. He was playing a role in which he had no heart. 'I'm going to my study now,' he said. 'Go down and make it up with Christina. She loves you. She wants the best for you. For *you*. Remember that.'

He went quickly from the room. He wanted no part in her confrontation with Christina. He was concerned about himself and about his own feelings. He was confused. He didn't know what he *ought* to be feeling, but he sensed that it was a long way from the almost illegal stirrings in his heart. At his desk, he found it hard to concentrate. He kept thinking of Miss Freeman. Not of her face. After thirty or so years, he could barely remember what she looked like. A faint smell of her still lingered like a long-pressed flower between the leaves of a much-loved book. Neither could he remember what she wore or even the room where their passion was spent. But what he did remember, and with utmost clarity, was the simple youthfulness of that green loving. And even now, his heart leapt at its recall. And he understood Amanda's happiness and her resolve to marry her Ian, as strong as his to take Miss Freeman to wife. Then he knew what he was feeling, whether he ought to be feeling it or not. He was jealous. He was full of envy and he did not like himself at all. This sudden spurt of self-disdain released him to his work. He accepted sadly that there was nothing in his life left for him to do.

The following day Amanda returned to Oxford promising to visit with Ian on the weekend. She had clearly affected a reconciliation with her mother for their parting was affectionate enough. For the rest of the week, both Christina and Walter avoided any conversation relating to Amanda. But Walter was pleased to note that Christina spent most of the days in the kitchen preparing food for the weekend. In the evenings, they looked at television together but they did not hold each other's hands. For Walter the screen was a means of escape and he was indifferent to which programme he was watching. He dreaded the weekend.

They arrived early on Friday evening. Christina had prepared a festive supper. She had perhaps gone a little overboard, Walter thought. Since Amanda's homecoming, he had nurtured a dislike for Ian, no matter how 'kind' he was. And he had no doubt that he would have greater difficulty in coming to terms with his putative son-in-law than would Christina. But he had to put a brave face on everything. It simply would not do to betray his true feelings. He must mind his every gesture and word.

When the bell rang on Friday evening, both Christina and Walter made for the door. Walter hung back. He did not want to overdo the welcome. So he waited in the living-room, standing like a clergyman with his back to the fire, shifting from foot to foot as he eavesdropped on the greetings at the door. He heard a murmuring and then a silence, and then. to his astonishment, a tinkle of laughter from Christina. It should have pleased him, but his wariness increased. He waited for them to enter the room.

He looked at Ian and knew that he had seen him somewhere before. He could not remember where. But the face was so familiar, and recalled pleasure, so that it was easy to smile at him and to greet him warmly. As he crossed the room to shake his hand, his eye fell on the silver-framed photograph of Tom. Tom in his uniform before he left for India. Now he knew the source of Christina's laughter in the hall and why Ian was Amanda's choice. All she had known of her father was set in a silver frame. All her life she had held it in her mind's eye and now she had freed it from its framing and given it life. The resemblance was remarkable. Ian could have been Tom's son. Walter shook his hand warmly. Ian's looks would ease his passage into the family. His coming might well bring peace to them all.

The weekend passed pleasantly enough. Walter did not allow his working routine to be disturbed. All Miss Freeman thoughts had mercifully faded. Ian was as much his step-son as Amanda was his adopted daughter. To all intents and purposes, Ian and Amanda were siblings, and in that light, Walter was able to view them without envy. Before they left, they discussed arrangements for the wedding. They wanted a quiet family affair in Oxford and perhaps a restaurant lunch after the ceremony. Ian's family numbered seven. Two maiden aunts, two sisters and a brother, his mother and hopefully his father, he added, who at that moment was estranged from his family.

'Let's hope the wedding will bring them together again,' Christina said.

'You must find yourself a nice flat in Oxford,' Walter said. 'It will be our present to you.'

'And I shall give you your honeymoon,' Christina said. 'You won't mind, will you Walter?'

Walter understood. She wanted to give them something in her own right. She wanted to give them the honeymoon that she hadn't had with Tom. Vicariously she

194

would be a bride again. Although he understood her motive, it saddened him. He wondered what he had been able to give her after all these years. He wondered indeed why she had ever married him. Tom could have died a thousand deaths, she would never have left him or let him go. For almost twenty years, Walter had been a stand-in. And now he saw himself robbed even of that role. For Ian would be called upon to play the understudy. For the rest of his life Walter would dwell in the wings, moving a prop or two from time to time, prompting occasionally from his own experience, and wondering all the time how the play would end.

During the weeks preceding the wedding, Tom's name was never mentioned again. There was no longer any need. He had returned and his return had obliterated nostalgia. Christina lashed out on an elegant suit for the wedding, and she insisted on Walter doing likewise. She would have wished for a greater splash for Amanda's nuptials, but she bowed to her daughter's modest wishes. Their union had miraculously lifted her burden of mourning. Her widowhood had been erased in Ian's coming. Now she could honestly consider herself as Walter's wife. It did not occur to her that in Ian's coming, Walter had lost his role and that for him, without Ian's removal, there was no other part that he could play.

About a week before the wedding, Amanda invited them both to Oxford to view their wedding present. She had settled on a small cottage on the outskirts of the city. Although he drew no attention to it, Walter saw the little house as an exact replica of the one in Camden Town where he had first seen her as a child. It was uncanny how deftly she was replicating the father she had lost and never known.

'D'you like it, Walter?' she asked.

This new term of address came as a shock. He had always been 'Daddy' to her. Now she was simply confirming the role that he had lost. The 'Walter' had fallen so naturally from her lips. As naturally as Christina would always be 'Mummy' or 'Mother', depending on her mood.

He tried to wear his new status with some style. He smiled at her and put his arm around her shoulder. He even kissed her cheek. As 'Daddy', she had grown too old for such handling, but as 'Walter' he felt himself free to be an affectionate stranger.

That evening they dined in the restaurant where they would celebrate their wedding. Walter approved of their choice and privately he made extra arrangements with the owner.

In the car on their return to London, Christina attempted signs of renewed affection. She placed her hand on Walter's knee and let it lie there for a while. It's too late, Walter thought to himself. It's too late for all that. I know you too well, and you have become a stranger. We never synchronised in our loving and now its timing is irrelevant. But he would be polite. Etiquette was now the most and the least that he could give her. When they reached home, he went to his study and he worked with heart-broken fury.

The day before the wedding, they went to Oxford and spent the night in an hotel. At noon they all gathered at the registry office. Ian's family made up the bulk of the party and Ian effected the introductions as they waited for the registrar. As they shook hands all round, both Walter and Christina knew that they were unlikely to meet the family again. It was clear that they were not their kind of people and Christina found herself staring at Ian and that uncanny resemblance, to reassure herself of the logic of her daughter's choice, and thus her future happiness. Mrs Smethwick, Ian's mother, was effusively polite, being painfully aware of her morganatic status. She almost genuflected in her greeting. But Ian's siblings offset their mother's deference with a certain arrogance, evident in their hard and confident handshakes and exaggerated bonhomie. The two maiden aunts offered a compromise with a gesture of greeting no more than a simple and synchronised nodding of heads. Walter had the uneasy feeling that every single one of them was doing the wrong thing. He looked at Amanda and silently prayed for her, and he saluted her honesty in her choice of dress. It was off-white and exactly translated her bridal status.

The ceremony was a conveyor-belt operation. A brand-newly-wedded couple emerged from the registry as Ian and his party were ushered inside. And their place in the waiting-room was immediately taken by the next pair of hopefuls and their families. Walter looked at them. Apart from the bridal pair, they all looked strangers to each other and like the Smethwicks and the Berrys, they were unlikely to set eyes on each other again.

They all assembled in the office. The Smethwick clan took up most of the near-side block of seats. Christina and Walter echoed hollowly on the other side. The marriage officer pronounced the full names of the new applicants for married bliss.

'Amanda, Stella Greenfield/Berry,' he read from his paper.

Walter knew that as Amanda's legal name but she had never used it. A simple Amanda Berry had been enough for her and this sudden assertion of Tom came as a surprise to him but nowhere near the astonishment that struck him as the registrar announced the similar details of Ian's baptism.

'Ian Adolph Smethwick,' he announced.

Amanda looked quickly at her intended, as if she too were hearing it for the first time. Walter shivered on her behalf. That baptism did not augur well. Ian was very much a post-war baby. Time had elapsed since the German defeat, but not enough time, Walter thought, nor ever would there be enough, to sully a new-born with such a blemished label. And he wondered what Mr Smethwick senior was made of. He was nowhere in evidence, and as yet no-one had offered a reason for his absence.

Walter suspected it would be politic not to enquire. So astonished was he at this latest revelation about his son-in-law, that he paid no attention to the ceremony itself.

When he dared to look at the couple, they were embracing, brazenly he thought, in such a public venue, and he understood that the formalities were over. He was glad that they could now adjourn to the restaurant. His growing anxiety was giving him an appetite.

The proprietor had put aside a private room for their entertainment, and had dressed it accordingly. Walter viewed the flowers and the ornate table-setting, and considered it all a sorrowful waste. He hoped he would not be called upon to make a speech. Every syllable would be a lie since his truth would be unspeakable.

There were no special seating arrangements around the table, and Walter noticed how the maiden aunts made a bee-line for Christina and had seated themselves on either side of her. Immovable. They cast a glance at Ian and smiled in triumph. Walter found himself next to Mrs Smethwick and he wondered what they could find to say to each other.

'I'm sorry your husband isn't here today.' It seemed to Walter polite at least to notice his absence.

'He's busy travelling,' Mrs Smethwick said. 'Did his best, but simply couldn't find the time.'

He heard the struggling adjustment of her accent. Her posh unpractised tones were applied like smudgy make-up. He sensed she would be relieved when the Berrys went home. At the far end of the table, Christina, by some telepathic sympathy, was also expressing her disappointment at Mr Smethwick's absence. The two maiden aunts gave a synchronised giggle. One of Ian's sisters, who had overheard Christina, offered her the same excuse as her mother had offered Walter, though with unpolished accent. Again there came a twin-maidenly giggle. But nothing more was said until the hors d'oeuvre was served. And then, under cover of the cutlery clatter, one of the aunts offered the reason for Mr Smethwick's absence.

'He couldn't find the time because he's doing it,' she whispered.

'Doing what?' Christina asked, whispering too, for she felt part of a conspiracy.

'Time,' the other maiden said.

'D'you mean he's in . . .?'

'That's right,' she said. 'In prison.'

'Whatever for?' Christina was indignant. It went without saying that Amanda's father-in-law had to be innocent.

'GBH,' one of the maidens growled, and Christina didn't know what she was talking about. She must remember to ask Walter. But one of the aunts was going to save her the trouble. She sensed that Mrs Berry did not move in GBH circles.

'That means grievous bodily harm,' she said, salivating a little. 'He beat up our sister something terrible.'

Christina shivered. Now that she knew the reason for Mr Smethwick's absence, she would not mention it to Walter, though she had no doubt that during the course of the lunch, the maidens would make it their business to apprise Walter of the information that his lunching neighbour would die sooner than impart. Christina looked across at Mrs Smethwick. She didn't look as if she'd been beaten up. There was still a possibility that poor Mr Smethwick was the butt of a gross miscarriage of justice. She wondered whether Amanda knew the truth, or whether she too had been fobbed off with the travelling story. She looked at her across the table and her radiance warmed her heart. It seemed that nothing could impede a happy future for both of them. The sight of them gave her courage to turn to the aunts and whisper, 'I don't believe you.' She returned to her plate and took a small slice of salami. She did believe them of course, but what she refused to take on board was the malicious inference that she heard in their words.

Walter concentrated on his food. Occasionally he looked up and smiled at anyone's glance he caught at the table.

'This is a lovely lunch Mrs Smethwick,' he said. 'Don't you think so?'

'I'm enjoying every mouthful,' she said, her mouth full of it and her accent inevitably slipping.

Three more courses to endure, Walter thought. He looked across at Christina. She too was concentrating on her food, and no doubt harbouring thoughts similar to his own. He thought that at the end of the lunch he might make a speech. Someone ought to give a toast to the young pair. Someone ought to endow the ceremony with a little formality. He began to prepare what he would say. He noticed that the wine-waiter, though doing regular rounds, found little cause for refill. The Smethwicks were not wine-drinkers. He whispered to the waiter to bring beer to the table. Its arrival was heralded by an empty beer glass at each setting, and a great sigh of joy and relief gathered around the table, and when the bottles came, there was much hasty pouring and salivation. Mrs Smethwick put her wine glass aside with some relief, together with her imported accent.

'That's better,' she shouted, and downed the beer in a thirsty noisy gulping. Slowly the spirits lifted around the table. Walter noticed that the maiden aunts clung to their wine glasses, sipping occasionally, but with little relish. He made a mental note to order port at the end of the meal.

By the time the dessert course arrived, the merriment looked as if it might get out of hand. Already pellets of crumbs were being flicked across the table and Walter feared that the plates could not be far behind. He decided not to wait with his speech. He rose from his seat and clinked his fork against a glass. All the guests fell suddenly silent.

'I'd like to drink a toast to our newly-weds,' he said.

'Make it short,' Ian's brother shouted.

Walter clenched his fists. A surge of violence overtook him, and he would, along with his toast to Amanda's happiness, have happily cursed the whole rotten Smethwick family. He wanted to take Amanda home, and then, after a while, back to her college and to pretend that the whole Ian episode had been a terrible dream.

'Just a toast,' he shouted and he felt the tears well in his eyes.

'To Ian and Amanda,' he said, his voice breaking. 'And to their happiness.'

The voices were subdued as they echoed his toast. The guests were embarrassed by his emotional display. In their circles, a man was not a man if he betrayed his feelings. There were no more toasts and the meal ended in relative silence. Farewells were taken, grateful on all sides. Walter's last farewell was reserved for Amanda and he decided to fashion it formally. He took both her hands in his.

'You know I wish you the greatest happiness,' he said.

He was lying. He wished her nothing like it. He would allow her a happy honeymoon and then he would watch the rot set in, and he would take her home again and she would call him 'Daddy'. At least, that's what he thought he wanted. But whatever it was, it was something different from what she had chosen. He decided not to kiss her, and suspected that he was using a hard-to-get technique. He was fairly disgusted with himself.

On their way back to London, Christina held her tongue on GBH. But it rattled like a mantra in her head. She recalled the old proverb. 'The apple does not fall far from the tree,' and she feared for her daughter's future. But Ian was the image of Tom. Almost cloned in his likeness. And Tom's gentleness had to be part of that cloning.

'She seems happy enough,' she said.

'You're right, my dear,' Walter said. His hands gripped the steering-wheel. It was precisely that happiness of hers that was breaking his heart.

Chapter 13

While I had been labouring to break up Walter and Christina's marriage, or what was left of it, my mother had been busy repairing her own. She had moved into Mayfair and was slowly coming to terms with Virginia, who presented her with greater problems of accommodation than did my father. It seemed that they were faring well enough. The apartment was large and allowed them their separate privacies. While I had been writing, they had actually taken a second honeymoon in Madeira, and they were still together when they returned. I was satisfied that all would be well with them, and neither of them were on my worry agenda any more. I thought I should try to finish my autobiopsy. But close as I was to the end, I was loathe to finish it. I remember Walter telling me that towards the closing chapters of a novel, he was overcome by feelings of regret and loss, and he would deliberately postpone its end. Perhaps I was assailed by those same feelings. In any case, Amanda was on my mind. I hadn't seen her since Frank Watson's party. I hadn't missed her because she'd been with me on every page every day. She had phoned from time to time and left messages on my ever-running machine. Now having lost her for a while in my fiction, I wanted to see her. I dialled her number which I now knew by heart and arranged to take her to dinner the following evening.

Meanwhile, I had time to kill. I went downstairs to my workshop. I felt the time was approaching when I could donate my present to little Simon expediently. I would finish Pegasus as my first bid for a future with Amanda. There was only the varnishing to be done and I applied it carefully and slowly, prolonging its finish. And when it was done, shortly afterwards, I phoned my childhood home and asked Violet if I could visit. She was overjoyed at the prospect.

'I've been waiting for you to come, Master Martin,' she said.

I would never break her of that habit. For Violet, I would be Master Martin in my dotage.

On my way to the house, I called in on my local estate agent and made arrangements to put my flat on the market. I was fortunate in that I didn't have to wait for a sale. I could move out as soon as I wished. I arranged an appointment with the agent to view the property and I drove to what I still considered my mother's home. I hoped that after a certain 'in-residence', I could learn to call it my own.

Violet was agog with welcome. She had cooked lunch and I insisted on her taking it with me. 'Like we did in the nursery,' I reminded her, seeing her reluctance to join me at table. I needed to talk to her. I needed to confide in her my future plans. I needed to tell her about Amanda. I didn't need her advice. In any case, she would never have offered it. I just needed to share the name with her, and I realised I had done it with no other. I had given no hint to Amanda of my intentions, but that I would remedy the following evening.

Violet should have been every boy's mother. In principle that is. For I suppose, had she been mine, that simple blood tie would altogether have modulated the love that she had shown me as my nanny. But that untempered love she could now give to Simon, and it was the prospect of Simon that excited her most about my proposal. After lunch, she suggested a tour of the house and how I could adapt it to my newly-expected status. We wandered together around the rooms and she was like a child in her reconnaisance. She recalled events in my childhood that I had conveniently forgotten, the traumatic ones in which my father had played a significant role. She reminded me of them gently because she thought I was happy enough now to accommodate the pain they had caused.

'Don't forget Master Martin,' she said. 'Your father had a father too.'

'And a mother,' I said. In family matters the mother might

not have been on the official cast list, but by God, she was pretty busy on the production side.

'I don't know anything about Simon's father,' I told her. 'I met him only once when I attended their wedding. But the marriage didn't last very long. I don't think Simon has any contact with his father.'

'Then you will have to make it up to him,' Violet said.

My mother had left almost all the furniture in the house. I was happy to live with it and all its reminders, painful or otherwise.

'When will you move?' Violet asked me.

'I would think in about a month,' I said, reckoning how long it would take me to finish my autobiopsy. Only then could I envisage marriage, or even living with Amanda. As long as she was my fiction, I could not seriously entertain her in the flesh. Now I had renewed appetite to finish my book, but I feared what I would discover about Amanda in my fiction. I had problems in separating my written word from the reality. I would have to close the book on Walter before I could view him as a fondly remembered friend. And no longer would I mourn him, for my grief would have been translated.

Once home, I went to my workshop and saw that Pegasus had completely dried. I was pleased with the carving. It was possibly the most successful figure I had ever made. I wrapped it in many tissues and then covered it in a gold-leaf wrapping paper that I had bought for the purpose. It had seemed to me right and proper that Pegasus should be clothed in gold.

There were still a few hours to go before I could pick up Amanda and I thought it was now the turn of Scarlatti whom I had neglected for some time. On my way to the piano I passed by the kitchen and I was sorely tempted to go to my freezer. But I resisted. I had a feeling that the next thought I would syphon would surely give me that long-awaited clue as to the nature of Walter's shame, and in no way could I put such a thought aside, even for one moment. I would have to deal with it straight away, for such a thought could not be kept waiting. So I quickened my pace past the kitchen door and I made for my piano. I did not play. I practised. And after an hour or so my fingers grew familiar with the Scarlatti mode, so then I played a whole hour for pure pleasure. There was still enough time left to shower and change my clothes and at eight o'clock precisely, I pressed Amanda's doorbell, Pegasus clutched firmly under my arm. It was a pyjama-clad Simon who opened the door. Amanda was just behind him.

'He was waiting up for you,' she said.

'And just as well.' I ruffled Simon's hair, 'because I've brought you a present.'

I followed them into the living-room. Simon clung to my trouser-leg. 'Let me see. Let me see,' he said.

Suddenly it crossed my mind that Simon might be a little disappointed. Pegasus was not a toy, and could not be played with. He was a myth, a story to be told, one of a winged horse, born of Medusa's blood, and hardly a bed-time story for a seven-year-old.

'It's nothing to play with Simon,' I said forestalling his disappointment. 'It's something to look at. Like a model vintage car. And I want you to have it because I made it myself.'

Sensing its special value, Simon opened the package very carefully, and when the whole of Pegasus was revealed in its winged splendour, he gasped with astonishment and pleasure.

'You *made* it?' he said.

I nodded.

'It's beautiful,' Amanda said.

Simon flung his arms around my neck, and I could not help recalling Amanda's first meeting with Walter in my Camden Town fiction. And it seemed logical to me that sooner or later, Simon would ask his mother if he could call me 'Daddy'. For I had learned that history tends to repeat itself, in fiction as well as in fact. Then I was surprised by Christina's sudden entrance into the room. I was slightly unnerved by her unexpected appearance, and she noticed the hesitation in my greeting.

'I'm on my way,' she said. 'I just gave a lift to the babysitter. And isn't that absolutely beautiful,' she said, catching sight of Pegasus on the table.

'Martin made it himself,' Simon said.

'So many talents,' Christina said, and she reached out her cheek for a greeting.

I had problems in adjusting to her. The last time I had had dealings with Christina, she had her hand on Walter's knee on the drive back from Oxford, and her head was throbbing with GBH. It required something of a physical effort to bring myself back to Amanda's drawing-room.

'You haven't been to see me for a while,' she said.

Then I used my mother for an excuse, as was my wont. But this time I used my father too, and briefly I told her the story of their reunion. Then for some reason, I asked after Frank Watson. It seemed to me a suitable enquiry to follow my parents' story.

Her blushing was answer enough. 'He's well,' she said. 'He's busy with Walter's last novel.'

Then it struck me that all of us were in the business of burying Walter for the last time. My autobiopsy would lay him gently to rest. Frank's completion would turn Walter in his grave. Christina would renounce her double-widowhood once and for all. She wished us both a very happy evening. And so did Simon, and earnestly, as if he himself could profit by it. And I urgently hoped that he would.

I had booked a table at a very exclusive restaurant. It was known to be intimate and quiet, and one used for special occasions. It seemed to me that the site of a marriage proposal was certainly special, and I think I sensed Amanda's antici-pation as we were led to our table. When she saw the oysters on the menu, she whooped with delight. And so did I, for oysters are my favourite too, and it was comfortable to accumulate those things we had in common. I took her hand across the table. She seemed in no way surprised, and she freely responded to my touch.

'I have wanted to do that for a long time,' I said.

She smiled, and then the oysters came and interrupted the first instalment of my proposal. But I was in no hurry. I had much to tell her before I actually posed the burning question. I had to tell her about my move to my old home. I had to describe its rooms to her and relate their associations. Above all, I had to tell her about Violet. I would do it for my own sake, but also perhaps to whet her appetite for my proposal.

Oysters were a good choice. We ate each others'. It was Amanda who initiated the mutual feeding. It was a gesture of extreme intimacy, and in her expertise, I suspected that she might have done it many times before. She could not have been short of suitors, and for the first time since I had entertained the thought of Amanda as Mrs Peabody, I was aware of her possible refusal. I had been arrogant in taking her acceptance for granted. I knew I had to woo her, but my experience in that discipline was strictly limited. Wooing is not required in a one-night stand, which was the tenor of my relationships to date. I did not know where or how to begin. Or perhaps I had already begun my wooing, or at least colluded in it with Amanda's lead. I would be happy to follow her in her strategy, since she clearly knew where to go.

'It was so sweet of you to make Simon that horse. It's beautiful.'

The air cooled between us and I was grateful for the respite.

'Christina's looking well,' I said, wishing to maintain the even temperature.

'She's happy. I think she's in love.'

'With whom?' I suspected it was Frank, but I wanted Amanda to tell me, and I would receive it as a surprise.

'Frank Watson,' she said. 'They're seeing quite a lot of each other.'

'How d'you feel about that?' I asked.

'I'd be overjoyed,' Amanda said. 'She'd have somebody else to concern herself with. She's too dependent on me and Simon.'

Since Walter's death I had noticed that dependency and Amanda's irritation with her mother's clinging nature, but I didn't want to probe further, 'I hope he makes her happy,' I said, because I had to say something.

By that time our oysters were finished, and the wait until the next course was likely to be a long one. It was one of those restaurants. If they didn't exactly cook food freshly on demand, then at least they pretended to. I suspected the latter but I was glad of the interval for it gave me the opportunity to tell Amanda about my mother's house which would shortly be my own. I heard myself talking like an estate agent. I gave her every detail, and would have added room measurements had I known them.

'It takes a lot of courage to resettle in one's childhood home,' Amanda said.

'I'm ready for it,' I said. 'I have forgiven.'

Which led to questions of what I had to forgive, and over our next course, I gave her a run-down on my childhood.

'Tell me about yours,' I said when the dessert arrived. Then I regretted having asked her. I knew all that. It's true I had invented it, but I wanted my story neither confirmed nor denied. I would be happy to live with my own brand of truth. I knew about her adoption. Walter had told me himself. And I knew about her failed marriage. That I had witnessed. I had also witnessed her drop-out from Oxford. The rest I had fashioned according to my own truth, which may or may not have been fiction.

'There's nothing much to tell,' she said. 'You saw most of it.'

I did not press her further. 'I remember that you were beautiful as a child,' I said, 'and have grown in beauty ever since.'

I heard what I had said, without rehearsal, and I knew that my style might have been labelled as 'wooing'. I took her hand across the table. 'Amanda,' I said, 'I want to ask you some-thing. It's a request. I don't want you to answer straight away,' I said. I could not have stomached an immediate rejection. 'I want you to think about it, and to take as long as you wish.'

'What is it?' she said.

I noticed that her hand trembled beneath mine. 'We have known each other for a long time,' I said. 'In many ways, I know you better than most. And in others, I know you not at all.'

I could have sworn she blushed at that, and such a response gave me courage to continue. But alas, just at that moment, our coffee landed on the table and in one move, broke the tension that I had been at such pains to build. Amanda laughed aloud and I joined her. It was the only way to deal with our mutual embarrassment. At last the waiter removed himself from our table, and to give me confidence, Amanda stretched out her hand for mine.

'The request,' she whispered.

Now I was obliged to come straight to the point. Any preamble would have looked like postponement and would betray a lack of assurance on my part.

'Amanda,' I said, tightening my grip on her hand, 'I'm asking you to marry me.'

Then immediately I feared rejection and I regretted my lack of preamble. I suspected that if a rejection was a possibility, then a prolonged proposal might have delayed that refusal, and during that delay, I could nourish a little hope. But now it was too late. The question was out. Straight, direct, and deserved no more than an unequivocal 'yes' or 'no' answer.

But Amanda parried. 'My life is so complicated, Martin,' she said. 'You don't know me at all. And if you did, I doubt that you would want to marry me.'

'Then why don't you tell me about it?' I pleaded. 'Whatever it is, I doubt whether it would cause me to withdraw my proposal.'

'Can I think about it?' she said. 'About telling you, I mean. If it were just about me, I would trust you enough to tell you. But other people are involved, and I don't know whether I have the right to share them with you. But Martin dear,' she added, 'you have made me very happy.'

'You will think about it though, won't you? D'you promise me?'

'Of course,' she said. 'But give me time. I can't say how long. My decision depends on factors that cannot be timed. Courage and loyalty mainly. It could be tomorrow or next year. Or never perhaps,' she added.

I considered it the most gentle refusal she could have offered, and the disappointment must have shown on my face.

'Be patient with me,' she said. 'We may yet make a life together, you and I.'

I wondered about my next move. Patience had never been one of my virtues, and I wondered whether an outright rejection would have been fairer. Then I could get on with my life, whatever that meant. But I had planned my future in such meticulous detail. It would not be easy to find a substitute for Amanda at my mother's dining-table, or a pupil for Violet under the mulberry tree. My mother's home held out less appeal without Amanda and Simon, but I would not waver in my decision to move, for that decision had less to do with Amanda than with my own growth and capacity at last to forgive. No. I would move. And quickly. It would give me things to do.

'But we can still meet,' I said to her.

'Of course. Whenever you like. I'd want that.'

Then I made a bold suggestion. 'Perhaps you'd like to go away for a weekend. Somewhere quiet. Both of us. Getting away from the site of one's dilemma, can be helpful,' I added lamely.

'There is no specific site,' Amanda said. 'The dilemma is inside me. I carry it wherever I go.'

'Does it sadden you?' I asked.

'No,' she said. 'I've learned to live with it. But just occasionally, like now, when opportunities arise, then it becomes something of a stumbling-block.'

I was very confused. I had no idea what she was talking about. But for some reason, I felt it all had something to do with Christina. I decided to let the matter lie. I had looked forward to ordering vintage champagne to round off our meal, but I only had hope to celebrate and hope calls for a numbing agent rather than one for jubilation. So I ordered brandy for us both, and I trusted that Amanda nourished hope as well as I. It was she who proposed the toast. Raising her glass, and clinking it with mine, she said, 'To us. And to our future.'

It was a toast vague enough to embrace both acceptance and rejection. I had to be satisfied.

I took Amanda home, but refused her offer of a nightcap. I was not too keen on running into Christina, who might have returned to run the babysitter home. In fact, the whole Berry family was becoming too much for me to handle. At least in flesh. And I had to get back to the fiction of them to regain my equilibrium.

Amanda promised to phone me. 'We must see each other soon,' she said. She turned to face me squarely and cupped my face in her hands. Then she kissed me. It was totally unexpected. Amanda was not a tease, and that kiss fed my hopes once more.

But I made no move to prolong the encounter. I felt that its development, however it turned out to be, would be ill-timed. I sent my regards to Christina. 'I'll wait to hear from you,' I said.

As I drove home, I realised that I had to busy myself during the waiting time, however long that time turned out to be. The move to my mother's house would certainly disturb me, and leave me little time to dwell on whom I would share it with. Then there was my autobiopsy. I knew I was close to its end. Though it had retained its perfect symmetry, the brain in my freezer was considerably depleted. And knowing I was so close to exhausting its wonders, the thought depressed me. Like Walter, I was loathe to come to the end of the book. I wanted to prolong its completion because I didn't know what subject I could tackle next. Or whether the old writer's block would once more assert itself. I worried too about how my autobiopsy would be received; and thoughts of such nature are fatal to any writer. I knew I had to dismiss these thoughts for they were not reason enough to delay the book's completion. I was tired too. Tired of my own expectations. Of my own dreams. I would go straight to bed, I decided, and wake up refreshed to my freezer.

But in the morning, refreshed as I was, I delayed that journey. I felt it would be my last. So I lingered over breakfast. There was no Pegasus to complete and I didn't have the appetite to start on a new carving. So it was Scarlatti. I did not practise. I felt I had to conserve that species of energy. I played. I played those sonatas in which I was fluent. I played for my comfort and my pleasure. And self-indulgent as I am, two Scarlatti hours passed and entirely cleared my mind of all Walter thoughts. And then the phone rang and broke the mood entirely. It was my mother.

'I'm just ringing to say hullo,' she said.

I listened to the cheer in her voice and each and every

syllable she had spoken was unladen. They meant exactly what they said. No overtone, no sub-text. Had I, in my growth, adjusted my hearing, so that it was deaf to any innuendo, or had she changed so radically that it simply wasn't there? Either way, I was content.

'I'm well thank you. How's Dad?' The label surprised me. It had slipped out of my mouth quite naturally. The 'Daddy', the 'Father' days were over.

'He's well. We're both fine. Come and see us when you've time,' she said. 'Just give us a ring beforehand. I've turned Virginia onto Indian cuisine,' she laughed.

'I'll come for that,' I said. 'Next week. I'll phone you.'

It was a miracle, I thought, as I put the phone down, and I hoped that some of my parents' luck would rub off on me. I went straight to my kitchen. But not yet to my freezer. First I would make myself some coffee. Not the instant kind. A proper filter, that takes a little longer. And a little longer to relish. Which I did. I drank all that I had made. Two and a half cups in all. Then I washed up the utensils I had used. I emptied the trash-can. I wiped down all the kitchen surfaces. I procrastinated as long as I could, as long as there was the slightest and most menial task to fulfil. Then 'Bugger it,' I said, and went to my freezer.

I was aware that it might be my last journey to that wondrous zone. I would do my best, if it were possible, to leave just one thought behind to give me reason to make that journey once more and to prepare myself for a sad farewell, before I buried Walter once and for all. My thumb would be very gentle, as gentle as the breeze of the approaching Angel of Death. I took Walter carefully out of the freezer and laid him on my kitchen table. And for a while, I looked at him. It seemed that the orb assumed eyes, a nose and a mouth. The ears were encased in the globe so that the perfect circle lay undisturbed. Did I see a smile linger on the lips? A light of admiration in the eye? And did they then close in a gesture of farewell? I caressed him then with a love that I knew I would never feel for anyone else in my life again. I suppose I was saying farewell, just in case my thumb overstepped its present purpose and I kissed him where I thought his brain's lips might have been, and I picked up my syphon in a feverish hand.

Again there was no waffle and a thought emerged immediately. My thumb quivered with love as the idea unfolded.

> *I can't write about it now. It's too soon. To*
> *write about it now would be mere therapy,*
> *and therapy makes for poor fiction. A*
> *writer must write in last year's blood,*
> *when that blood has cooled and allows for*
> *perspective. But in this respect, even when*
> *the blood is cold as ice, the words will burn*
> *the page with their infamy. God help me.*

Quickly I removed my thumb. I felt sure there was at least another thought to come. I would save it for another journey. Besides, I had signposts a-plenty. I caressed Walter with infinite gratitude and returned him to the freezer. Then I settled down to the closing stages of my autobiopsy.

... it was precisely that happiness of hers that was breaking his heart.

On their drive home to London, they were silent for the most part. Then Christina spoke.

'Well, they seem happy enough.' But in the silence that preceded this opinion, she had considered all the reasons why her daughter had perhaps made a mistake and the GBH syndrome was at least part of it.

'In spite of everything,' Walter said.

'What d'you mean?'

'Well, they're a pretty ghastly family aren't they? Beer-swilling louts, the lot of them.'

'I think Ian's different,' Christina said.

'Well let's hope to God you're right.' Walter was glad he was in the middle of a novel. He would throw himself into his work and concern himself with something other than Amanda's future. But he found it difficult to concentrate.

One morning they received a card from the honey-mooning couple. Both wrote that they'd never thought such happiness possible. A week later Amanda phoned. They were back in Oxford and settling into their new home. Ian was building bookshelves and she was making curtains. And what would they do, Walter wondered, when the shelves were done and the curtains made? He looked forward to the time when nothing more could be done to their little house, when the testing time would begin. Then he would stand on the sidelines and watch the boredom and the rot set in. He hated himself for such thoughts. He knew that his only solution lay in work and he returned to it, locking himself in his study, forcing every dry syllable from his reluctant pen. And slowly he became involved, and no Amanda thought disturbed him.

When she phoned and invited them both to Oxford for a house-warming, he declined. 'I know you'll understand, Amanda,' he said, 'but I'm close to the end of my novel. I daren't leave it at this stage. But Christina will go down. And she'll bring back all the news. You sound wonder-ful,' he said.

'I'm happy Walter. I've never been happier.'

'Then that makes me happy too,' Walter said. At the time he knew that he meant it. At bottom, all he wanted was her happiness. He simply didn't trust anyone else but himself to give it to her. But he looked forward to Christina's report.

A week later he was working in his study and awaiting her return. His book was going well. Its end was in sight, and he decided that as soon as it was finished, he would go alone to Oxford and take Amanda to lunch. Ian too, if she insisted, and he would try to persuade her to return to her studies. He was on the last sentence of his penul-timate chapter when he heard Christina's key in the front door. Excited as he was, he forced himself to finish the sentence and then he answered her call.

'How was it?' he shouted, coming out of his study.

'They missed you,' Christina said, 'and it was wonderful.'

They met in the drawing-room. Walter poured a drink for both of them. 'Now tell me all about it,' he said.

'Well, the house is beautiful,' Christina began, 'and they've made it all themselves.'

'With a little help from us,' Walter could not help adding.

Christina chose to ignore his remark and continued. 'It seems that Ian's a pretty good cook. He made a very good lunch.'

'And what did they drink?' Walter asked. 'Don't tell me. Beer.'

'Oh Walter, do stop it,' Christina said. 'Yes, they drank beer. They're different.'

'Who was there?' Walter asked. 'Any of Amanda's college friends?'

'I didn't meet any. They all seemed to be Ian's. Old friends but now of course, Amanda's friends too. And thank god,' she added, 'no-one was there from his family.'

They laughed together at that, and then, after a while, 'Is she happy?' Walter asked.

'She looks radiant. And I must say, I'm getting to like Ian more and more.'

As a Tom-clone, Walter thought, Ian had a good start. 'Did they say anything about coming to London?' he asked.

'I asked them, but Ian has little time off, and I think Amanda's looking for a job.'

'D'you think she'll ever go back to her studies?' he asked sadly.

'That's not Ian's world,' Christina said, 'and I think Amanda knows it.'

'Well I hope she knows what she's doing.'

The news depressed him. He poured himself another drink.

'They want to see you,' Christina said, 'They were sorry you couldn't come. But Amanda understood. She told

Ian she knew your pattern. She'd lived with it long enough.'

'I'll go down when I've finished the novel,' Walter said.

'Are you close?'

'Another week or so.'

But it was to take much longer. What Walter called the 'last chapter paralysis', came upon him shortly after Amanda's house-warming, and though he sat at his desk every day, the page in front of him remained blank. He was not worried. With the last chapter of almost every novel he had confronted that same numbing hurdle. He knew he could overcome, this time as all other times. He regretted his visit to Oxford would be delayed, but whenever Amanda phoned, he spoke to her warmly. And even to Ian if he was at home. Then one morning, while he was staring at his now familiar blank page, marked only with his daily desperate thumb-prints, he received a letter from an Oxford university debating society inviting him to be guest speaker at the end of term lecture. They left the subject to his own choice. The date was in a month's time. He was certain he could finish his novel by then and he wrote and accepted the invitation. When Amanda next phoned, he told her the date and the time and he hoped he would see them both at the meeting. 'Then the three of us can go out for a slap-up meal,' he said.

'I don't know about Ian,' Amanda said, and Walter thought he missed the cheer in her voice. 'He works late most nights.'

'Then it'll just have to be you and me,' Walter said. 'Like old times. Don't forget. Put it down in your diary.'

'I'm not likely to forget,' she said. Then she paused. 'Walter, it's so long since I've seen you.'

'Are you alright Amanda?' he whispered.

'Yes,' she said quickly. 'I'm fine. Why shouldn't I be? I'm very happy. Everything's working out well.'

It was as if she was reading from a piece of paper in front of her. 'I'll see you soon then,' Walter said. When he put the phone down, he still heard the echo of her parroting voice in his ear. He knew that things were souring for Amanda. Yet he took no pleasure in it. He simply felt an outrageous anger towards Ian, that Tom-clone, who had seduced not only Amanda but her mother too. But perhaps it was merely a passing phase. Perhaps it was just a bad day. God knows he had enough of them with Christina. Thus he tried to comfort himself, though he could not rinse her plaintive voice out of his ear, and he went back to his empty page now with an extra incentive to finish his work.

The break-through came a week later, and thereafter he finished the novel with ease. He passed it to Christina for her typing and as she was doing so, he prepared his Oxford lecture.

Lately Amanda's calls had become less frequent. Christina didn't comment on it. Perhaps she didn't even notice and Walter did not want to bring it to her attention. A few days before he was due to go to Oxford, he rang her himself. She sounded cheerful enough and said that she was looking forward to seeing him. She added hastily that Ian would be working and that there would just be the two of them. He asked her to book a table at a good restaurant and he asked her, too, to come early to the lecture so that they might have a little time together beforehand.

Walter was satisfied. Amanda had sounded well enough and he was glad that Ian was working overtime. He decided to go to Oxford by train. He needed the time to look over his notes. He had chosen to lecture on the decay of language in the modern English novel. It was a subject he felt very strongly about. The neglect of cadence and rhythm in novel language and even syntax and basic grammar, offended him. But what offended him most was that writers got away with such neglect, and were even praised for it, so that a new standard of mediocrity threatened to hold sway for future generations. In the train, he studied the examples he had chosen: they appalled him, and he alighted at Oxford station imbued with an evangelical passion to return to a linguistic reverence. Even thoughts of Amanda did not cross his mind, and it was only when he arrived at the hall, a good half-hour before the lecture was due to begin, that he remembered their appointment. He looked around the faces of those who had already gathered, but he could not see her. No-one in authority seemed to be there to greet him, so he took an inconspicuous seat at the side of the hall and waited for Amanda to arrive.

The hall began to fill. Walter looked at his watch. It was already ten minutes to eight. At that moment he was approached by the Dean of the college. He was profuse in his apologies for not being there earlier to greet him and quickly he ushered him into a private room at the back of the stage. Walter took a last look around the hall, but there was still no sign of Amanda. He was disappointed but he was sure that she would turn up for the lecture. In the private room, he was greeted warmly and was introduced to other academics who declared themselves honoured by his presence. Sherry was taken and as the bell rang for eight o'clock, they all rose in unison and accompanied Walter into the hall. Only the Dean ascended the platform with Walter. His colleagues settled themselves in the front row where seats were reserved for them. There was a great welcome of applause, and when it faded, the Dean rose to introduce the guest. While he was speaking Walter took the opportunity to look around the hall in the hope that he could spot Amanda among the audience. But the hall was crowded. People were even standing at the back, and in such a mass, that all faces looked the same. And he couldn't see her. He was sorely disappointed, but he was still hopeful that during the course of his speech, she would make a tardy appearance.

He heard the Dean speaking but he did not listen to his words and he knew it was over only because he heard the clapping. Then he rose, and he began to speak, and he heard his dead words and he wondered where they came from and who was responsible for their delivery. For all the passion that he had felt in their preparation, all his rage against the misuse of language, had evaporated, and in their place simmered a wretched anxiety as to Amanda's whereabouts. He did not take his eyes off the door at the back of the hall. If she came, he would perhaps begin to relate to what he was saying, to *feel* the anger and offence of his words which were now falling from his lips like a tired and much worn recital. For a moment he took his eyes off the door, and looked at his audience and he was appalled at the almost unanimous look of boredom on their faces. Usually when he lectured, he was happy to respond to his audience's animation, and now he felt ashamed. He would not look at the door again. He wished he could start at the beginning. But he would make it up to them. He decided to dispense with his notes. He would talk to his audience as if they were a gathering in his own drawing-room. And immediately his tone became familiar, and he felt how his audience began to respond, leaning forward in their seats, laughing with him occasionally, and sharing his disgust with their sighs. Towards the end of his speech, they were cheering his every sentence and when he sat down, they begged for more. Once again he looked at the door at the back of the hall. She might well have entered when he wasn't looking. But it was as he had left it at his last gaze. He looked back at his audience and their expectant faces and he asked if any of them had any questions. A multitude of hands shot in the air and the Dean had to organise the order of questioning. Walter satisfied as many questions as the time allowed and he was grateful to the Dean when he offered an effusive vote of thanks and closed the meeting. Walter hung around on the platform for a while. Perhaps he had missed her in the audience and she would join the autograph-hunters who were milling the stage. They formed an orderly line at the table and Walter looked into each face before signing his name. But there was no sign of Amanda. Now anxiety beset him once more and he was in haste to get away. In time the last of the autograph-hunters left satisfied and the Dean led him away.

'You must take a little supper with us,' he said.

It would have been impolite to refuse but he needed

desperately to contact Amanda. 'Do you have a telephone?' he asked.

'In my study,' the Dean said, and he led him to his office at the back of the hall. Before leaving him he told him the way to the supper-room. 'We'll see you shortly,' he said.

Walter dialled the number in a frenzy. It gave the engaged signal. Well at least she was at home, Walter thought. There must have been some very good reason why she hadn't kept their appointment. He waited a while, then dialled again. Again the tone gave engaged. He was wary of keeping his hosts waiting and he began to curse them for their oh-so-decent hospitality. And he was irritated by Amanda's loquaciousness. He tried once more, with the same engaged response, and then the Dean knocked on the open door. Walter apologised and left with him for supper. He managed courtesy and responsiveness during the meal, but he was impatient to return to the phone. He looked at his watch. It was a good half-hour since he had first dialled. She surely must have said all she had to say by now. He excused himself once more and made for the Dean's office. And dialled with fury. And his step-daughter was still talking. He decided to try the operator. Perhaps there was something amiss with the Dean's phone. He was relieved that the operator, at least, was not engaged but he, or perhaps she, was taking an inordinate time to answer his call. He hung on for what seemed an eternity and then, his anxiety mounting, he shouted, 'Hullo' into the mouthpiece. But his word was a mere lyric to the burring accompaniment. At last a woman announced herself.

'You take your time,' Walter said.

'And you your turn,' the woman answered, a phrase she had no doubt intoned the whole evening. 'We're very busy.'

Walter gave her Amanda's number. 'I've been trying all evening,' he said plaintively, 'and it's engaged. Could you test for talking?' he asked.

She didn't reply, but shortly he heard the engaged signal which was no news to him.

'Hold the line,' the woman's voice instructed.

Again he hung on, panting for her verdict, and it took some time to come.

'The receiver has been left off,' the woman said at last. 'I'll put a blower on it.'

Walter quickly put the phone down. Now it seemed his anxiety had cause. He hurried back to the supper-room and gave his excuses.

'I'm spending the night in Oxford and my host is expecting me,' he said. 'I don't want to keep him up.' He was careful with the pronoun. He didn't want to ignite any gossip.

They thanked him again. Profusely. One of them offered him a lift. 'It's not far,' Walter said quickly, 'and I could do with a walk.' Once outside the college, he looked around for a taxi, and out of the blue one came, as if heaven sent. He gave the cabbie Amanda's address and sat forward in his seat, loathe to relax. He didn't know why, but he had fearful feelings about what he would find. Her failure to meet him could somehow or other be explained, but that, coupled with her unhooked telephone, were facts full of foreboding. He felt in his pocket for change. He wanted to lose no time before he rang her bell. When the cab stopped at her door, he rushed out and handed the cabbie far more than the fare was worth, and he rushed to the door. And there he lost his nerve. For all the lights were on in the house, but somehow they spelt an emptiness. Timidly, he pressed the bell and held his finger there as he listened to its echo bouncing round the house. Occasionally he took his finger away simply for the relief of the silence. He thought he heard a noise inside and he quickly lifted the flap of the letter-box. Through the hall, the living-room door was open, and through it he saw the beginnings of a sofa and a head lying on its upright. Around the head an arm was draped, and around its wrist, a gold bangle full of gold and silver charms, charms that he had given Amanda on each of her birthdays. He yelled her name through the box. The hand moved and the charms tingled into life, 'Amanda,' he screamed again. 'Open the door. It's Walter.' He banged on the woodwork.

'No,' he heard suddenly. 'You can't come in.'

He waited. Then he said in a voice that was painfully controlled, 'Amanda, if you don't open the door, I shall call the police.' He saw her feet touch the floor. He straightened himself and waited. The door opened very slowly, and only to a narrow crack. He saw half her face and that was partially covered with her hand. Then he himself gently pushed the door open. She turned her back on him quickly, as if she did not want to be seen and he followed her into the living-room. There, he held her tenderly from behind and slowly, fighting her resistance, he turned her to face him. He had to take stern control of himself, for what he saw horrified him. One eye was entirely closed, and bulged blue. The other had taken the burden of all her tears and was swollen with sorrow. On one cheek lay a dried crust of blood.

'Who has done this thing to you?' he whispered. 'And where is he now?' He would find Ian and kill him without scruple.

'He's gone,' she said. She put her arms around his neck and wept like a child. As she did so, her loose sleeve slipped from her shoulder and on her flesh he saw a stuttering line of bruises. So symmetrical were they, that it seemed they had been inflicted with infinite care and with an artist's precision. He held her close and said, 'I'm taking you back to London. You have no reason to stay here. We'll buy you a flat and you'll make a new life for yourself.' He let her cry for a while, holding her all the time. Then he asked her where her cases were.

'In the bedroom,' she said.

'Come,' he held her apart. 'Let's pack. I'll help you.'

He followed her up the narrow stairway. In her bedroom he helped her take her cases from the top of the wardrobe. He put them on the bed and watched her as she collected her clothes.

'When did all this start?' he dared to ask after a while.

'On the honeymoon,' she said. 'I thought it was a game. That's what he said it was. After a while, he didn't even bother to call it a game.'

She bent down to pick up her shoes, and in doing so, she bared one leg. At first Walter thought he imagined it, that imprint of an angry purple brand on her calf, the seared weals on the flesh, the clear footprint of an iron. He stared at it, swallowing his bile. No imaginings. It was there. Undeniably there. Rooted in his retina. And it broke him.

As I wrote about those injuries, I was infected with Walter's outrage. I viewed them with his horror, and I shivered as he must have done. I shivered as much with loathing as with discovery. For I suddenly knew, and with absolute certainty, what shame had quivered on my mentor's dying lips. I knew what Walter was going to do, and had I been in his position, I should have done exactly the same. But certain as I was, I rushed to my freezer for confirmation. And there it obliged. The first clear syphoned thought.

    I'll kill him.

I patted Walter's shrinking skull and re-nested him. I would write about the murder of Ian, and I relished it. I would have Walter return to Oxford after settling Amanda in London. He would lurk outside the cottage, Amanda's keys in his hand. He would ascertain that Ian was at home. Preferably with the television blaring. Ian would be scoffing a take-away and his back would be to the door. Then Walter would let himself into the cottage, gun in hand. I'd have to cook up some story as to how he came by such a weapon. Perhaps it could be a left-over from his soldiering days. Walter would open the door of the sitting-room. Unseen and unheard. I'd fix it for the television show to be a western with endless gunfire, so that even Walter's shot would not be heard. But felt it would be, certainly, as it travelled through Ian's rib-cage direct to his heart. Yes. That's what I would do.

I thought I would make myself some coffee before committing my story to paper and revealing, once and for all, the cause of my mentor's shame. But as I waited for the kettle to boil, it struck me that my fabrication was not such a good idea after all. Somehow it didn't fit. It wasn't right. In my wildest dreams I could not imagine Walter as a killer. The image of him holding a gun, leave alone pulling the trigger, was utterly ridiculous. Yet the last thought that I'd syphoned clearly indicated a murderous intent. But I recalled how often in the past, especially in my childhood, I had thought exactly the same towards my father. And not only thought it, but said it aloud to myself. Each buckle greeting was met with that whispering cry, 'I'll kill you'. And no doubt Walter had felt the same. But there are a million miles between the whisper and the fire. No. It would not do at all. I skipped the coffee and went straight back to my desk. I had left Amanda half way through her packing. I had to complete that episode before I could explore further.

... Undeniably there. Rooted in his retina. And it broke him. Then she started to cry again. Once more he held her, soothing her with whispers he would have used to a child. And then, in the silence of the room, and the throbbing of her hurt, she said, 'It was only because I knew I couldn't marry you.'

He let the words rest on the silence for a while. He was trembling. He didn't know what to say. He should have laughed it off, and teased her gently. That would have been the decent and moral response. But he was too thrilled with her declaration and in no way did he wish it muted. She must have taken his silence as encouragement for he felt her hand on his chest and the throb of a shirt-button as she peeled it from its moorings. And then a second button. And still he did not move or utter a word. Later, when he thought about it, and he thought of little else, he told himself that it was she who had initiated all that was to happen to them, and that without her move, he would have held his passionate tongue. For ever, perhaps. But at the same time, he had to admit to himself that he had *allowed* the buttons their freedom and perhaps, with his ardent breathing, he had facilitated their release. Even when she brought his hand to her naked breast, he rested it there and offered no resistance. His silence and passivity had been collusion. Thus he let her lead him to the bed, to lay him down, and slowly and gently to lay him bare. And she did not turn away as she slipped her clothes to the floor, and let him view her bruised and assaulted body in its entire.

And it was then that Walter made his first self-motivated gesture. He took her in his arms and laid her beside him, her tears mingling now with his own. And he held her for a long time.

'I have made love to you so often,' she told him.

'And I to you,' he said.

Then he took her, with all the love that Miss Freeman had nourished in him, with all that ardent instruction that had lain so long unused, so long unpractised. Then they slept, and in the morning, they underwrote their love once more.

'For ever?' she whispered.

'How could it be otherwise?' he said.

In silence they dressed. She completed her packing and she left the house with not one look behind. She knew she needed no reminder of her marriage home, neither as a torture-chamber, nor the site of a blissful release.

On the train back to London, he held her close. He didn't mind what onlookers thought. For some reason he felt strangely innocent. He wondered whether he would be able to forsake his writing now that the glorious prospect of living had been offered him. He was determined to give it a try. He was glad that he had finished his novel. He would be happy for it to be his last. He took her once again in his arms. Then, because he couldn't help himself, he thought of Tom. And for the first time in many years. And it surprised him for he thought Tom had almost been forgotten. It was not that he had called his name to mind. Rather, it seemed that Tom, in a certain violent intrusion, had claimed a reminder, and his name, with its single accusing syllable, broke into that closed door of Walter's memory and drenched him in a pall of shame. And with that uninvited thought, all Walter's sense of innocence faded. And for ever.

He loosened his hold on Amanda. He dared not look at her, else he see a glint of Tom in her eye. He knew he could not touch her again. Ever. After what had happened between them, even a smile would compound his shame.

'God help me,' he cried to his raging heart.

Chapter 14

I put down my pen and smiled. Once again I blessed that magic of fiction, that oh-so-rare miracle, when the words fall spellbound onto the page and explain everything. Walter's rude confession from his dying lips was the sin of shame. The terrible shame of betrayal. Not so much of Christina who had already, in her own way, rejected him. But of Tom, the closest friend he had ever known, whose goods he had inherited and now abused.

I knew I was close to the end of my book, or maybe, like Walter's it would be left unfinished. I came out of my fiction and faced the reality, and as always, I was deeply confused. I thought I might go away for a while to escape from both. But I had much to do. The estate agent had received a very good offer on my flat. I had accepted, and within a month I was bound to move. I had to organise my packing, and I decided to make a start on my books. The phone rang on my way to my study. It was Amanda. Her voice threw me a little and I was on the point of asking her whether she was back from Oxford for good. I was still floundering around in my fiction. Then I realised that it was a long time since I'd heard from her. A whole month in fact, while I was writing that last chapter. Now, suddenly I recalled everything. Our dinner together and my proposal which still hung in the air.

'Can I see you?' she asked.

'Of course. When?'

'Soon, if you can.'

'Tomorrow?' I said. I needed a little while to rinse the young and bruised and ecstatic Amanda from my sights, to unravel her from my fiction, and to accept the grown and beautiful woman whom I had asked to share my life. I invited her to supper. 'I'll cook for you myself,' I said.

When my mother phoned a little later, I had no problems of readjustment. She had never figured in my fiction. They were giving a flat-warming, she told me. A week hence. 'You must come Martin,' she said. 'And bring a friend if you like. It's so long since we've seen you.'

I was happy to accept. I told her about the move and the selling of my flat. And my visit to Violet.

'I know all about that,' she said. 'Violet told me. She's so excited.'

'How's Virginia?' I asked.

'He's like the dish-washer that Violet refused to let me buy. I don't know how I lived without him.'

I laughed with her. 'How's Dad?' I said.

'He's well. He sends his love.'

When I put the phone down, I could not help but feel a little envious. The thought of moving into that large house alone saddened me. I wondered what decision Amanda had reached. She'd had a whole month to consider my proposal and I had no doubt that, one way or another, she had made up her mind. That was why she had asked to see me. In a way, I wished she had taken longer. Her delay would have given an extended life to my hopes. But tomorrow, they might well be shattered. I was now in great danger of indulging in a bout of self-pity and to offset it, I busied myself with sorting and dusting my books. Almost the whole day passed in this activity. I had catalogued and cleaned about half of my collection. It had been a pleasant task, discovering those books I'd thought I'd lost and recalling the stories of some I had read many years ago. I would ration myself with such a pleasure, I decided. I would do a little each day, eking it out, until I moved.

I made an early night. I knew that the following day was a critical one, and I intended to spend it doing very normal things. In the morning I would go for a walk, then I would shop a little and come home to cook. A very simple meal, I thought. I did not want to make a production of what in any case could well prove to be a drama in its own right.

I woke up refreshed, and followed out every item of my plan. It was a lovely day and it cheered my spirits. I found myself counting my blessings, but I was well aware that I was gearing myself for disappointment. While I cooked, I cheered a little more. My mood oscillated between despair and hope all through the day. When she arrived, it was hope that held sway.

I was delighted to see her, and relieved too that there was no longer any trace of the bruised girl I had left on the train to London. She seemed very much at her ease. I was careful to avoid any reference to the unfinished business of our dinner together a month ago. We talked of Simon, and Christina. And I dared ask after Frank.

'Wedding bells, I think,' she said.

'How d'you feel about that?'

'A little jealous,' she laughed.

So I shared with her those feelings I had towards my own parents, but now we were getting dangerously close to that topic that both of us were at pains to avoid. I told her that supper was ready, and we went into the dining-room. Over the meal, our talk was of trivia, and it was not until the dessert that a silence fell and I knew it as a prelude to the introduction of that theme that I had both dreaded and hoped for.

'Martin,' she said.

Then I knew for sure that she had come to a decision. I noticed that she kept her hands on her lap, a gesture that did not bode well.

'You haven't forgotten our dinner a month ago,' she said.

'Of course not. I've been trying not to think about it. About all the words left unsaid.'

'I've thought about it,' she said and she laid her hands on the table. I was tempted to take one of them but I didn't want to push my luck.

'You asked me a question,' she said.

'Yes,' I mumbled.

'I . . . I want you to ask it again.'

229

This time I took her hand. 'Will you marry me Amanda?' I said.

She nodded. I could hardly believe it. 'Say yes,' I said.

She nodded again. 'Yes. But . . . there are lots of things that I must tell you. But one thing you must know now.'

'I'm listening,' I said.

'It's about Simon. It will come as a shock, I'm afraid.'

I was anxious. Perhaps Simon was ill. Perhaps he did not have long to live. I steeled myself.

'It's about Simon's father,' she said.

She paused before telling me. 'It's a secret and must remain so between us. Even Simon doesn't know.'

'What is it?' I asked.

Again a silence. And then she said, 'His father was Walter.'

I felt a giggle well inside me but I stifled it. 'I know,' I said.

She was astonished. 'How?' she almost shouted.

'Magic,' I said. It was that fabulous magic of fiction.

'But how?' she insisted. 'Nobody knows.'

How could I explain that magic? How could I tell her about the book that I had purloined? How could I tell her about my writer's block that Walter's death had broken? So I brought the simple power of instinct to my aid. 'I just had a hunch,' I said. 'I often thought that Simon looked like Walter. I just guessed it.'

'Please,' she said. 'It's just between us. Christina must never know.'

I said nothing. It seemed to me that Christina must have known all along. She could not have been blind to Simon's likeness to Walter. Perhaps it might even have pleased her. Amanda had given Walter what she had been unwilling to give, and in her twisted way, she might have thanked Walter for making Tom a grandfather.

'I promise I won't say a word,' I said. Then I took her in my arms.

'Tomorrow I'll take you to the house,' I said. 'Our house. Simon's too.'

When she had gone, I sat and gathered the silence around myself, and let my happiness overwhelm me. A new life was

230

beginning, but a sense of unfinished business nagged at me. I knew its nature well, and I went willingly to my freezer.

I had to make sure that I had exhausted my mentor entire. That that rich vein had been fully mined. Then I could truly pronounce him brain dead, and give him my own loving and private burial. I laid an embroidered cloth on my kitchen-table. A prepared shroud. I had it in mind to take him to my mother's house and bury him under the mulberry tree, so that he could watch and hear his son at play. Then I took him gently from my freezer for the last time.

I laid him on the cloth, and caressed him, as was my wont. Again I thought the orb assumed each facial feature, and its symmetry, though shrunken, was astonishing. In all my probings, Walter had remained steadfastly as round and as solid as the earth. I kissed him, then took up my syphon. As I pressed my thumb, I listened to the silence within. Even at this stage, after all my plundering, I was still loathe to let Walter go. Then a sound came, a breathing, a beginning of a thought.

> *Forgive me Amanda. Be certain that I*
> *cannot forgive myself. Oh Tom. Dear Tom.*

And that last cry for Tom blended into a hissing sound, like a straw that sucks the last of a liquid from a glass.

And afterwards, a silence.

THE ELECTED MEMBER

Bernice Rubens

Norman is the clever one of a close-knit Jewish family in the East End of London. Infant prodigy; brilliant barrister; the apple of his parents' eyes . . . until at forty-one he becomes a drug addict, confined to his bedroom, at the mercy of his hallucinations and paranoia.

For Norman, his committal to a mental hospital represents the ultimate act of betrayal. For Rabbi Zweck, Norman's father, his son's deterioration is a bitter reminder of his own guilt and failure. Only Bella, the unmarried sister, still in her childhood white ankle socks, can reach across the abyss of pain to bring father and son the elusive peace which they both desperately crave.

'She has a large compassion, and an intelligence which makes her compulsively readable'
New Statesman

'Splendidly sane, compassionate and often grotesquely funny'
Daily Telegraph

'The writing sparkles and flickers and blazes'
Jewish Chronicle

Winner of the 1970 Booker prize

MR WAKEFIELD'S CRUSADE

Bernice Rubens

'My name is Luke Wakefield and I am a failure ... My ability to miss out, to fall short, to come to grief, amounts almost to a talent ... Even my failure is a failure. My life has lurched from one catastrophe to another ...'

Until one day a different kind of catastrophe occurs: the man in front of him in the post office queue suddenly drops down dead. Instinctively, Mr Wakefield's hand snakes out and slips the corpse's unposted letter into his pocket. With one impulsive act he launches his crusade, ostensibly a search for Truth and Justice – and the identity of the mysterious 'Marion' – but eventually an irresistible adventure which takes him through a labyrinth of risks, clues and blind alleys to lead him triumphantly – if a little haphazardly – to hilarious success.

'First-class entertainment'
Listener

'We are left with that warm feeling that follows a good read that is also much more than that'
Daily Telegraph

'For sparkle ... go for Bernice Rubens's
MR WAKEFIELD'S CRUSADE'
Sunday Telegraph

'The tale skips and bounces and loops back upon itself with dazzling agility while the hero stalls and bumbles about hopelessly. Once again Bernice Rubens demonstrates that she is one of the cleverest and funniest novelists writing in England today'
Punch

☐	Mr Wakefield's Crusade	Bernice Rubens	£4.99
☐	The Elected Member	Bernice Rubens	£5.99
☐	A Solitary Grief	Bernice Rubens	£5.99
☐	Go Tell The Lemming	Bernice Rubens	£4.99
☐	Brothers	Bernice Rubens	£5.99

Abacus now offers an exciting range of quality titles by both established and new authors. All of the books in this series are available from:

Little, Brown and Company (UK),
P.O. Box 11,
Falmouth,
Cornwall TR10 9EN.

Alternatively you may fax your order to the above address. Fax No. 01326 317444.

Payments can be made as follows: cheque, postal order (payable to Little, Brown and Company) or by credit cards, Visa/Access. Do not send cash or currency. UK customers and B.F.P.O. please allow £1.00 for postage and packing for the first book, plus 50p for the second book, plus 30p for each additional book up to a maximum charge of £3.00 (7 books plus).

Overseas customers including Ireland, please allow £2.00 for the first book plus £1.00 for the second book, plus 50p for each additional book.

NAME (Block Letters) ....

....

ADDRESS ....

....

....

☐ I enclose my remittance for ....

☐ I wish to pay by Access/Visa Card

Number ☐☐☐☐☐☐☐☐☐☐☐☐☐☐☐☐

Card Expiry Date ☐☐☐☐